HALLOWEEN HORROR

Volume 2

Edited by
Zach Friday

DBND Publishing
Visit our website at www.dbndpublishing.com

Cover art by Luke Spooner / Carrion House
www.carrionhouse.com

This book is a work of fiction. Names, characters, places, and incidents either are products of the author's imagination or are used fictitiously. Any resemblance to actual persons, living or dead, events, or locales is entirely coincidental.

Printed in the United States of America

First Printing: October 2020
DBND Publishing

ISBN-9798687076371

CONTENTS

HALLOWEEN HORROR

VOLUME 2

PUMPKIN SEEDS

KEVIN DAVID ANDERSON

HALLOWEEN JACK-O'-LANTERNS DECORATED the Linden's front porch. Their soft glow illuminated Mark Linden's dazed expression. Sheriff Kinkade tried to appear positive as he put a gentle hand on Mark's shoulder. Having no family of his own, Kinkade could only imagine what Mark was going through.

"Is there anyone we can call?" Kinkade hunkered down a bit so his thick six-foot frame didn't tower over Mark as much.

Mark's eyes were shut and Kinkade waited patiently for him to speak. He knew Mark was an educated man, the kind that had been keeping up with current events. Mark would know that his wife wasn't dead. Not yet.

The *Daily Gazette* article had been very detailed, more so than Kinkade liked, about the M.O. of the Riverdale Snatcher.

Mark's eyes opened. "How long do we have... till she's found?"

The time between abduction and the discovery of the bodies, ritualistically pinned up like a frog on a dissection slab, varied from two to five days. Away from the press, the FBI had shared with Kinkade that it really depended on how much gratification the Snatcher was deriving from the current victim.

"We're gonna find her," Kinkade said. "Long before..."

"I just took the kids out trick-or-treating. We were only gone a half-hour. I can't believe—oh, God, Karen." Mark sobbed into both hands.

"We'll find her." Kinkade tried to remember what church the Lindens attended. It wasn't St. Andrews because that's where he went. "Do you go to First Community?"

Mark nodded, his hands still covering his face.

"Would you like me to call Pastor Johansson? I'm sure he c—" From the corner of his eye Kinkade saw one of his deputies waving at him from the sidewalk. "Excuse me a minute, Mark."

Kinkade started down the porch steps. By the time his foot hit the grass he was angry. Whatever reason Deputy Simon had for interrupting, Kinkade knew it would be either trivial or just plain stupid. Most of Kinkade's deputies were kids fresh out of high school, and not one of them had enough confidence to handle anything on their own. To a veteran like Kinkade, a man with fifteen years as a city cop and two tours of duty in the Marines, it was infuriating.

Kinkade met the deputy in the middle of the lawn. "What the hell is so goddamn important you need to interrupt me every ten seconds, Simon?"

Looking down, Simon seemed to be searching for words in the vicinity of his shoelaces. "You know how you told me to take pictures of the crime scene?"

Kinkade was hoping to get some shots before the FBI showed up and shut him out again. "Yeah. Did you forget the camera?"

"No, Sir, I brought it," the Deputy said. "Batteries are dead though. Been meaning to swing by the Walgreens for some new ones."

Kinkade shook his head. The day he first laid eyes on Simon's resume, he saw no bullet points that listed idiot or first-class moron as his characteristics. *Why did I hire this guy?*

"I have a camera in my trunk, so never mind that. Here's what I want you to do," Kinkade said.

Simon nodded, taking out a notepad.

"Take Mark inside to be with his kids. Then, call Pastor Johansson. Tell him what's happened and ask him to come over. Then call Karen Linden's sister. Think she's in Idlewood. I'm sure Mark would want her here. Times like this a man needs the support of the Lord and his family."

Simon stopped writing, and then started reading aloud. "Uh, take Mr. Linden inside, call Pastor Johansson and sister in Idlewood. Got it." The deputy slapped his notebook shut and marched off toward the house.

Kinkade felt an eye roll coming on but he stopped it, sighed instead, then headed to the street. His squad car, parked at the curb, had a disposable camera in the glove box, but he was hoping that he'd left his digital in the back compartment. When he reached the rear of the car, he paused a moment remembering the huge mess he'd left in the trunk. To find his camera he was going to have to dig.

Glancing back at the porch, Kinkade wanted to make sure Simon was following instructions. The orders seemed simple enough, but that had never stopped Simon from screwing them up before. Simon escorted Mark into the house. He shut the door, leaving the porch vacant, save for three jack-o'-lanterns, eyes glowing orange.

Their devilishly carved eyes cast an almost knowing stare at Kinkade. A chill crept over his neck, and he slapped it away. He'd never liked jack-o'-lanterns. Damn things gave him the willies.

He popped the trunk and peered inside. Yep, it was a full-on mess. *Jeez, the camera is probably all the way at the bottom.*

He reached in and lifted Karen Linden's bound feet off the spare tire, and then tried to roll her further back. She still appeared to be unconscious from the blow he'd delivered to the back of her head.

No sign of the camera.

When Kinkade grabbed a fist full of her hair to lift her head, her eyes popped open. She tried to scream through her gag—a sock shoved so far down her throat only the torn fringes of the toe section dangled outside her bleeding lips. Kinkade leaned in, putting his face inches from hers. "Don't even think about it. Make one sound and I'll pull that tongue right out of your pretty little head."

Karen Linden blinked and sunk back into the trunk.

"That's better," Kinkade said. "Besides, there will be plenty of time for screaming later." He released her hair and slammed the trunk closed.

He glanced back at the Linden's porch, prepared to meet the watchful leer of the glowing jack-o'-lanterns. But there were two more sets of eyes staring back at him that he hadn't prepared himself for.

Mark and Deputy Simon stood on the porch, looking astonished.

Kinkade shook his head. *Simon, you're such a screwup.* The instructions were simple. Take Mark inside, call Johansson, call the sister. What the hell were they doing on the porch?

The deputy went for his gun but had trouble releasing the holster strap.

Kinkade knew that hiring deputies that made Barney Fife look competent would prove beneficial at some point. He cocked his head and swiftly pulled his revolver, leveling it at the deputy. Before Simon could get his weapon free, Kinkade fired.

The deputy was hit square in the chest and fell back against the house. As he slid down the wall, he finally managed to unholster his pistol. The gun fell into his lap when his butt hit the porch.

Kinkade turned the revolver on Mark. The frightened man dove out of the way. Kinkade fired twice, trying to hit Mark in the air, but his shots shattered the living room window instead. Mark landed out of sight, toppling a few uncarved pumpkins off the porch banister.

Screams came from inside the house. *The kids,* Kinkade thought. *Jeez, I'm in no mood to kill kids.*

Neighborhood dogs started barking, porch lights came on, and behind him, across the street, a screen door squeaked open. *Damn.* He lowered his weapon. *Time to move on.* This town was about tapped out anyway.

Kinkade stepped around to the driver's side of his squad car and reached for the door handle. A speeding glint of orange reflected in the car window. When he turned, the pumpkin hit him in the face. The blow knocked him back against the car. His head cracked against the lights on the roof.

He slid down onto the grass, wiping pumpkin guts from his eyes. The juices stung. Pumpkin seeds slid down his cheeks like unwanted tears. His fingers grazed his nose and he winced in pain. It was probably broken.

Kinkade should have been angry, but he wasn't. Mark was now fumbling around Simon's body.

Nice throw, big guy.

Kinkade searched for his gun in the pumpkin innards on the ground. His piece had fallen into the gutter, hammer still cocked. He clasped it as Mark came down the steps, holding something out in front of him.

Kinkade's eyes focused with a suddenness that made him blink. He brought his revolver up. Mark had Simon's gun and was rushing across the lawn, pointing the weapon, and frantically searching for the safety.

Kinkade chuckled. *That's the spirit. Fight for it.* Kinkade took aim and pulled the trigger.

But nothing happened.

He pulled again. Nothing.

He examined the revolver and couldn't believe his eyes. Pumpkin seeds, wedged in like a doorstop, were keeping the hammer from falling. He pushed the seeds out with his thumb then brought the revolver up again, fast.

A pistol shot boomed and flashed before his eyes. The first shot hit his chest like a baseball bat to the ribs. The second and third pierced his gut with the burning intensity of branding irons.

When the shots ended, Mark stood in front of him, silhouetted in the porch light. He was still pointing Simon's pistol at Kinkade's chest and, shaking like a child, kept pulling the trigger. Click, click, click.

"Good job, Cowboy," Kinkade said, choking up blood. He brought his hand to his face. Pumpkin juice dripped down his fingers, mixing with splatters of crimson.

Kinkade convulsed and pulled in a last shallow breath as he glanced up at the Lindens' porch. Maybe he was hallucinating, but he swore that the jack-o'-lanterns were grinning at him. Twisted grins with glowing malevolence.

Then, just before he died, Kinkade remembered... he didn't actually see Mark throw the pumpkin.

THE CANDLE GAME

BEN HURRY

THE CANDLELIGHT DANCED BEHIND me, warping the shadows on the wall and creating fantastical shapes in my periphery as I stared into the mirror on the vanity. That's the reason why I didn't believe my own eyes when I caught a glimpse of it the first time, a shadow not like the others sitting in the corner of my vision. I glanced down at the piece of paper beside me, printed instructions that my older brother had left explaining the ritual. A method he pulled from the internet on how to peer beyond the confines of our world and catch a glimpse of someplace else. Some other world, or dimension, or universe where all the things that live under our beds come from. You could try it any night you wanted, but the instructions were quite clear that the old Celtic holiday Samhain, celebrated today as Halloween, was the best time to do it. It explained that tonight was a night where the border of our world and the Otherworld are at their thinnest. Ghosts were said to come back and visit their loved ones and much, much darker things are said to use the shadows of Halloween night to stalk our world, at least for a little while. It was silly, of course. Nothing more than a way for bored teenagers at a sleepover to scare each other, at least that's what I told myself. In my case, it was a way for one bored teenager to scare his little brother while he sat in the next room with his friends and cruelly snickered at how scared I must have been in the dark and all alone. But I was desperate to win their approval like all little brothers are, and prove I was old enough and brave enough to sit with them and watch the horror movie marathon.

The ritual itself was simple enough. Sit and stare into a mirror in a dark room with a candle burning just behind you. After a few minutes, the reflection in the mirror stops reflecting your world and starts reflecting the Other. The instructions warned in big, bold letters that it was not a game, and you should do this for no more than ten minutes at a time, or else you risk making the connection between worlds strong enough for any manner of beings to come through. If it worked though, then you might start seeing a reflection of yourself as you really are, or you might see the monsters that sometimes sneak into our nightmares, or if you're really lucky you might catch a glimpse of a friend or loved one who has passed along to the other side. It was clearly a game designed to creep you out and make you think you see things that aren't there.

But there it was again, a shadow that seemed out of place. The flicker of the candle cast the shadows in one direction as this shadow seemingly glided in the other. Just for a moment, of course, just enough for me to notice and for my eyes to glance to that spot in the reflection. Nothing there, no monsters lurking in the corner. A sharp thud on the closed door behind me sent a shock down my body and I jumped violently in the chair.

"How you doin' in there?" my brother called out. I could almost hear the smirk in his voice, could almost sense the grin over his shoulder at his friends as they waited to hear my trembling voice cry out.

"Fine. Nothing is happening," I lied. I did well to hide the little shake I felt in my chest as I nervously watched the shadows behind me. I heard the muffled voice of my brother say something, and then the faint laughter of his friends. It was obviously some joke at my expense. I thought back to that afternoon. To our fight. He took me Trick or Treating late in the afternoon, the sun hadn't even gone down yet when we began our journey around the neighbourhood. But he wanted to get that childish stuff out of the way early so he could race home and hang out with his friends. I wanted to hang out with the older boys too, play videogames, watch the horror movies on TV, listen to them talk about the girls they were into and the mischief they got up to when they disappeared after school. My brother didn't want me around them, he was probably worried I'd tell on them or something, and things between us got heated. In the end, we came to a compromise. He had found this silly game online, and his original plan was going to play it with his friends to scare them. But suddenly he had a much better target to scare. I could hang out with them, my brother said, if I could last for 10 minutes in a room by myself playing the candle game. Simple.

An icy gust swept through the room as the wind picked up outside and crept through the cracks in our ancient house, causing the candle flame to flicker and almost extinguish. The shadows behind me were thrown around wildly, bouncing off the furniture and causing strange, angular shapes to form and disappear from one moment to the next. As I watched the shadowy dance behind me my eyes lost focus for a second and that's when I saw it again. A shadow not moving with the rest, almost hiding in the back corner beside the large wardrobe. I tried to let out a gasp but it caught in my throat, coming out instead as an almost silent squeak of shock and fear as an icy chill ran down my back and goosebumps began pricking at my neck. My eyes never left that spot as the light flickered around the room, and when that spot was momentarily illuminated and I saw that the shadow remained, a low moan of fear escaped my lips. I tried to yell out, but my voice came out in a hoarse whisper as my body was flooded with a very primal sort of fear. I swallowed and tried to call out again.

"How much longer?" my voice came out shaky, unsure of itself. The fear in it was unmistakable. That shadow in the corner, silently standing in the blackness of the corner had my full attention. I couldn't make out any shape or form, almost like it was wearing the darkness as a cloak to hide from prying eyes. But it was unmistakably there. I wanted to look behind me and see it with my own eyes but a glimpse down at the rules of the game confirmed what I half-remembered reading earlier—acknowledging the presence of something from the Otherworld was dangerous and might be the invitation it wanted to stay permanently.

"You still have two minutes left," my brother yelled from the other side of the door. The safe side. His voiced changed to a mocking tone.

"Why, are you scared?" He laughed and I heard his friends laughing too. I couldn't answer him. I desperately wanted to, so I could tell him that I was scared more than I had ever been in my life. That my heart was pounding so hard I could hear the blood in my ears. That my stomach felt like an empty hole, like a void in my very person filled with nothing but dread and despair and pure, abject terror. But my voice had failed me again because there, a few steps away from the first shadow, another one had appeared. It too was a silent sentinel, looming in the shadows as if watching me. My vision was clouded now as tears welled up in my eyes, and my vision darted around examining every inch of the refection in the mirror. I saw a third figure on top of the wardrobe. Then a fourth by the window. A fifth was now on the bed where just moments ago nothing had been. Every passing second seemed to bring more and more figures. The howling wind began slamming against the outside of the house, forcing its way into the room and kicking the candlelight into a frenzy. Despite the light flying haphazardly around the room, the shadows behind me stood still and silent and tall as they, whatever "they" are, continued to mass together into a wall of black shapes. It seemed as though every shadow behind me now was one of them. The more I looked the more I realised I didn't even recognise the room behind me anymore. It was different, not in any way that I could point to physically, but it had begun to seem alien to me like it was no longer the room I had grown up in. Another long howl from the wind caused the shutters outside to slam shut against the window and I jumped violently. A sharp cry escaped my throat when my reflection didn't jump with me. I pulled my eyes away from the shadows and slowly glanced at my reflection. It shifted, almost imperceptibly at first. The eyes narrowed, the nose stretched a bit thinner. For the briefest of moments, I could have sworn I saw my Aunty Beth who passed away last year. She was sitting and staring at me from where my reflection should have been for just long enough for me to recognise her, and then she was gone. I opened my mouth to cry out, to beg my brother to save me, to turn on the light, to break me out of wherever I now was. This wasn't meant to be happening, I kept repeating that to myself almost like a mantra. This can't be real, this can't be happening. This can't be real, this can't be happening. This can't be real, this can't be happening.

The wall of shadow behind me flickered then, letting itself get picked up by the light of the candle and thrown violently around the room. The stretching shadows were lashing at the walls and ceiling and had begun to take on sinister shapes, monstrous, animalistic, claw-like shapes tearing at the light. I tore my gaze away from the mirror, determined to break its spell, but from the corner of my eye saw that my reflection once more refused to follow my movements. Slowly I looked back to find my reflection still staring forwards, dark-eyed and seemingly furious, watching me from the other side of the mirror. The shadows behind me were frantically throwing themselves around the room, and I could hear a low howl rising from somewhere in the room. At first, I thought it was the wind again, but as it built in intensity, I could make out dozens of individual howls coming together and building in a crescendo until it was all I could hear. The wailing shadows seemed to be everywhere now looming over me and all around. I could even see them in the corners of my eyes now, no longer confined to the mirror, they had reached out from wherever they were in an attempt to reach me in my world.

I gave in to my fear then, and the paralysing spell of my terror that held me glued to the chair and the mirror finally broke. I screamed. A low, loud groaning shriek of fear from deep in my chest. I tried to push the chair back, away from the mirror, but it caught on the carpet and tipped, throwing me onto the ground with a crash. Behind me, the door flew open and light flooded the room as my brother burst in. He ran over and pulled me into a hug, checking to make sure I hadn't hurt myself in the fall.

"You okay little bro?" he asked. I nodded into his chest. I don't remember exactly what I said. Some excuse about how I leaned back to far and fell. He laughed and let me go, helping me up to my feet. I looked around. No shadows. No monsters. Just a room. I was still trembling with fear. Had I imagined it?

"You lasted twelve minutes, I forgot to get you earlier," my brother told me. "The rules do say anything longer than ten minutes is dangerous and I guess in your case it was!" he said laughing, rubbing the back of my head where I had fallen and hit it.

"Funniest thing though," he said thinking. "For a split second then when I came in I could have sworn I saw your reflection still staring at me in the mirror."

LAST'S THE BEST

J.C. RAYE

First's the worst.
Second's the same,
Last's the best of all the game.

ON MISCHIEF EVE AFTERNOON, a small squadron of concerned parents were gathered on Temy's front porch when he opened the door. He recognized almost all of them immediately and was ready for the encounter. Two men, three women. All the color of cream cheese, donned in their mall boutique bests, and not a hair out of place. Worry and wealth were painted across their botoxed brows. The one man Temy did not know was of course the poor soul the others had put up to the knocking, the cowards, and the knocking became more like pounding when the little preppy posse realized his doorbell was on the fritz. Instead of inviting them in, Temy stepped *out* to meet them, closing the wooden door behind him, and folding his arms defensively. They all took one surprised step back into the hearty October gusts when he did this, involuntarily establishing what might have appeared at a distance to be the perfect holiday caroler formation. Right there, he knew he had offset the first stage of their well-thought out plan, and he absolutely loved it. Two points, Temy Grozel.

He wouldn't give this bunch the satisfaction of inviting them in for tea, or smoothies, or whatever the hell these perfect people tend to do when they gang up on you, ever so politely and sickeningly, suggesting their playbook of rules for how everyone else should live. He wouldn't allow them to hungrily scope out his messy apartment and report back to their little mom-bot associations about stacks of newspapers, the brown plaid sofa patched with gaff tape and yesterday's lo mein fork stuck to a smudgy glass coffee table. Temy was admittedly sloppy and proudly antisocial, but held a legitimate, full-time job landscaping for the county parks commission, always paid his taxes, and certainly was not the low-life they had already decided he was years ago, when *they* moved into *his* neighborhood.

Temy could see they had not expected to deliver their grown-up scolding on the *outside* porch, and were already looking at each other awkwardly for some sort of a regroup. Maura Niles, 40-something, divorced, tan salon aficionado, yoga pants and smooth chocolate pony-tail, did not hesitate. She bravely stepped into the center of the group to face him, clearly establishing her leadership, and the high probability that she was the ringmaster who had suggested the parent-parade down Washington Road to Temy's in the first place. They were certainly in new territory walking down this way. His was the last home before the Millstone River cut off and the only apartment building in the gentrified village of Rocky Hill. The structure, a lopsided, two story duplex, was battleship gray with a charcoal-blue trim, and still bedecked with original cedar panels. The countless determined borings of carpenter bees freckled the wood, and a low-growing lime carpet of mildew was encroaching from the side of the house which faced the Millstone and woods beyond. The only remaining charm of the place was its large porch, though crooked, skirted with cracked gray lattice. The porch spanned the full width of the building and was sheltered by an equally lopsided balcony nestled between two century-old, charcoal-blue, columns. Staring at the shivering parents, Temy knew his place was the bane of their existence, and the eyesore of Rocky Hill, a town once made famous by revolutionary colonials and historic grist mills. He also knew, as a renter, he wasn't planning on doing a damn thing about it. His next door neighbor in apartment A, Terry Schroder, had been dumped into some upscale assisted-living place by her family two years ago, and her half of the building had remained empty. Temy supposed her middle-aged children, his new landlords, were just holding on to the building for a tax write off.

"Mr. Gurzel," Maura Niles began.

"It's Grozel," Temy countered. And then, just to be a dick, he smiled, and added, "Graaa-Zeeelll."

Maura rolled her eyes and sighed dramatically, as if mustering the patience to deal with a sulky kindergartner. One nervous hand went to her hip and the other rose to gently pat the front of a silver charm dangling from a dainty chain round her neck. "We've only come to ask," she paused, looking to the others for any nod of encouragement, "if you could perhaps not scare the children so badly this Halloween... uh... tomorrow night. The last two Halloweens, you were pretty rough on the kids. I mean, those were kind of *adult scares*, you know?"

Gemma Niles, Maura's older sister, stood furthest from the front door. Her crystalline eyes, the color of jade, were unwaveringly fixed hard on Temy. "The rats?" she said. "The real rats you had loose on this porch, if you don't remember?"

Temy, determined to yank her chain, raised his eyebrows to feign surprise. "Whatever do you mean Ms. Niles? I mean isn't Halloween about trick-or-treating and things that go bump in the night? I'm only trying to be a part of the neighborhood as you and some of your friends have often remarked to me that I should. You know? Just getting into the *spirit* of the holiday."

"Listen buddy..." the knocker started, "there is no reason to get defensive about this."

"And you are?" Temy turned, dropping his arms to his sides, ready for a tussle if need be.

Rose Dupont, the cheerless and ancient Mary Jacobs Memorial librarian, protectively touched the knocker's forearm and took a half step forward, as if to say, *I've got this dear,* and turned to Temy. "Temy, this is Don Pentner, Lisa Pentner's husband. I'm sure you've met her and their two boys. They live in that lovely olive-colored, gingerbread house across the street from the library. I think her oldest son delivers your paper, right?"

"Oh, sure," Temy replied, "I know the boy." He refolded his arms and leaned back on his door. "Nice to meet you." Temy looked old Donny up and down, only now noticing the guy's backwards hat, button-down oxford shirt and lace-up hi-tops, and devilishly added, "Borrow your kid's clothes today Pentner?"

Temy saw a fiery flash in Don's eyes, which he almost respected. But it was quickly replaced by a shrug, a downcast face and small cough. Temy had seen this reaction a thousand times from the married guys at his job. The dull capitulation of a man who'd already accepted that he'd not only lose in any physical scrap, but then be subject to further humiliation, having to answer to an angry hen at home who stole his balls years ago.

Chocolate ponytail Maura recaptured the flag and spoke again in a low and purposely soothing voice. "Mr. Grozel. We did not come down here to fight with you. And we realize that there is some tension here, which you seem to have been harboring since we all bought houses on this street.

"Lady..." Temy started.

"But," Ms. Niles interrupted, holding her hand a few inches from his chest in some kind of weird peace-sign benediction move, "your decorations and animations are just too scary. The kids come home crying after they have been here. That thing you pulled two years back with the cannon shooting worms from the bushes was dangerous, and I'm not even sure if it was legal."

Temy shook his head impatiently, a move he had been resisting, lest they know that they were getting to him, which they were. He unloaded on the group. His tone was bitter, and he made a point to eyeball them all equally. "Look. Here's the deal. You people never give me the time of day except to tell me that I have to clean up my front yard, or pull in my recycling bins one minute after the damn truck comes. Oh! Right! And to drive zero mph down the road so I don't run over any of your precious little spawn who prefer to play manhunt in the street rather than in their own Great Adventure backyards. Halloween is a national holiday. HAH-LEE-DAY. And I have a right to enjoy it. It's my holiday too. And I can choose to celebrate it in any fucking way I damn well please.

"There's no reason to get vulgar, Temy," Rose admonished, the timbre of her voice hushed and embarrassed.

Pentner powered up again. "Look man, this was just a friendly visit. Don't turn it into something it's not."

"Dude. I don't even *know* you," Temy said, straightening up, "and where the hell you people get off lecturing me about Halloween decoration choices is truly hilarious. Like it's okay for you to line the streets with those stupid-happy-face inflatables? Sure, your kids may get scared, but that's the whole point! It doesn't seem to stop them from gobbling up my candy every year, does it? Now if you don't mind, some of us get up for work at 5am, and I'd actually like to continue eating my dinner."

After ferociously slamming the door on them and audibly snapping the bolt, Temy stepped over to the front window and lifted one of the slat blinds. The group seemed to have stopped halfway down the porch steps. Maura, clearly not happy with the encounter, was whispering rather urgently, frenetically waving her skinny arms about as if to call them to further action. It wasn't working. One by one, each the of the unwelcome wagon looked at

17

their phones, feigning appointments or kids play-dates, and dejectedly ambled back up the street to their six-figure, restoration homes. Game. Set. Match. Temy Grozel.

He toasted his win with a shot of Baccardi in the apartment's aging eat-in kitchen and headed down the basement to gleefully unpack his toys. Nothing was going to impact his plans this season. He had been researching haunted house DIY sites since April, and built quite a new array of terrorizing animated contraptions, which he had meticulously tested in the weeks prior. This year's blueprint for horror was totally awesome.

First, he'd back his truck down the driveway. This was for two reasons. The vehicle would partially block the view from the west end of Washington Street and thus, the activity immediately in front of his house. Kids would not be able to see what was going on until they were already on the property, when it was far too late. Second, from the shadows of his truck cap, the clear view could help him orchestrate the remote-controlled circus of fear planned for the little buggers. And oh, did he have the goods this year.

A life-sized angel of death, made out of cheesecloth, wire hangers, and a mannequin head would plunge down from the second floor balcony and land dead center on the front walk. Getting the measurements correct had taken half a day, and its first flight was a crash and burn, well, without the burn part. Donned in a white flowing wig, glow-in-the-dark paint and red devil eyes, the high-speed pulley mechanism on eight-pound fishing wire, as well as the inhuman screeching of the specter, would drive the kids backwards for sure.

Now, if in their hasty retreat, they stepped to the right of the front yard, a dead body, Temy lovingly dubbed, Mr. Creepy, would greet them from behind. Mr. Creepy was a pvc-formed half-torso, three feet wide, dressed in bloody flannel, with a realistic skull mask and poseable werewolf hands. On cue, it would spring from its open grave and drag itself over the grass, growling like a dog. The sound was amplified by a car equalizer. It was pretty horrible.

Now, if the angel drove the children left into the front yard, they fared no better, because reaching from the shadows, a six-foot grim reaper, complete with sickle and maniacal laughter track was sure to make them pee their pants.

Of course the frights did not stop there. Those were just Temy's newest biggees. He'd still be using the dead grandma in the rocking chair, the shaking coffin wrapped in chains, tons of strategically placed blue and purple spotlights, a whole collection of rubber wonders (heads, severed arms, and the ear pizza.) Topping it off, Temy would douse the entire area in black cobweb and ketchup-corn syrup handprints. And like jimmies on an ice cream cone, he'd sprinkle an army of rubber spiders along the pathways and picket fencing.

There was only one hitch to what would be Temy's Ultimate Trick-or-Treater Homestead Scarefest tomorrow night. The snapping skeleton candy bowl had not yet arrived in the mail, even though the company had advertised three-day delivery, and Temy had ordered it early last week. He'd found it online, a place called the *Prank Warehouse* in Wichita, Kansas. He never saw anything quite like it before. Motion sensitive, it was a skeleton's upper torso, head and arms which snapped close around little hands seeking treats. Of course, animated candy bowls were not a new idea. Over the years, he's seen the mummy hand, the monster hand, and a bat bowl that spread its wings and squawked with piercing red, LED eyes. And they were all great. But this one, the one Temy purchased, was brilliant. Because in addition to the movement, this candy bowl delivered a small electric shock to the child's interloping paw. Temy would be truly disappointed if it did not show up in time. Still, though, he did have one more day.

Temy rinsed out a cleaning bucket from the basement, ran a double-wide piece of masking tape across it, and wrote *TAKE ONE* with a black marker. He then set about gently carrying all the large animations up the basement stairs, one by one. He checked each one for motion and for scare. If needed, he touched up evil face paint or changed out clothing with some recent picks from the local thrift shop. By midnight, Temy was exhausted, more with excitement than anything else, and decided to hit the hay. He would have a few hours tomorrow after work to set the stage out there. It should be an easy set-up, as he had already marked everything out. Mostly it would be running wires and plugging in cords. That night he fell asleep hard, but content.

Temy arrived home in the afternoon, around half past four, on Halloween. Pulling his Ford into the crumbling driveway, he became downright giddy spotting a package on the front porch nuzzled up against the door. It had arrived! Temy entered the house so quickly trying to manage his toolbox, coat, lunch thermos and the box, he nearly fell through the doorway. Dumping everything onto the couch, he placed the package on the coffee table and tore into it, scissors be damned. It was smaller than he expected. When he broke through the cardboard flaps and reached the bubble wrap, he could already tell the company had made a mistake. Temy unraveled the item from the wads of excess plastic and set it on his lap. It was a fake hand, withered, dry and somewhat fragile. Temy's heart sank. A small piece of red paper was taped inside the palm that explained what the prop was: *The Hand of Glory is the dried and pickled corpse hand from a villain who has been hanged on the gallows. Enjoy!*

Temy groaned angrily and wrenched the last pieces of bubble wrap from the inside bottom of the box, desperately seeking an explanation for the mix-up. As if to answer his call, a plain white business envelope dropped onto the floor. Inside, Temy found a single piece of letterhead with the *Prank Warehouse* return address.

Dear Mr. Grozel,

We regret to inform you that at the time you placed your online order for: Halloween Merchandise: Grabby Bowl, we were out of stock. We apologize for the inconvenience, and have already refunded your purchase on the credit card that was used. As a show of good will, we have sent you a similar item from our Halloween Decorating Center free

of charge to let you know we appreciate your business. Please contact our
service department with any questions you may have.

Thank you,

"Damn!" Temy shouted, and threw the box across the narrow living room, nearly missing the table lamp. It was a disappointment to say the least, but the hand was damn creepy, so maybe it wasn't all bad. He decided to set it up in the windowsill, next to a resin black cat with twinkie lights twisted around its neck.

Temy spent an hour carving out his usual hard rock-themed pumpkin design, set it on the porch, and lit the white candle inside. Looking towards the Millstone River woods, midnight blue sky was impatiently pressing down upon the last feathery streaks of orange light. Way up the street, he heard a few children happily shouting. It was almost time. He had just about an hour to set up the yard.

As he walked inside, he tripped over something, fell, and crashed through the glass coffee table. Shards of glass painfully introduced themselves to his right cheek, arms, hips, and upper thighs. No sooner had he hit the floor, he protectively bounced into a pushup posture on hands and knees. It was the wrong move. More glass pushed into the already shredded flesh on both his palms. Temy then used all his lower body strength to lift himself to a kneeling position, without the use of his hands again. Also, a pitiful choice. A thousand needles of fire poked through the thin denim covering his bony knees.

Temy knew he had to stand. Using his left arm, he reached for the plaid sofa, only then noticing that half his view was awash with blood, and under the blood, a searing twinge, growing by the second. A shard was in his eye.

He considered yelling for help, but only considered it. He never actually had the option. A swaggle of bubble wrap came swiftly flying around his head and closed in tightly on his face. Temy's hands instinctively rose to his neck, and he tried to free himself, air immediately becoming an issue. But not only was he being choked, he was being shaken, side to side, forward and backward, with a force so strong, so violent, his mind could not fathom who or what might have the sheer power to do it. What made it all so dreadfully ironic for Temy was that his only witnesses were the silent audience of Halloween animatronic figures, assembled in the living room, still wrapped in their cords. None of them able to save their creator.

Slipping on his own blood, he again fell into the pond of broken glass and shrieked in agony. As he writhed in the barbs, with his one working eye, he saw a dribble of clear liquid wash down the outside of his plastic face and detected a faint odor of rum. Then he felt the burning. Then he screamed.

* * *

On the morning of November 1ˢᵗ, Maura Niles walked east on Washington Road. It was a brisk walk, energized by the bright, unusually warm fall sunshine on her shoulders, but also by the contents of the handwritten note tucked into the plastic shopping bag under her arm, addressed to Temy Grozel. The street was noticeably quiet. No doubt all of her neighbors were still recovering from their Halloween escapades the night before. While children were still waking up with Frankenstein grease paint on their cheeks and chocolate candy smudges in the corners of their mouths, their poor parents were guzzling that second cup a joe, and surveying the holiday combat zone for an impending and monumental cleanup. Torn orange streamers and deflated vampires. Tipped scarecrows and muddy Styrofoam gravestones. Trails of sticky candy wrappers and stomped on tubes of purple eye glitter. Thrown away? Packed away? Scary artifacts, to be assessed by for damage, and the potential for repair to last just one more season.

Certainly she was not the only parent, speculating in the crisp, morning-after-fray, whether all that time, money and energy was worth it, for just one wonderful night. But Maura's misgivings quickly dissolved as she strode past Mary Jacobs Library. She could not help but giggle remembering how Rose had extended library hours last night and treated the children to riveting fireplace reading of *The Legend of Sleepy Hollow*, complete with cocoa, marshmallow ghost pops and free black cat "Meow-loween!" bookmark. This year, the librarian had even convinced a local farmer to ride past the big library picture window as none other than the Headless Horseman himself! So much fun. The faces of the children as he howled by, and their delight in petting the horse afterwards, made it all worthwhile. Of course, Rose's old witch costume was getting a little tight these days and more than a few children sniggered when the safety pins holding it closed over her backside dramatically popped during the story.

A cluster of crimson leaves whispered across Maura's feet as she walked past Brolia's Antiques & Curiosities, and then further down, past the Rocky Hill Inn, where daily lunch specials were posted in white plastic lettering on black swinging sign: *Troll Burgers and Dragon Scale Chips! Cauldron Curry! Bat-Wing Chili!* Now past the post office where Gemma worked, and finally crossing over Princeton Street, Maura arrived at Temys.

It was just as the children and other parents had said. Temy had heeded their request and decorated rather sparsely this year. There was a burnt out, lone pumpkin on the top step of the tilted porch, swathed with fake cobwebs and carved with a few alphabet letters, A, C, D, C. There was (just one) fake, zombie-skeleton-type creature laying face-down on the front lawn. It's exposed patches of bone shone white in the morning sun against countless flaps of blood-coated, charred skin. The zombie did not come to life or try to grab her ankle as she stepped over it and up onto the steps. In fact, none of the usual over-the-top frights were present, which had caused so many children in recent years to disband their trick-

or-treating romps early, and in tears, inconsolably scamper home to confused parents and a ruined holiday. Nothing moaned, wailed or screeched as she reached the top porch step. Nothing spidery or clutchy dove down from the balcony, and she wasn't squirted with red goo as she reached for the door handle. A large, yellow plastic paint bucket next to the door marked, *TAKE ONE*, held a few remnants of last night's candy selection: two caramel lollipops and an individually packaged licorice rope. Maura snatched up the licorice packet, found it dry, and pocketed in for later.

Pulling the thank-you note, written by herself on behalf of the neighborhood, from the plastic bag, she tucked it into a crevice in the doorjamb and turned for home, pleased.

As the young mother was mentally tallying her morning errands, she remembered something, gritted her teeth, and snapped her fingers in self-reproach. Turning back, she stepped into the front yard and removed the Hand of Glory from Temy's dead hands and stuffed it into the plastic shopping bag.

THE MURMUR OF THEIR TINY HEARTS

PAUL STOLP

IT'S KARA'S TURN TO mind the house this Halloween and Ryan is already in full-blown complaint mode.

"You said yourself no one has lived in that house for nearly a decade. Why on earth you and Kelly won't just sell it, I can't understand."

He is right about that much. He doesn't understand and she is tired of hearing about it. There is no way she or her sister are going to sell the house they grew up in. They'd agreed on this eight years ago with a squeeze of hands while standing in front of their mother's coffin before the funeral. Words weren't necessary, a concept Ryan will never grasp given the way words rarely stop pouring from his mouth.

"Even in a recession, the house could make both of you a nice sum." He sits stiffly in the passenger seat, a never-ending fountain of advice she has neither asked for nor listened to. She feels her irritation rising and tamps it down. Patience, patience.

They've been together 18 months and there will not be another 18. Arguing with him now would be little more than an exercise in futility.

"We aren't having this conversation again. Kelly and I aren't selling."

"Fine." She hates the petulant tone, the sound of a child not getting what he wanted. "So you want to hold onto the house for sentimental value—"

"It's for more than sentimental value. It's our history—"

"Ok, fine, family history, whatever. That still doesn't explain why you go there every Halloween and greet trick-or-treaters."

"I told you it's not just for trick-or-treaters and it's not every Halloween. Kelly and I alternate. Don't you even remember last Halloween? We carved pumpkins and did a movie marathon at my apartment."

"Right, that's right. I'm sorry, my bad." His tone suggests it is anything but. "That was a fun night."

It had been a fun night. First, they carved the pumpkins. While he cleaned up the pumpkin remains, she made eyeball pasta—penne with mozzarella and olive eyeballs in the sauce. They ate and killed a bottle and a half of wine while watching three horror movies. They were still on the upswing then, buzzed with the wine and drunk on each other. The levelling off didn't begin until after the winter holidays and the downswing didn't go into effect until last summer—gradual at first but really picking up steam this last month. She knew it; he knew it. So why had he been so eager to accompany her in the first place?

Curiosity, probably. He's never seen the house. She's made it clear it is nothing special as far as houses go—a split-level duplex sitting in a neighborhood that has seen a steady influx of tech money over the last decade. She and Kelly split the costs of having it maintained via a housekeeping service, visiting only once a year, on Halloween. Maybe he remembers the cookies Kelly brought over last Halloween, just before they finished the third movie. He certainly fawned over them (and her) enough. She'd sensed her sister's instant dislike, later confirmed via multiple texts and phone conversations. She'd written it off as too much wine, no big deal. She shouldn't have. Kelly was good at seeing through bullshit.

It didn't matter now. Like the song says, all she needs is just a little patience.

She pulls the car into the parking lot of a big box supermarket. Once inside she begins by loading up on candy. Kelly reported less than a dozen trick-or-treaters last year, but Kara buys enough for four times that amount; she believes in being extra generous when doling out candy. She considers grabbing decorations for the house but the selection on the endcap is pathetic, already thoroughly picked over. A few desultory plastic pumpkins and mini cauldrons are all that remain. No big deal, she can get by without decorations. The two carved pumpkins currently sitting in the trunk should sufficiently alert trick-or-treaters that the house is occupied. Besides, the trick-or-treaters aren't the important thing.

Ryan pauses behind her as she makes her way down the baking aisle. She doesn't need to look at him to feel his confusion as she adds bags of flour and sugar to the basket dangling from her right arm. She offers no explanations as she selects bottles of food coloring, sprinkles and sparkles. He's a big boy, he can put one and two together. He remains silent all the way through the checkout process, but once in they are in the car and moving again, he speaks up.

"So—what's with the baking stuff? Are you going to make cookies?"

"Yep."

"Guessing that means no cookies from Kelly."

"Yep."

When she offers no further details he surprisingly doesn't press her, perhaps realizing for once he won't get anywhere. Instead he leans back in his seat and stares out the passenger window. The quiet, uneasy on his side, is for her a relief. Traffic is light and the steady hum of the car is soothing. Her mind drifts, filling with memories of her mother.

How she loved Halloween! Every year the season of the witch began with the decorations going up in mid-September. (She let Kelly claim all the Halloween decorations after their mother's passing, something she still regretted.) By the end of the first week of October, costumes had been discussed and agreed upon. By the middle of the month they were watching horror films nearly every night. And then, best of all, on Halloween day their mother baked cookies. So many cookies! Extra cookies went into the freezer, taking them all the way through Christmas. Their mother believed Halloween cookies tasted better than Christmas cookies no matter what ingredients were used. Neither she nor her sister disagreed.

She learned just how special those cookies were when she was eight and Kelly was nine. Cancer had robbed them of their father only three months prior and the girls were hardly even aware it was October. No decorations had been unboxed, no costumes discussed, no horror movies watched. Between them existed an unspoken expectation that Halloween was, in effect, cancelled. Yet on Halloween day they came home from school to find the house decorated and wonderful, sugary smells emanating from the kitchen. Kara exchanged a glance with Kelly. Her sister's face looked as shocked as she felt. They dropped their backpacks and followed the sweet fragrance into the kitchen.

"Girls! I bet you'd each like a cookie." Their mother brought a plate to the kitchen table. Ghosts, bats, skulls—the frosting detail on each completely unique, a cornucopia of expressions from zany to spooky, happy to sad. There was nothing rushed about the decorating job, either. Tiny drops of bright red blood dripped from vampire teeth, multiple blades of grass crawled up the surfaces of cracked grey tombstones. Grim reapers wore purple robes from which skeletal hands emerged, each bone lovingly crafted. Had she been doing this all day? Kara looked at her mother, who wore a huge grin. It was the first genuine smile she'd seen on her face since Dad died. She pulled out a chair opposite her sister.

"Put your ear close and listen, girls. Do you hear that?"

They leaned in towards the plate, each holding their long hair back so it would not brush the delicate frosting. Kelly heard it first.

"I hear it!"

Kara closed her eyes against the look of wonder on her sister's face. Kelly was always first and it was the most annoying thing in the world. She concentrated. She heard the ticking of the kitchen clock on the wall behind her, the low humming of the furnace and the quiet breathing of her sister. She squeezed her eyes shut tighter and listened harder than she ever had listened before. *Lub-dub. Lub-dub.* The other sounds of the kitchen faded away. *Lub-dub. Lub-dub.* Like what the doctor heard through his stethoscope in the funny movie they'd watched on TV last week, but unlike the movie these heartbeats weren't booming loud. They were soft but strong.

"I hear it too," she said.

"Now that you've heard it, you'll always be able to hear it if you listen close." Their mother spoke with a clear and slightly stern voice, the one she only used in Important Moments. "You will always hear the murmur of their tiny hearts."

The girls raised their heads and looked at the each other. A sense of love and mystery flooded through Kara, overwhelming in its intensity. She could tell her sister felt the same. The magnificence, the hugeness of the gift they'd just been given danced in the air between them. Kara felt light with the wonder of it all. Then a shadow darkened Kelly's face and she raised her head towards their mother.

"But mama, if we can hear their hearts, then won't it hurt to eat them?"

"It's ok dear, they're just cookies. Special cookies, but cookies all the same. They want to be eaten. That's why their hearts beat—

they are excited." Mom smiled at them both. "Even things that aren't alive can have heartbeats."

They accepted this even though they didn't understand it, in the way that you accept wisdom from your mother. Especially when she was using her Important Moments voice.

"These special cookies can only be made in this kitchen on Halloween day, girls, and they can only be made for us. You may each have one."

Kara looked at the plate for a moment before selecting a vampire bat with red eyes and horizontal veins on its wings. It was the most delicious cookie she'd ever eat. Even the others on the plate, and the ones their mother baked every Halloween day after, were never as good as that first one. They tasted just as fine, but the extra ingredient of mystery and discovery was a once in a lifetime experience, never to be replicated.

That Halloween began the traditions that remained until their mother passed away. Mom took Halloween day off from work and spent the day in the kitchen baking. Kara and Kelly never again donned costumes or went trick-or-treating, preferring to stay at home and give out the store-bought candy to the neighborhood trick-or-treaters while waiting for the real treats. After the trick-or-treaters died out for the night, their mother would turn out the lights and disappear. Sitting on the couch and giggling as often as not, the girls held each other tight, a plate of cookies on their laps.

"Trick or treat!"

The girls screamed as their mom jumped up from behind and crashed onto the couch beside them.

"Give her cookies! Give her cookies!"

Screaming with laughter, they pushed cookies at her until she could eat no more. Then, laughter finally dying down, they listened to the heartbeats of the remaining cookies before eating them up. *Lub-dub. Lub-dub.* It never got boring, that sound, never seemed anything less than a miracle. Eventually the lights came back on, signaling bedtime and a wave of sadness that the evening had passed.

There will be no selling of a house where such magic happened. Not so long as she and her sister draw breath.

As Kara turns the car into the driveway, she is pleased to see the housekeeping service is doing a nice upkeep job. The grass is uniformly cut and the rhododendron bush by the front window has been recently pruned. The light blue siding is clean. Leaves from the surrounding maple trees dot the lawn and driveway as per the sisters' request; the service has been instructed not to rake the yard the week prior to Halloween. The leaves provide a bit of natural decoration—ambience, as Kelly would say—since no one lives in the house and can otherwise decorate. Kara is glad she skipped the cheap grocery store decorations. Nature doesn't need her assistance.

She pops the trunk and takes out one of the jack-o-lanterns. It is as big as her chest. Carefully cradling it, she walks to the porch and deposits it to the right of the front door. She returns to the car for the second one and finds Ryan peering in the trunk.

"Wait, there's two? You didn't—I could have carved one."

"You worked late, remember? And you didn't want to come with me last Sunday when I chose the pumpkins."

She grabs the second jack-o-lantern and carries it to the porch before he can reply. Truth is, she wouldn't have let him be part of the pumpkin activities even if he'd been available. Not with how things currently stand between them. As is, she's nervous bringing him into the house. What if the hearts don't beat with a stranger present? It's a chance she's willing—has to—take, but that doesn't stop the thought from sitting uneasily in the back of her mind.

She pushes doubt aside as she unlocks the house. A seasonally appropriate musty smell pervades the interior. The odor doesn't bother her, it enhances the Halloween mood and soon enough it will be replaced by the smells of baking. She catches Ryan grimacing out of the corner of her eye. Seems about par for the course but there's no need to say anything, to ruin the lightness that settles in as the walls of her childhood home wrap their welcoming arms around her. Setting three plastic bags of groceries down, she glances at her phone. About two hours until trick-or-treaters start arriving, just enough time to do up a couple of batches of cookies.

"So what's the plan?"

She tenses, the lightness in her chest momentarily turning to heaviness. She lets out a quiet deep breath before turning and speaking.

"I'm going to bake. You can light the jack-o-lanterns and then sit and watch TV or whatever. There won't be any trick-or-treaters for a while, but it would be nice if you could hand out candy when they do arrive."

"There's a working TV here? Why am I not surprised? And probably a full set of cookware too. You two really have kept this house like a museum. What are the dinner plans?"

"There are none."

"You're just going to eat cookies? Kara, good grief—"

"Ryan." The tone in her voice stops him. "This is my evening, not yours. I'll not have you ruin it. You can play along or you can get in the car and leave and I'll figure out another way home. I don't really care, but I'm tired of the interrogation."

If only she could frame the shocked look on his face! So many times they've argued of late, always his head too far up his own ass to hear a word she says. Whether it's the unfamiliar territory of the house, her refusal to engage him since they left the store, or something else, that look says he is hearing her right now. Before he can argue she turns back to the counter. He won't take the car and leave. He'll stick it out, if only to spite her. She hears him shuffle out of the kitchen. Moments later the muted sound of the TV wafts in from the living room.

She lets out another deep breath and turns her attention to baking. She pulls out the cookware and begins unpacking the groceries. By the time she finishes the tension is gone, replaced by a feeling of serenity she has only ever felt in this kitchen.

For the next two hours she measures, heats, stirs, bakes and frosts. Sweet smells fill the air, driving away all traces of mustiness. The combined heat of the stovetop and oven brings a pleasant flush to her cheeks. Her mother's presence fills the kitchen, wrapping around her like a well-loved blanket, guiding her movements.

After the first batch sufficiently cools and are decorated, she puts half a dozen on a plate and sits down at the kitchen table. She leans in, closes her eyes and listens. For a moment she hears nothing and then: *Lub-dub. Lub-dub.* A surge of relief floods through her. Her mother has guided her to the magic once again. She picks up a vampire bat cookie, the beady red eyes betraying no hint of knowledge that she's responsible for the tiny pulsating heart lying somewhere in the tangle of sugar, flour, butter and eggs.

The doorbell rings, shattering her reverie.

"Kara, trick-or-treaters are here!"

"Can you get them? I'm busy!" Really, she has to ask? He's right around the corner from the door!

She hears the muffled thump of his feet. What she can't hear is the swearing she is certain he is doing under his breath. The sound of the door opening informs her that at least he's passing out candy. Kids shouldn't be denied treats on Halloween just because the house is occupied by an asshole. Maybe they'll think acting like a monster is part of his costume. She smirks at the thought, but anger has settled in her chest. Just a little patience, she reminds herself. She sets the cookie back on the plate and returns to baking.

Soon the doorbell is ringing every ten minutes or more. He answers a few more times before informing her that he'd like to see how the movie he's watching turns out. It's bullshit and she knows it but once more chooses not to argue, reminding herself that this is how she'd be doing it if Ryan wasn't here anyway. For the next hour and a half, she runs a steady loop between the kitchen and the front door as the trick-or-treater volume crests and then gradually dies down. She ends up with far more than Kelly had last year, three dozen at least.

At last, the final batch of cookies decorated, she leans against the kitchen counter and checks her phone. It's past eight, the trick-or-treaters and her baking are done. She's earned her treat.

In the cabinet above the fridge she finds the bottle of cognac she bought the Halloween before last. She fills a wine glass quarter full and takes two pleasantly burning sips before setting it on the counter and retrieving her purse. Rifling through the tubes of makeup, pens and other odds and sods, she finds what she's looking for at the bottom. She returns the purse to the counter before stepping into the living room where Ryan sits, eyes glued to the TV. He doesn't turn as she walks up behind the couch.

"Are you done yet? I'm not planning on spending the night here."

"Almost done," she says cheerfully, leaning over his shoulder and with both hands ramming the syringe of gasoline into his heart. Quickly she depresses the plunger and pulls away. Ryan lets out a single weak scream and reaches for the syringe, but his hand freezes halfway up and he slumps over. She watches as his body spasms and convulses before turning still. A small part of her is disappointed that a half-assed scream is all she gets. She was hoping for at least a window-rattler.

She goes to work.

The body is stripped and positioned lengthwise on the couch, arms at the side. White frosting is smeared across his face (she regrets the sloppiness but it's the best she can do) and two bags of powdered sugar dusted across the rest of his body. She carefully lays candy corns on his abdomen in the shape of three phases of the moon: quarter, half and full. Removing the syringe, she places over his heart three freshly baked cookies: a black cat with lime green eyes, a sparkling pumpkin, and a simple white ghost. She leans in. *Lub-dub. Lub-dub.*

"Happy Halloween, Mom."

Though she will not be here to witness, she is certain her mother will enjoy her treat. It's a step up from the stray dogs and cats they'd been leaving up until now and she appreciates not having to kill an animal this year. She smiles at the one-upmanship over her sister. Kelly has a whole year to dwell on it and figure out how to top the offering next Halloween.

She checks her phone for the third and last time. There's just enough time to finish her drink, pack up the cookies and clean the kitchen. Then it will be off to her sister's, dozens of tiny heartbeats filling her ears.

THE UNINVITED

KELLI A. WILKINS

JIMMY SWATTED A LOW-HANGING rubber bat out of his face as he bit into his third chocolate cupcake. He'd been at the party for over an hour and nobody had talked to him yet. He watched the other costumed kids across the room. They were laughing and joking with each other, ignoring him.

He hated starting over at new schools, and this was the third school in two years. The kids at the other elementary schools had picked on him all the time, too. They called him names like Fatso and Gimp-boy. After a month of half-hearted attempts, he'd abandoned the idea of making friends inside the brick walls of Addams Elementary. All the kids in this town were stuck up and mean. They made fun of his limp and laughed at him when he couldn't keep up in gym class.

Jimmy looked around the small basement and fingered the orange paper tablecloth decorated with white ghosts and black cats. Jennifer's mom had done a good job with the decorations.

THE UNINVITED

Black balloons and streamers covered the ceiling. Bats, skeletons, and owls danced on strings overhead. An inflatable Frankenstein's monster stood in one corner. Paper Jack O'Lanterns, ghosts, and devils swirled everywhere. Mrs. Wilbur had set out trays of pumpkin-shaped cookies, cupcakes, caramel apples, and fresh hot apple cider. A tape of haunted house sounds—screams, howling wolves, wind, and demonic laughter—blared from the stereo. The only illumination in the cellar came from strands of orange party lights and lit candles.

If it wasn't for his homeroom teacher, Mrs. MacGregor, he wouldn't even be here. Two weeks ago, Mrs. MacGregor had allowed Jennifer to pass out the party invitations in class. He'd waited anxiously for his as Jennifer pranced across the room. "Here's yours, Kathy. One for you, Michael."

All of a sudden, she had finished and sat down without coming near his desk. He'd glanced around the classroom and saw all the other kids chatting excitedly as they opened their orange envelopes. Well, *almost* all the other kids. Becky was staring down at her barren desk. Her bottom lip jutted out and she looked like she wanted to cry. Everyone had been invited to the party except them. They were the outcasts, the uninvited, the misfits.

He'd shrugged off the slight. He had his built-in excuse ready. He was the new kid in school and didn't have any friends. But Becky, nobody liked Becky.

Becky was short, rail thin, and pale with stringy, ink-black hair. A large, blood-red, leaf-shaped birthmark covered her right cheek. She wore the same faded blue flowered dress and tan shoes every day. The kids said she stank like cat piss and teased her whenever the teachers weren't around. She hardly ever spoke, but they always ate lunch together. Mostly because nobody else would sit with them, the freaks.

The day after the Halloween party invitations had been passed out, Jennifer had marched over to his desk.

"Here!" She threw two, half-crumpled orange envelopes at him. "Mrs. MacGregor called my mother and said it was unfair of me to invite everyone but you two mutants," she sneered. "Give one to your girlfriend, Beastly Becky. Come if you dare."

Jimmy took a cookie off a paper plate and sighed. Mrs. MacGregor hadn't done him any favors. The last place he wanted to be was at this stupid party. His mother had found the invitation in his school bag and insisted he try to make friends with the other kids. No matter how hard he begged, she wouldn't let him stay home and watch horror movies or go out trick or treating on his own.

She had left him standing on Jennifer's porch with the devilish Jack O'Lanterns, scarecrows, and skeletons whirling in the wind.

"I hope there won't be any trouble tonight," Mom had said.

He just nodded. Deep down, he hoped so, too.

Jimmy grabbed a handful of candy corn—it was the good kind with the chocolate bottoms—and stuffed it into the front pocket of his farmer costume. He wore blue overalls, a red and white plaid shirt, a straw hat, and sneakers. His second-rate outfit made him feel even more out of place, but it was the fastest, easiest, and cheapest costume his mother could find.

He'd read somewhere that Halloween was the one night of the year you could be whatever you dreamed. That was stupid. He didn't want to be a farmer. He'd wanted to come dressed as the Masked Executioner and scare everybody, but Mom had protested.

All the other kids had great costumes. Steve came as a pirate and had a talking mechanical parrot perched on one shoulder. Mike was dressed up like a vampire and his teeth squirted fake blood. Red-haired Bobby wore a devil outfit, and Phil came as a glow-in-the-dark skeleton. The girls wore fancy dresses. Jennifer became the perfect princess with her long, curly blonde hair, big blue eyes, a pink ruffled dress, and a gold glitter crown.

Jimmy glanced up from the dish of candy corn and saw Becky standing alone in the corner. When had she come downstairs? The windowless cellar only had one door. Becky wore a white ballerina outfit, tiny pink slippers, and white tights. She looked even paler than normal. He started to walk over to say hello, but Jennifer spotted Becky first.

"Oh, look who came after all? Beastly Becky." The Princess laughed and pointed. Everyone in the basement turned and stared at the thin girl in the ballerina costume. "You shouldn't have come. You didn't really think we wanted you here, did you? You should be out trick-or-treating and begging for candy like the rest of the poor kids. You don't deserve to be at *my* party!" Jennifer spat.

Becky bowed her head.

Jimmy's blood boiled and he clenched his fists. Jennifer had no right to say those things. He bit back his fury and fought the urge to scream, to tear down the decorations and hurt them, hurt them all. He hated them, all of them. They were just like the kids at all of his other schools. Those kids had been mean to him and they had gotten what they deserved. Someone should teach these brats a lesson.

He closed his eyes and counted to ten. The counselor had told him to do that whenever he felt like hurting people. Sometimes it worked, but other times... After a minute, he calmed down a little and limped over to Becky. His uneven gait and huge size drew some of the attention away from her. He pretended to ignore everyone's cold stares. Now that Becky was here at least he had someone to talk to.

"Hey, Becky. I didn't think you'd come. I'm only here 'cause my mom had to work at the diner tonight. Don't listen to Jennifer and her snotty friends. They're mean."

Becky stared straight ahead. Her gaze was fixated on Jennifer and her friends giggling in the corner.

Jimmy studied Becky's pale face. Something about her seemed creepy. It was hard to see clearly with nothing but orange lights and lit candles in the basement. Shadows leapt out from the corners, distorting reality.

A few minutes later, Jennifer started handing out pumpkins to everyone. The largest and best-looking ones went to her closest friends. Jennifer dumped two pathetic gourds on the table in front of Becky.

"Here! Unwanted freak pumpkins for unwanted freak guests."

Jimmy stared at his half-green, lopsided pumpkin, then glanced at Becky's. Hers looked even worse. The tiny gourd was squishy and caved in on the bottom. A large, dark bruise marred one side. His heart went out to her. This was no way to spend Halloween night.

"Wanna trade?"

Becky looked at him with sad, brown eyes and shook her head.

"Okay, then." He started to carve his pumpkin with a flimsy plastic knife. It bent as he tried to shove it through the leathery skin. The unripe gourd was impossible to carve. He gave up and sat next to Becky. She was looking in Jennifer's direction again.

"I should've stayed home." Jimmy reached into his pocket and pulled out a piece of caramel candy. "Channel 45 is showing monster movies all night."

All of a sudden, a wet, slimy blob landed on the side of his face.

"What the hell?" He wiped cold, sticky pumpkin meat off his cheek and saw wads of stringy pumpkin guts in Becky's hair. "Hey! Cut it out!" he cried out into the shadowy room filled with monsters.

"Shut up, you dumb, fat slob," Jennifer shouted.

"What's the matter? Afraid your girlfriend won't like you?" the pirate yelled.

The Devil pelted Jimmy in the eye with a glob of pumpkin seeds. A second later, everyone joined in and threw handfuls of pumpkin innards at them.

"Stop it! Stop it or else you'll all be sorry!" he screamed.

The howling wind from the sound-effect tape drowned out his words. Jimmy's temper flared, and he marched across the basement and punched the pirate in the face. The pirate yelped and crumpled to the floor.

A vampire elbowed Jimmy in the stomach. Jimmy fell back against the table and knocked the food, candles, and Jennifer's Jack O'Lantern to the floor. The pumpkin smashed to bits. Its carved mouth crookedly grinned up at him. Jimmy slipped on the wet pumpkin mess and landed hard on one knee. He felt his pants split up the back.

Jennifer threw a cup of cider in Becky's face. "I hate you. I wish you were dead. You and your fat friend ruined my party! You're a horrible, ugly thing. Go home!"

Jennifer shoved Becky hard. Her soft ballerina slippers slid on the pumpkin innards and she stumbled backward. Jimmy watched the side of Becky's head crack against the edge of the table. He heard a heavy thud as she crumpled to the floor.

Demonic laugher from the haunted house tape filled the dark basement.

Jimmy spotted a small flame lapping at the paper tablecloth near the cupcakes. A black votive candle had rolled behind the dish of candy corn. He was about to put the candle out when Becky struggled to her feet and started walking toward Jennifer. In the feeble light it looked like she was crying blood.

Becky reached out a thin, white hand and grabbed Jennifer's wrist. The Princess struggled and screamed.

"Get her off me! One of you jerks get her off me!"

Becky placed her hand on Jennifer's right cheek. Jennifer shrieked and thrashed. Her crown toppled to the floor.

"Make her let me go! She's cold. So cold..."

As Becky pulled her hand off Jennifer's face, Jimmy saw bits of meat and skin stuck to Becky's hand. The disfiguring purple-blue mark Becky left on Jennifer was impossible to miss, even in the dim light.

"You will remember me forever," Becky stated.

Jimmy hobbled toward the stairs as fast as he could. He had to get out of here, now. Something was wrong with Becky. She looked dead. He glanced back over his shoulder and saw Becky fading into the shadows. None of the other kids were moving to help Jennifer.

Jimmy flung the cellar door open and shuffled into the kitchen.

"Mrs. Wilbur, there's a—"

Jennifer's mom sat at the kitchen table. Her makeup was smeared, and her nose was red from crying. Jimmy closed and locked the cellar door behind him. He smirked. That would teach them. He pulled a red bandanna from his back pocket and wiped off the doorknob.

"Is something wrong?" he asked in his sweetest voice.

"My husband just called from the police station. He had an accident a little while ago." Mrs. Wilbur wiped her eyes with a tissue. "There's going to be a scandal, an investigation, maybe even a trial. We'll be ruined! I have to get to the police station..."

Jimmy cocked his head toward the basement door. He heard faint screaming coming from downstairs, and he knew it wasn't from the sound-effect tape. It was the voices of the terrified monsters trapped in the cellar. Soon, they would pound on the door and beg to be set free. But nobody would ever hear them until it was too late.

Mrs. Wilbur continued rambling as she gathered her purse and coat. "He had a few drinks with a client and was coming home for Jennifer's party. He hit and killed a girl walking along the road in a ballerina costume."

LAST TREAT OF THE NIGHT

CULLEN MONK

"HERE YOU GO, little princess, Captain America," Mrs. Caplan said, dropping her treats into the bags. "My last ones."

Peter grinned seeing the full-size Snickers disappear into his Halloween bag. Another full-size candy bar. What a haul!

"Thank you," Peter said in unison with his sister, Katie.

"Happy Halloween, kids," Mrs. Caplan said as she closed the door.

Peter and Katie sprinted away from their neighbor's house. Peter figured they could dump their candy at home and keep going down the street. He was going to be able to tell everyone at school he got the biggest load.

Dad waited for them on the sidewalk. He had a weary smile on his face. "Anything good?"

"Yeah, big Snickers," Katie said.

Dad's smile turned into an annoyed frown. "There seem to be a lot more full-size candy bars this year."

"Yeah, it's great!" Peter put his bag down and flexed his fingers.

"Oh, what's the matter, Captain America?" Dad asked. "I thought you were tough, yet here you are, defeated by a bag of candy?"

"It's heavy." Peter lifted the plastic Captain America mask off his face and wiped sweat from his eyebrows. "Can we dump this off at home and keep going?"

Dad looked at his phone. "Nah, we need to head on home. It's late."

"Please?" Katie said in that high-pitched squeal of hers.
"Come on, Dad, just a little more?" Peter asked.

Dad shook his head. "Nope, we gotta get home. Come on."

Katie's shoulders slumped. "Aww."

Peter smirked at how silly she looked. What kind of princess went moping around like that? A six-year-old princess, that's who. Still, she didn't complain any further. Neither did Peter. His feet ached, and he tried and failed to suppress a yawn. It'd be good to go home and sit down. Maybe they could talk Mom and Dad into letting them stay up and watch a movie while they sorted through their candy.

The sidewalks were emptying fast. Everyone seemed in a hurry to go home. And just like that, trick-or-treating was over. Peter never understood the rush to go home on Halloween. Didn't other kids in other towns stay out all night? The little kids should be sent home, sure, but the big kids? Come on, that was stupid. Why couldn't the big kids—and Peter counted himself among the big kids—stay out later?

They arrived home after a short walk from Mrs. Caplan's house. Three jack-o-lanterns greeted them on the porch. Two of them had dark eyes and mouths, but the third still had the flickering glow from a candle too stubborn to blow out. Peter smiled. At least something from Halloween remained alive, at least for a little while. As he passed by, Peter caught the faint whiff of baked pumpkin. Mom and Dad put real candles in the pumpkins, and that smell was one of Peter's favorites.

Inside, Peter glanced in the orange plastic bowl, hoping for more candy, but it was empty. Mom had been busy. Peter told Mom and Dad they needed to have more candy ready, and no, it wasn't just so he could raid the leftovers. Word got around fast if a particular house ran out of candy early. And when that happened, those people had better watch out! Of course, he never actually heard of anything bad happening to anyone who ran out of candy, but still....

Peter and Katie ran into the living room and promptly dumped out their candy on the table. Pepper, their black and gray cat, hopped up on the table with a meow. He sniffed at the scattered candy. Peter gently pushed him back. Even if cats were allowed to eat chocolate, Peter wasn't about to share his hard-earned stash with Pepper.

Peter made sure to keep his stash from mixing in with Katie's. His mouth watered as he took in the grand sight before him. Six, no, seven full-size candy bars lay buried among the dozens of fun-sized bars and bags of other candies. Fun-sized—they really should swap the names between fun-sized and full-sized.

"We're home," Dad called as he walked past the stairs. "Sarah?"

A moment later, Mom came downstairs. She already had her pajamas on. "How'd it go?"

Dad came back from the kitchen with a beer. "I think we set a record for houses visited. Looks like you had a lot of visitors yourself."

"Yeah, pretty steady and—hey, no candy, you guys. It's late." Mom rushed over and pulled a fun-sized peanut butter cup out of Katie's hands.

"Aww, come on, Mom," Peter said. "It's not that late."

"Please?" Katie chimed in.

"It *is* late and you both need to go to bed."

"But it's Friday night. Can't we stay up and watch a movie?"

"Maybe tomorrow. Now, off to bed."

Peter dropped his candy back on the coffee table and frowned at Dad. Katie did the same. Dad glanced at them and sighed.

"We don't have school tomorrow, couldn't we—"

Mom shook her head. "No." She lowered her voice, but Peter could still hear her. "I want them in bed before the final one arrives."

The last one... they'd said something about a final trick-or-treater last year too. Why were they so concerned about a latecomer? There wasn't any candy left anyway. If they turned the porch lights off, people would know not to ring the doorbell.

Dad grimaced. "I guess you're right. Okay, put the kids in bed, and I'll prepare the ... you know."

Mom turned and smiled at Peter and Katie. "Okay, you two, upstairs. Out of those costumes and into your jammies. Want me to read a Halloween story?"

"Yeah," Katie said through a yawn.

Peter narrowed his eyes at Katie. Her resistance to bedtime was pathetic. Maybe he could convince Mom and Dad to let him stay up while Katie listened to some stupid story. But before he could say anything, Dad had already vanished back into the kitchen while Mom followed Katie upstairs.

It was over.

Yeah, they would probably watch a movie tomorrow, but it wouldn't be the same. Halloween had a sort of magic to it. So do other holidays. Watching fireworks on June 4th wasn't the same as on July 4th. Same with Christmas and birthdays. Watching a scary movie the day after Halloween wasn't the same.

With heavy steps, Peter climbed the stairs and went to his room. He slid out of his Captain America costume and put on his pajamas. He put his costume on the chair and sighed. So long, Halloween.

Peter went to Katie's room where Katie was already tucked in and half-asleep. Mom sat on the floor next to her bed with a book in her lap. Peter sat down next to Mom. The book, he saw, was *Five Little Pumpkins*. It was more Katie's speed. He'd long outgrown something so juvenile, but at least it fit for Halloween. As Mom opened the *Five Little Pumpkins*, Dad came in.

"Hey, uh ... where's the ... last treat?"

Mom stared at him. "Didn't you get it?"

Dad's eyes widened and his jaw clamped together. He spoke through gritted teeth. "I told you I couldn't. I said *you* had better pick it up on your way home from work."

"You never—I didn't—whatever." Mom dropped the book and pulled herself up. "Do you want to go out or shall I go?"

Dad huffed. "No, I'll go." And he stormed off.

"Please hurry."

"Yep," Dad said from the stairs.

"Mom?" Katie asked, her eyes closed. "Where's Dad going?"

"Oh, he's going to the store for something."

Peter heard the front door open downstairs. A few minutes later, Dad's car started and he pulled away. Peter's brow furrowed. Normally, the familiar sound of Dad's car wasn't so loud. Unless....

"Okay, let's see," Mom said, picking up a book. "Five Little—"

"Mom?" Peter said. "Did Dad close the door?"

"I'm sure he did. Five Little Pumpkins."

"I don't think he did."

Mom grimaced. "It'll be fine."

"But Pepper could escape."

Mom huffed. "Fine, I'll go check." She put the book down and stomped out of the room A few moments later, her muffled voice traveled up the stairs. "Pepper? Pepper, where are you?"

Peter jumped up and ran downstairs. The front door stood wide open. Mom climbed over the back of the couch to see if Pepper was hiding back there. Peter went to the door and stared out into the night. The lone lit pumpkin's face still flickered orange. The sidewalks were completely empty. Pepper wasn't anywhere he could see.

"Peter," Mom said coming up next to him. "I think Pepper's outside somewhere. I tried treats, he didn't come."

"Mom, we gotta find him."

"Don't worry. He couldn't have gone far." Mom grabbed the second set of keys off the table and went to the door. "Peter, I'll go find Pepper. I'm locking the door behind me. You go up and wait with Katie."

"I want to help."

"You can help by staying here with your sister. Dad will be back in no time. We'll find Pepper, I promise."

Peter watched as Mom went outside and closed the door behind her. The door locked with a metallic thud. He considered going out there as well. Two people looking for Pepper had a better chance of finding him than one, right? But, what about Katie? She'd been asleep, sure, but what if she woke up and couldn't find anyone? No, he should stay inside.

He went to the window and looked out. He caught a glimpse of Mom before she melted away into the darkness. Any moment, she'd return with Pepper in her arms. For what must have been five minutes, Peter stood waiting, but Mom never returned. Pepper must have gone up into a tree or hidden where Mom couldn't see him. The longer Pepper remained missing, the more likely he'd get hit by a car or eaten by a dog.

Why did Dad have to be so clueless? He knew he couldn't leave the door open. If anything happened to Pepper…

Peter took a deep breath. Mom would find Pepper. It'd be okay. He turned to go back upstairs and froze, his eyes drawn to the pile of candy on the table. Dad was gone. Mom was gone. Nobody would know if he had a candy bar… or three. Peter went over and picked through the pile. He glanced at Katie's pile and considered moving some of her pile into his, but he couldn't do that to her. She might be annoying sometimes, but she was still his sister.

There were a lot of KitKats, his favorite. He'd have one of those to begin with. Peter tore off the wrapper and popped the bite-size candy bar in his mouth, delighting in the chocolate crunch. What next? Oh, how about a—

Someone knocked at the front door. A second later, a deep voice grumbled from outside. "Trick. Or. Treat."

Peter froze. Mom had left the porch light on to find Pepper, but still, trick-or-treating had ended for the night. Whoever it was would go away when no one answered the door. Peter remained silent and waited. He flinched when the person knocked on the door again.

"Trick. Or. Treat."

Peter swallowed. Maybe Dad was playing a prank. But that voice sure didn't sound like Dad. The voice had a deep rumble to it, and it sounded... well, old. Old, like grandpa when grandpa got grumpy.

Peter couldn't help but picture an old man with a walker on the other side of the door. Only, instead of a kindly grandfather, this guy was mean. The old man pounded again, shaking the door in its frame. What old man could hit a door such force?

"Trick. Or. Treat."

Peter backed further into the living room. He was safe, he knew he was safe—the door was locked—but he still felt the cold chill of fear gripping him. The doorknob rattled but remained locked. With a loud grunt, the man again knocked.

"Trick. Or. Treat."

Peter stared at the door, hoping Mom would come back and send the old man away. If only Dad hadn't left the door open, allowing Pepper to run away. If only Mom had gotten... whatever it was supposed to buy from the store for the... final one... final trick-or-treater?

"Bah!" The old man gave the door a single slam. Heavy footsteps thudded from the porch as the old man went down the steps. He left, thank God.

Peter exhaled and felt his shoulders relax. He smiled—scared over nothing. But, what was Halloween without a good scare? He froze as he heard a noise outside the living room window. Something brushed up against the window. A few seconds later there came a familiar snapping sound. Peter knew the noise—the hedges, or rather, the snapping of twigs from the hedges as someone walked through them. Where was the old man going?

"Trick. Or. Treat," the old man said from outside the window as he passed. He passed by the second window and again muttered, "Trick. Or. Treat."

Peter's stared at the wall, where on the other side the man continued. He rounded the corner of the house outside. The next door neighbor's motion-activated floodlight flicked on. It didn't deter the old man one bit. When he emerged in front of the side window, Peter caught a glimpse of his shadow projected against the curtain and it didn't look at all like an old man. The creature's head had an odd shape to it, like an egg tilted one way, and the lower jaw jutted out in front of the rest of the face. And he hunched over and had spindly arms and long fingers.

"Trick. Or. Treat."

Peter shook his head. It had to be a costume—a really good costume. Oh, where were Mom and Dad? Peter stepped back towards the stairs. His foot knocked his Captain America shield and it went skittering across the hardwood floor. Peter froze. So too did the creature outside the window. The way he moved his head from side to side it seemed he was trying to peek through the narrow gap in the curtains.

Mom, come home. Please come home!

The thing snarled and continued his progress along the side of the house. Peter glanced at the shield. If he had really been Captain America, he would have gone out there and fought off the creature.

Perhaps it was time for him to be brave. It was up to him to protect their home, to protect Katie, and even to save Mom and Dad from being attacked by that thing when they returned. He had to be brave.

"Trick. Or. Treat," the thing said from further away. The creature edged towards the back of the house now.

Peter took a deep breath. Yeah, time to be brave. Time to stop being a scared little kid. He could—no, he *would* defend the house against that creature. Peter crept over to the shield and picked it up. Yeah it was plastic, but it would still hurt if he threw it at someone... or some-*thing.*

Out back, the thing would have to climb up the steps onto the back porch. But with all the windows and doors locked, it couldn't get in. Peter would make sure it stayed out back. That way, Mom and Dad could get home safe. Then, the three of them could confront the thing. Peter entered the kitchen and swallowed. Heavy feet clomped on the wooden porch steps.

"Trick. Or. Treat."

Peter gripped his shield. He imagined all the times where Captain America fought and defeated bigger and stronger enemies. If Captain America could do it, so could he.

"Trick. Or. Treat." The creature knocked on the porch door.

"Go away," Peter said. He instantly regretted speaking. His words came out shaky and high-pitched—not exactly the commanding tone of a superhero.

"Trick. Or. Treat." The thing banged on the door.

Peter took a step back.

The creature shook the door knob ... and the door clicked open. Coldness gripped Peter. He'd gone out back after school to play in the treehouse. Mom told him to lock the door, but he'd obviously forgotten. The door groaned as it opened. Peter saw a gnarled gray finger creep around the edge of the door. Then another finger appeared. That was all Peter had any wish to see. He turned and fled from the kitchen.

"Trick. Or. Treat," the creature bellowed into the house.

Peter took the stairs two at a time. He entered Katie's room and slammed the door behind him. Katie lifted her head from the pillow and blinked. Peter turned the lock on the doorknob and stepped away.

"Pete?" Katie said. "What's going on?"

He ignored her. He listened as muffled thumps grew louder. The thing was coming up the steps. Peter's heart pounded. He expected to see the door broken down any second. And then? He couldn't even think of what to do.

"Trick. Or. Treat," the thing said with a firm knock on the door.

Katie whimpered.

Peter glanced at her and realized how scared she must be— more scared than him. He jumped on the bed and pulled her close to him. The creature banged on the door.

"What is it?" Katie cried.

"I don't know," Peter whispered.

"Trick. Or. Treat."

Pictures on the wall rattled with a new round of banging from outside. Katie trembled in Peter's arms. He had to do something. Maybe... maybe they could climb out the window. If he held on to Katie and lowered her down, she could jump into the bushes below. Then he'd... he'd have to take his chances and hope he could land soft enough to not break a leg.

"Trick. Or. Treat." The thing snarled. The pounding on the door louder still.

"Go away," Katie shouted.

"Leave us alone," Peter said as he hugged Katie even tighter.

"Trick. Or. Treat. Trick. Or. Treat. Trick... or..."

Peter heard another voice.

"Hey! Hey, leave them alone," Dad shouted up the stairs.

"Trick. Or. Treat."

"I have it right here," Dad said.

The thing grunted. Heavy footfalls trailed away, followed by the thing's old man voice, saying, "Late. Don't. Like. Waiting. Next year. Don't. Be late."

Peter listened as the creature's heavy feet thumped away from the door and down the stairs. It let out a short shriek.

"Yeah, here's the treat," Dad said. "Now, go on."

"Be. Ready. Next year."

"We will."

A few minutes passed. Someone knocked on the door—a much softer knock. "Kids? It's Dad. Are you okay?"

Peter slowly released Katie and saw tears on her cheeks. He nodded to her and went to the door. He turned the lock and opened the door to see Dad waiting. Peter ran forward. Dad crouched down and caught him in a hug. Katie joined them, sobbing.

"Oh, Pete, Katie, it's okay now. It's okay."

Peter spoke into Dad's shoulder. "W-what was that?"

"Oh... nothing, Peter. Just another trick-or-treater. The final one of the night."

"Guys?" Mom called from downstairs.

"Up here," Dad said.

Mom ran up the steps. "I saw... did you... give out the treat?"

Dad sighed. "Yeah, I got the last one in the store. He was in the house though."

"Oh, geez."

Peter turned his head and looked at her. Her hair was all messed up, but she held Pepper in her arms.

"Looks like Halloween wasn't quite finished with you guys, huh?" Mom said, petting Pepper.

"Who was that?" Katie asked.

Mom grimaced. "Well, you know how Christmas has Santa? Halloween has something similar... just not as nice."

Peter blinked. He knew how Santa worked—how Santa *really* worked. At least, he thought he knew how Santa worked. After this, though, he wasn't sure.

"But who is he?" Peter asked.

Mom cocked her head. "Maybe next year, I'll let you give him the last treat of the night."

QUEEN OF HALLOWEEN

TIM MENDEES

SUZIE FLINCHED AND BALLED her fists as piercing wolf-whistles and lewd comments from the procession of teenage boys in cheap plastic masks grated on her already mangled patience. "I should have never let you talk me into this, Jane. I was quite happy having a quiet night in with some old Hammer Horror films." She sighed and pulled down the ridiculously short hem of the tacky blue nylon princess outfit as far as it would allow. As she had only finally agreed to go to Marsha Edwards' Halloween party earlier in the day, the only costumes she could find that fit within her meagre student budget were a range of shoddily-made Disney tie-ins. Suzie sighed, it could have been worse she supposed, it was either what she was wearing or Princess Leia's gold bikini.

"For God's sake, Suze." Jane laughed. "Just because you're a goth, it doesn't mean that you have to be so bloody miserable all the time."

"Hey, I'm not miserable… I just don't like dressing like some dumb blonde from a kid's film." She fussed with the irritating blonde wig. She had no idea what it had been made out of but was pretty certain it had never been near a natural fibre. "I don't know why you wouldn't just let me vamp it up?"

"Because that's how you always dress. You've got to put in the effort on Halloween… like me." Jane grinned and did a twirl.

Suzie rolled her eyes. Jane looked stunning as a vampire. As well she should, she was wearing Suzie's clothes. "You cheated… You just decided to be me for a night. How's the corset feel?" Suzie's lips twitched into a sadistic grin. "Can you breathe okay?"

"Yeah, it feels fine."

"Damn… I'll have to pull it tighter later. If I'm suffering, then you must suffer as well… it's the rules." Suzie was indeed suffering. Aside from feeling like a prize plum in her glitzy outfit, it was freezing cold and raining horizontally. November in Cornwall wasn't the ideal place for wearing skimpy outfits.

Marsha Edwards lived on the outskirts of town in a large house on the road to High Bend. The bus ran infrequently at best, so they were forced to slog from one side of the town to the other. Jane was in high spirits, as always; Suzie, however, was cold, wet and getting more cheesed off by the second.

As they passed one of the only shops that was still open, a grimy off-license that sold tins of dented vegetables and trashy Euro-porn magazines, a trio of half-cut lads came shambling out of the door clutching cans of super-strength lager. "Hey, princess," one of them slurred. "Come 'ere, I'll thaw out yer *frozen* bits!" This was followed by raucous laughter from his knuckle-dragging compatriots.

Suzie's eyes flashed and her fists clenched. Jane quickly put her hand on her friend's wrist. "Easy... We don't want you getting locked up, do we?"

At that moment, a night in the cells would probably have been preferable... and so incredibly worth it. Suzie flashed the yobs one of her patented 'I'll rip your nuts off' smiles and looked at the baskets of cheap Halloween tat outside the shop. "Right, that's it..." Suzie tore the awful blonde wig off her head and stuffed it in a dustbin.

"Hey, what're you doing?" Jane put her hands on her hips. She knew her friend was temperamental, but this took the cake.

"Elsa is dead..." Suzie spat as she gathered up some assorted junk and stormed in the shop.

Five minutes later, she appeared with a carrier bag in one hand and a large bottle of cheap vodka in the other. She motioned Jane over to a neighbouring adult shop whose blacked-out windows made a good mirror. "Hold this," she muttered as she thrust the bag into her friend's hand then proceeded to fish an eyeliner pencil out of her bag.

Jane watched in amusement as in a matter of minutes, Suzie had gone from squeaky-clean cartoon princess to Halloween queen from hell. Her straight black hair was immediately immaculate and her eyes two pools of inky black. Using the cheap make-up from the zombie kits she gave herself a livid gash across the throat and a cadaverous tint to her skin. Next, she handed Jane two tubes of fake blood that she had just torn open with her teeth.

"What the hell do you want me to do with these?" Jane asked in bemusement.

"Spray me with them, of course..." She took a plastic axe off its cardboard backing and stuffed the handle through the sparkly belt of her costume. "I'm thinking more Lizzie Borden, less princess ice-lolly."

"Okay, whatever you say." Jane chortled and let her have it with both tubes. The fake blood splattered Suzie from head to toe.

Several passers-by looked at them like they had just dropped off the moon. Suzie looked at herself in the shop window and grinned... much better.

Suzie put the remaining tat in the bin and took a long pull on the vodka. "Right... Let's party!"

* * *

Miss Edwards' party proved to be just as tragic as Suzie had feared. While she and Jane were the closest of friends, they ran in completely different social circles. Jane was of the trendy new-folk brigade and usually ran with the hipster crowd, while Suzie skulked in smoke-filled basement clubs with the goths and rivet-heads; not that there was many of them in Betyls Cove. Most of the attendees were the types of people that Suzie considered vacuous and superficial, the host included. Most of the boys were sporty types that considered her a weirdo and the girls, well... they would have been right at home in the princess outfit, let's put it that way. The house, on the other hand, was spectacular...

Marsha lived in a sprawling Victorian manor that looked like it had been ripped straight out of a survival horror game. It sat away from the road, nestled in a patch of dark woodland. Though it was only around half a mile from town, it seemed like it was in a different direction. Suzie had found herself gazing in awe at the gabled windows and ivy-choked facade as they crunched down the twisting driveway passing the vodka between them. Her spirits had lifted somewhat, due in no small part to the booze, but soon got slapped back down when the door opened.

"Hi, girls!" Marsha simpered with faux enthusiasm, her smile as sickly-sweet as the sugar-based blood that periodically dripped onto her lips. "You're just in time. I've got *spooky* cocktails on the go and a *scary* movie lined up... Oh, and games."

Suzie rolled her eyes.

Jane elbowed her in the ribs. "Sounds great! ... Love the costume!"

"Thanks..." Marsha was wearing a princess outfit similar in style to Suzie's but in yellow. It came complete with a plastic crown and sceptre. "I'm the queen of Halloween!" She beamed as she did a twirl. "Anyway, come on in." She moved to grant them entry then shouted to the assembled guests. "Hey guys, look who it is! ... Jane has come as a sexy vampire and... err... her *friend* looks like she has been in an accident." The crowd cheered drunkenly as Marsha trotted off towards the bathroom.

"You'll be in a fucking accident in a minute..." Suzie grumbled under her breath and took a step after her.

Jane grabbed her arm, again, then gave her one of her looks. "Please behave... She isn't that bad."

"Not that bad?" Suzie replied incredulously. "You wear my clothes and you're a *sexy vampire,* I wear them and I'm a freak! ... Queen of Halloween... bloody cheek. I'm the queen of Halloween every damn day of the week, you lot are just part-timers. Anyway, what's Halloween about *that* outfit? She looks like she belongs on the top of a fucking Christmas tree..."

Jane looked around uneasily. Suzie had a big mouth. Even when she was trying to be quiet she was like a foghorn. She needed to stop her ranting, and fast. Luckily, she spied a good distraction in the kitchen... people Suzie actually liked. "Hey, look. Pete and his droogs are in the kitchen."

Suzie looked, "Thank Gygax for that!" She took the bottle of vodka and hurried over while making a mental note to congratulate Jane later; not only did she reference *A Clockwork Orange* but she did it in an entirely apt way... kudos.

Paul was the leader of a small tightly-knit group of role players, of which Suzie was a proud member. Her heart lost some of its sharp pointy edges as she spotted that they were all working on a new *Dungeons and Dragons* campaign. Each one of them was wearing an identical blood-spattered cheap suit and a Donald

Trump mask complete with glittery red devil's horns and fangs... droogs indeed.

It didn't take them long to turn the kitchen into their own private party. Suzie commandeered the stereo and put on a *Depeche Mode* CD that Pete just *happened* to have in his rucksack. The booze flowed as they discussed hit-points, initiative rolls and slime children, things were definitely on the up. That is until Marsha Edwards made her presence felt.

"Okay, guys!" she called out in a shrill voice as she turned off the music.

Suzie bristled, she had turned it off, right in the middle of *Stripped...* who does that?

Marsha clapped her hands in the direction of Jane and her friend who was still giggling about something or other. "If you would all like to grab a fresh drink... It's Movie Time!" She grinned and waited for a round of applause. It eventually came but was far more half-arsed than she was hoping. Her right eyelid fluttered almost imperceptibly and her fingers twitched but the manic grin stayed firmly in place.

After a few minutes, everyone gathered in the spacious living room. It was tastefully decked out in keeping with the age of the property and had two large arched windows on the west wall that hung open to let the marijuana smoke out and the fresh air in. The trio of stoners on the sofa barely noticed as multiple bottoms fought for the remaining seating next to them. Jane sat cross-legged on the floor next to a bookcase and was superstitiously checking out the impressive collection of encyclopedias. Suzie hung back and leaned against the door-frame taking swigs from her vodka... she had no confidence in Marsha's taste in movies. It was probably going to be a crappy Hollywood remake of something that really didn't need to be remade. "Dear God, please don't let it be the bloody Nicholas Cage *Wicker Man*." She whispered as she crossed the fingers of her free hand behind her back.

The entirety of the north wall was taken up with a huge home cinema set-up complete with digital surround sound and all the bells and whistles. It put the two-screen dive next to the bingo hall in town to shame.

Marsha turned on the screen and turned off the lights that were already dimmed to little more than pin-pricks of illumination. She stepped front and centre and held up a DVD case emblazoned with a strange yellow squiggle. Suzie squinted to see what it was, but the design was so blurred that it seemed to move like a liquid, slipping and sliding away from her scrutiny.

"Right, guys," Marsha chirruped with excitement burning in her eyes. "This film is banned in Europe! My uncle had a copy hidden with the rest of his video nasties from the eighties. I... ahem... *borrowed* it when he was in the bathroom."

The room cheered as Marsha giggled like a naughty toddler.

"It's supposed to be really fucked up... It's French so there will probably be subtitles..." She turned around and pointed the remote control at the screen. "Okay, folks. Here's is the notorious *Le Roi En Jaune!*"

Nobody clapped or whooped with excitement... nobody had ever heard of it. Suzie's interest was piqued, she had a comprehensive knowledge of gore movies that the BBFC had taken exception to, so to get the chance to see one that had somehow slipped her net was an opportunity to good to miss. Maybe the party didn't suck too much, after all.

A cacophony of discordance burst from the speakers as the film flickered into life. The bass notes sat heavy in Suzie's gut and made her wish she had gone easier on the vodka. As the first grainy shot appeared on the screen, the soundtrack switched to a scraping fanfare that sounded as though it had been played on rusty medical equipment. It sawed and grated into the eardrums, gnawing on the edges of the brain like a hungry rodent as a dim shot of a crumbling colonnade choked by sickly-looking creepers faded into view.

The film was grainy to such an overwhelming degree that it seemed to ooze filth and infection. The camera flickered, its sepia images evidently captured on antique equipment. Film scratches and spots made the image jump and twitch unnervingly. Thick shadows covered the far end of the shot. As a poorly tuned viola screeched a twisted melody, a pale face materialised in the gloom. It hung as though disembodied and though completely passive, radiated with sadness.

As the camera cut away to a fleeting silhouette of an oddly twisted bird, Suzie took another swig and grumbled to herself. "Great, bloody *art house* crap." She couldn't see Marsha in the sickly yellow glow that radiated from the screen, but she felt her furtive eyes upon her like poisonous insects. Suzie grinned into the gloom and focused back on the screen.

A low skewed angle shot of a brutalist factory spewing its poison from two phallic chimney stacks rippled with a time-lapse shadow that distorted into strange angles and eventually eclipsed its bulk. Hunched figures stood in line outside what looked like a public toilet but in Greek-classical style as bodies were stretchered from the rear of the structure. A once-beautiful woman in a flowing gown removed a creepy owl mask to reveal a face ravaged by venereal disease. Her cracked lips parted as she gazed through the camera and into Suzie's soul.

"Êtes-vous prêt pour la vérité?" The woman's voice was like hot tar, sticky and toxic.

Marsha had been wrong, there were no subtitles. Suzie's French was rudimentary at best, she had dropped it in favour of German... lots of cool bands were from Germany. Her brow creased as she tried a rough translation. "Am I ready for the truth? ... What truth?" she whispered then bit her bottom lip. The film was strangely gripping. No, it was more than gripping, it was intoxicating.

A closer shot of the line outside the chamber revealed men and women in a variety of disturbing masks. Dull eyes that showed no spark of life stared out through the holes in visages of grinning satyrs and leering dog-faced ghouls. Each one watching the unmoving head in front... waiting.

Suzie gasped as a handsome man in the dress of a faux fifteenth-century courtier removed a striking harlequin mask to reveal chiseled features blemished with patches of rat-gnawed skin. He grimaced at the camera and gestured for someone to move closer. Suzie felt oddly compelled forwards, she took a cautious step before stopping herself and shaking her head. She looked around the room. Everyone she could see was entranced. Their rapt attention fixed on the disquieting cinematography.

The frame shook as another female glided across to the courier as though on a cushion of air. Her gown glimmered in lemon and golden hues as the flickering candlelight caught the material. She wore no mask and had a face like porcelain. She kissed her lover warmly then started to dance. Her movements were strange and spasmodic. Her limbs jerked like a badly wired marionette.

Unseen by the lovers, the yellow drape at the far right of the shot twitched as it was caught by the wind, revealing the rage-contorted face of the first woman. Clearly, she was a jilted lover of some kind. Though there was little dialogue, and what little there was happened to be in a foreign language, Suzie knew exactly what was going on. Everyone knew exactly what was going on.

Zooming in on the head of the queue, the next in line removed his mask, a feminine goat, to reveal a look of abject terror as he pushed open the door and walked inside. The screen flared with yellow brilliance like the light from a solar flare as an agonized scream joined the squealing strings and throbbing drums. The camera closed in on the door. Above it was a sign ringed with flashing carnival bulbs that blinked in various shades of grey in the monochromatic light. The sign read: *Chambre de Suicide.*

Another distorted avian shadow fluttered across a pile of discarded masks. The factory shook as the smoke billowed in frenzied gusts. The images were picking up pace now. The scenes cut with jarring regularity. It was as though the filmmaker was twisting a spring tighter and tighter, sooner or later it was going to burst and take somebody's eye out.

Filth-encrusted black feathers of some nightmare marriage between bird and snake filled the frame as it swooped down and plucked up one of the discarded masks in its fanged beak. The largest of the two chimneys started to split down the centre like over-ripe fruit. The first woman held a curved blade to her lips and licked a dark and viscous substance off the tip.

Suzie started to feel light-headed. Everything had faded into oblivion as the insidious film filled her mind. She couldn't help cheering on the diseased woman. After all, she was the rightful queen. "Dim Carcosa..." The words fell like liquid ice from her lips. They crystallised as they tumbled, eventually shattering on the laminate flooring of the manor.

The pilfered mask wept blood as the monstrous bird tore it to shreds and fed it to its young. The chicks snapped and scratched hungrily at the tasty titbits. The chimney started to crumble as hugely bloated maggots burst from the gaping wound in its side. The line moved quicker and quicker as an endless procession went to their self-inflicted doom. Hundreds of bodies fell past the camera and into a lightless lake without causing so much as a ripple.

"Êtes-Vous prêt pour la vérité?" the woman, who Suzie knew as Cassilda, asked again as she pouted seductively at the audience. She brushed the tip of the blade against one erect nipple and shuddered at the icy touch of the cold steel. Between her breasts, a wound in the shape of the symbol on the box oozed with vile yellow pus that sparkled like putrid diamonds.

Suzie wobbled as the flicker of the film rose in intensity until it was as frantic as a strobe-light. Each flicker was punctuated with subliminal images... The bird... The bodies... The masks... The knife.

The flicker reached such a pitch that it seemed to stabilise. The cuts were so fast that the naked eye was incapable of registering them. Every molecule in Suzie's body vibrated, her blood surged and her breath came in ragged gasps. The *truth* was close at hand.

A spectacular ballroom with people dancing like mannequins froze in position. The only movement was the gentle drift of the tattered robes that covered the regal figure standing upon a raised dais to the rear of the decadently decorated room. The bird screeched and the chimney toppled, then the happy couple took centre stage. The courtier and the porcelain-faced woman walked arm in arm towards the king. He motioned with his skeletal hand for the wedding to commence.

After a jarring sequence of underwater shots depicting slowly drifting faceless corpses, the courtier leaned in to kiss the bride. She stopped him with the wagging of one taloned finger and gestured that he should remove his mask. The courtier did as asked then fell to his knees as his bride did the same. Her immaculate face came away with a disgusting *slurp* to reveal Cassilda's cadaverous and blood-caked features.

The music reached a crescendo as the courtier cut his own throat with a serving knife from the buffet table that was piled high with rancid and maggot-infested food. The king faced the camera as Cassilda asked the audience: "Tu as vu le signe Jaune?"

"Yes, I have seen the yellow sign," Suzie whispered as the strange arabesque symbol flickered on the screen, suppurating like a festering wound.

Pressure started to build in Suzie's head. It was almost as though her brain was boiling in her skull. She stumbled and covered her ears as the camera zoomed in on the pallid mask under the king's crown. It shook and vibrated as he reached up a hand to remove it. There was nothing beneath except an ink-black liquid. Nausea rose in Suzie's throat as something started to wriggle and writhe in the black fluid.

Like a punch to the gut, Suzie doubled over in pain then ran from the room. She knocked empty beer-cans off the kitchen units as she clattered through the back door and into the garden. As she retched, her head throbbed and pulsed. With a crack like a bull-whip against tender young flesh, the yellow sign flashed before her eyes. Suzie vomited violently into a pot of petunia's then collapsed into a comatose heap...

* * *

Suzie wasn't out long. The gentle rustle of windswept autumn leaves tinkling past her head awoke her gently. It took a moment for her to figure out where she was... then she remembered the film. "What the fuck did I just watch?" she asked the tumbling leaves... they didn't reply.

Getting to her feet slowly, Suzie made her way back inside. She was more than done for the night. She was going to go inside, rinse her mouth out, grab Jane and call a taxi. For her, the party ended when Cassilda ginned triumphantly after claiming her victory. The sickness just put the exclamation point on her decision.

Crossing the threshold, the kitchen appeared to have become swathed in complete darkness. She flicked the light-switch but nothing happened. The room beyond was filled with voices that sounded strangely distorted under the strangled wail of some god-awful music that blared from the speakers. It sounded like one of the saccharine pop songs that clogged up the British charts but played both backwards and forwards simultaneously. It sounded exactly like a migraine felt and was the last thing that Suzie needed at that moment in time. Soon, her eyes had adjusted sufficiently for her to move forwards and not break her neck.

The world swam and drifted as she tried to navigate the cramped rectangle. The kitchen tap dripped steadily with metallic scented water that appeared black in the darkness. Following the column of half-light towards the exit, she paused to grab a can off lager off the side, open it, took a swig to rinse her mouth then spat the liquid onto the chequered tiles. Next, she took a tentative gulp. It stayed down, so she took another, then another. Soon, she was ready for the ball.

Yellow from the film had invaded the room. Everything was bathed in a sepia filter and had taken on a gritty aspect. Suzie stopped in the doorway and surveyed the scene. One of the droogs had his arms in a bucket of what looked to be real eyeballs. The three stoners whacked a plump boy with hockey sticks in the belief that he was stuffed with sweets like a huge pinata. Finally, she found what she was looking for; Jane was in the centre of the room ballroom dancing with Marsha Edwards.

Somehow, while she was unconscious, Jane had changed into the dress of a wealthy courtier... Marsha was still dressed as a queen.

Suzie raged and boiled when she saw where Marsha had her hand. "Get your hands off her, Camilla, you filthy harlot!" She hissed through gritted teeth as she stormed across the room, replacing her plastic axe with a kitchen knife as she went.

Marsh grinned as Suzie approached and gave her bottom a cheeky squeeze before taking her hand away. "Ahh, Cassilda... How pale you look. Are you feeling unwell?" She tipped her head back and roared with laughter. "Poor sick one... You should be more careful who you let lie beside you at night."

Several other guests turned around and joined in the laughter. They had all been bobbing for razor-blade-laced apples. None of them had lips any more, but that didn't stop them laughing.

Suzie started to weep as Jane turned to reveal that her once beautiful open face was now a shredded mask of blood.

Marsh laughed again and held a bloodied object out in her hand. "Apple?" Points of yellow light glittered off the sharp metal embedded in its flesh.

Suzie reached her hand down to her belt, the blade flashed as she first cut Jane's throat then plunged it into Marsha's cold heart.

Looking down, Marsha saw to her horror that her yellow dress was turning a deep crimson. "No!" She wailed. "I can't see the king like this!" She screamed so shrilly that the windows rattled and expensive wine glasses exploded in showers of cut crystal. With her dying gasp, she simpered: "My beautiful yellow gown..."

Suzie was about to finish act two of the dreadful drama that was unfolding and take her own life when a voice drifted to her on the wind.

"Come to me, my child..."

The voice was deep and sonorous, it filled her with beautiful sorrow. It was time to go home...

"Come with me to the lake of Hali..."

Suzie followed the voice out into the night, walking the crazy-paving path towards the large duck-pond at the rear of the property. She fell to her knees as she saw the king. He drifted on the water on a cushion of algae encrusted tentacles. His regal robes fluttered in the wind as he reached out one of his cadaverous hands and beckoned her to join him.

"Come with me, back to dim Carcosa, my queen..."

Suzie grinned with ecstatic joy, she *was* the queen after all. She was the queen of Carcosa, that had a much better ring to it than 'queen of Halloween' ever did, and it suited her well. As he plunged face-first into the chill waters, the smile never left her lips. Even when the water flooded her lungs... Suzie kept on smiling.

TRICK'R TREATS HIMSELF

DANIEL HALE

HERE IS THE MOMENT that Jack loves the least: waking up in his grave.

He has never been sure what mechanism it is that calls him back when the season is at risk. It is not a summoning, exactly, nothing that requires actual agency. More like lightning rushing out of the sky to fill a hole in the clouds, a sudden aligning of circumstances that results in him. Something goes wrong, or something arises; something that only his chilled hands can correct. Another aspect of his role that the wise women of yore failed to brief him on.

First there is the process of rebecoming, a slow creeping back into the world, bit by venous bit as he sloughs off the blazing womb where he resides: the scorching, hidden heart of the Hallowed Realm, flickering atop so desolated a plain that none but the most dim-witted of the hollow children would dare to slink upon it.

So, born again comes Jack, his flesh filling out in the secret places set aside for such occurrences. It is a profoundly uncomfortable experience, to suddenly come to be in the cramped, dark ground. If it had been up to Jack, he would have liked to have had a mirror and perhaps a candle waiting for him, if only so he could see what it looks like when he comes back together. After the eyes fill out, obviously.

Once it is done, there is the briefest moment of peace to enjoy, the sure embrace of the darkened dirt, the cooling refreshment of soil and icy worms.

It is the next moment—briefer still but nonetheless upsetting—that hurts him, when his lungs forget themselves and he tries to breathe.

* * *

The cemetery goes back a long way, longer than anyone knows. The bodies go deep, and stones wear away. Jack has a plot in all of them, in a space between the graves, with nothing more than a pile of gravel or a withered stump to mark its place.

Once he's pulled himself together, Jack claws his way up to the surface. No need to draw breath, no painful bleatings from his heart, not even a single twanging nerve to give him pause. Jack grasps for a purchase in the dirt, pulls up on roots and the rotted timbers of coffins, the workout doing much to reacquaint himself with his body. Finally, his fingers breach the grass and he pulls himself out of the earth, kicking back the dirt and grass to refill the hole he left behind.

No melodramatic gasping for air, no animal whine at the discomfiture of anatomy. That was for a younger Jack, still unused to the weight of his crown and the burn of his lantern. Now Jack stands, still and stiff as a corpse, and takes only one breath to smell the rot on the air.

These are the set asides, the indeterminate hours, the time between the resting of heads on pillows and the discovery of presents beneath the tree or a quarter under the pillow, the sound of alien creaking on the stair or knocking in the closet, when the minders of little miracles and insomniac phenomena have their way.

But none are about here but Jack. It is Halloween night—*the* Halloween night, whatever the local trick r' treat hours might have been—and the air should be frigid with goblins about their wicked work. The froggy-skinned sons of the Hallowed Realm, that most wretched corner of creation, never missed the call of the doors that opened on this night.

They should be everywhere, in pursuit of their earthly plunders as they sneak beneath the doors and windows of the unmarked homes, fouling the floors with their dirty feet, tasting the food with their nasty little tongues, snatching whatever shiny keepsakes caught their eye. Even if no such treasures could be found, better a night in the chill autumn air than another year of uninterrupted murk. This place should be writhing with them.

It is a sprawling neighborhood of large, slightly rundown homes that were once clearly of high-quality, all made in smugly similar styles that had so taken vogue in these times. Most are decorated for the holiday: cheery plastic skeletons hang from doors and fake cobwebs blanket the hedges. Spider webs strung with purple lights hang in windows and wreathes of glittering, vinyl bats while plastic ghosts hang from gutters.

None of the houses are explicitly marked, however. The only jack o' lanterns that Jack can see are of the plastic light or window vinyl variety, which offer no protection under the pact. No pumpkin, no grin, no flame. No protection. Then where are the goblins?

Jack decides that a test is in order. He chooses a house to set the trap, finds a suitable shrub by which to crouch, and sets to searching through the pockets of his jacket for the bait.

He pulls it out of his pocket: a small, untarnished silver spoon, glinting prettily in the moonlight. Jack flicks it with his finger, hears it ring, then tosses it carefully towards the path to the door, where it lands with a tinkle. *Come along, gobbly,* he thinks. *I've a nice shiny spoon for you to taste.*

Jack does not have to wait long before an odd little chill snakes into sudden sight. He smells the rot of marshes, the tartar breath of a goblin with the scent of something sweet on his tongue.

It shows itself like the swirling of oil over water, all viscous swirls congealing into something greasy and slick. It curls itself out of the air, all green skin and warts, long in the talons and teeth, grinning at its discovery shining on the ground before it. It lopes forward, moving ape-like on its boney knuckles...

And finds a hand grabbing it from behind and pulling it into the shrubbery. There is no need for Jack to press the creature too firmly to the ground—it has gone still, knowing the touch of its tormentor as well as all its brethren do—but Jack holds it tight regardless, feeling the same nausea for these damned abominations that he has always known.

"Nice night for it," he whispers in the goblin's ear. "Very nice night indeed. So nice, in fact, that it strikes me as quite odd that there aren't more of you about."

"Leggo," says the goblin quietly. Jack cannot help but feel gratified that it is trembling. "Leggo."

"You've a name, friend?"

"Grockus. Leggo."

"Not very friendly. I'm just asking some questions, after all. A conversation, yes? You know what one of those are?"

"I dunno about it," the goblin moans. "I dunno."

"I haven't even asked it yet. Now pay attention. Where are the rest of your brothers? Why aren't there more of you about? I've yet to see a single place around here where the pact stands. What's wrong with this place?"

"Nuthin here," it says. "Nuthin for us."

"Nothing for you?"

Jack pauses, thinks about it. Of course, the hollow ones take and wreck for sheer joy but that wasn't the point. Anything they did, the victims would not notice or perceive; not consciously, at least. The shit on the floor, the missing valuables, the taste of piss and phlegm in all their drink and food would only register on the most fundamental of levels as a soupcon of dread or bitterness that eats away in increments. And the awful little freaks would scamper off back to their home, content to have sewn a little unhappiness in their wake.

It was small, petty stuff, not exactly the greatest evils, but it added up and brought worst things. But if there was nothing to spoil...if the prospective home was so thick with misery already...

Jack squeezes a little harder, to keep Grockus from struggling. "I see. That's interesting. Then it seems I have some looking around to do. Thank you, Grockus. Now, if you don't mind..."

The goblin begins wriggling, apparently aware of what Jack was about. But too late: Jack presses his fingers into its flesh, eliciting a gurgling whine that cut off abruptly as the creature bursts apart with a sulfurous flash, a nasty smell and a pile of greasy bones lying in a puddle of black liquid. Jack bends down to get to work. The bones must dry quickly, before—

Vwoop.

Jack straightens up quickly, stashes the bones away in his pocket. The police car's lights are flashing behind the two officers. They scowl at Jack with bull terrier suspicion. The older of the two, a squat, potbellied sergeant with glasses more befitting of a librarian, asks: "You wanna tell us what you're doing out here, sir?"

There's a light on in the house behind Jack, peeping out the curtains. He must have made more noise than he thought.

Generally, he can do as he pleases in the non-time of night without fear of discovery, provided he doesn't spend too much time making too much of a racket in one place. There's always the risk of pushing the natural laws too far, especially in the presence of light sleepers.

Jack smiles his jolliest, allows a slight swaying to show through his stance. He speaks a calculated grogginess: "I'm sorry, officers. Think I got a little lost."

"You live here, sir?"

"Oh, no. Buddy of mine... Carl... he's putting me up for a few days. Said he'd pick me up from a bar over that way." Jack waves his hand with the vague emphasis of a drunkard towards the direction of the east. "Never showed up, though. Thought I remembered the way to his place but, I dunno, think I got turned around somewhere." Jack frowns, as though starting to sober up slightly. "Hell. I've not forgotten myself, have I? Broken a window or something? I knew I shouldn't a gone out, I'm sorry, but I thought the walk would do me good."

The younger cop is sneering. Jack sees his hand flexing vaguely, as though in yearning for the weight of his gun. They train meaner now, he knows. Train them to be nervous.

The older cop his smiling, pats his young partner on the shoulder. "Maybe you ought to come with us, sir. You can sleep it off at the station while we look for this friend of yours."

Jack slurs his agreement, allows himself to be helped into the back of the car. They leave off the cuffs, nothing bothering to waste time fitting them over Jack's bulging wrists. The young officer still looks unhappy. Jack gives him an especially imbecilic smiling, quietly delighting at the sight of his rising hackles.

"Lovely town you folks got out here," Jack murmurs. "Gotta love the fall colors."

Neither cop replies. The older one is driving. The younger one stares out the window.

"Reminds me of being a kid, you know? Halloween. Trick r' treat. All of that. Not so many places are doing that now, though. That's a shame. Nice place like this. Looks like practically all the houses are decorated for it, too. Bet the kids love that."

Jack settles back, sighs, and proceeds to snore. He hears the front seat shift as the younger cop turns to look back at him.

Jack doesn't need to sleep. He cannot help but feel a little soothed by the whispering in front:

"We should check his details, just in case."

"Christ, Alan. Calm down. He's just a bum."

"So what? You heard him talking about the kids—"

"Goddamn it. Don't start that again. You gonna start suspecting every drunk you pick up on the job? That's a good way to get yourself disciplined. Maybe even dismissed. I want to catch the bastard too, but that's not the way to go about it."

"So we don't even check?"

"What the hell for? You never hear of innocent until proven guilty?"

"Doesn't mean... what the hell?"

"Goddamn. Where's the road?"

Ah. Jack opens his eyes.

A solid wall of fog roils outside the windshield. The two cops peer confusedly into the murk, probably wondering how they missed this in the forecast.

Another aspect of his service the witches failed to mention to Jack was how the Hallowed Realm would stretch to keep him safe. Finding himself at the mercy of a mortal was enough for the greasy substance to come pouring after him. Long enough and it would bring the hollow children along for the ride, thrashing about in its tendrils like trout under a waterfall. Usually it wouldn't have to go that far—just the presence of the Hallowed Realm's concentrated chill was enough to put off Jack's aspiring captors— now and again, however...

"Fuck it. Let him off here. He won't care."

"You're right, there." Jack opens the door before the officers can react, forces the lock with his corpse-cold muscles and lets the fog roll in.

Jack stays awhile to watch the realm at its work, forcing its way into their lungs, pushing out their pains and dreads and manias to the surface. When it is done, the young officer is bleeding from a bullet hold in his skull. The elder is staring out the window, trembling as tears stream from his face.

"What was he called?" Jack asks. "The one who hurt people here? And what, precisely, did he do?"

The elder does not look at Jack, but he answers in a quiet tone that seems better fit for a little boy beneath the covers. "He took kids. Every year, one would be taken around Halloween. Ten years."

The old, fat cop draws a shuddering breath. "We kept it quiet at first. He'd send letters, before he did it. Signed them as *Trick'r*. And...there was a little girl. He didn't... didn't take her with him. Left her in the bed..."

The fog swirls hungrily about this pathetic, whimpering wreck, lapping at his tears and tasting his despair.

Jack does not need to press him further. He can imagine how it went: the same tragedy, year after year, the same season, festering suspicion and distrust and poisoning the metaphysical air in their homes as effectively, if not more so, than a visit from the hollow children. Paltry excuses from the police and empty pledges of vigilance from public officials losing their savor, dread giving way to a horrible, sick resignation. At heart these small towns are all the same: so used to things going on as they do, so at one with their identities and so used to going without support from the wider world, that it becomes a point of pride to think such things could not—and do not—happen *here.*

Jack pats the old officer just once on the shoulder before leaving the car. The fog rolls away, taking the car with it. He waits until he is sure the last shreds of it have faded away before taking the bones out of his pocket and beginning his work.

The anatomy of the hollow ones most closely resembles insects in nature. Beneath their slimy skin their insides are mainly fluid and bone. The fluid, once exposed to the open air, evaporates almost instantaneously, leaving behind an oily residue that adheres to the skeleton, which remains intact through some arcane tissue that Jack has never been able to identify.

Jack crushes Grockis' skull beneath his boot, an old superstition from his early days having long given way to spiteful habit. He has wiled much of his time away exploring the bodies of his hated subjects with great determination and enthusiasm. After nearly two-hundred years of dissection and vivisection he has learned all of their inner secrets, developed techniques to preserve their skin and—as he does here—adjust their puzzling skeletons to take on a new shape, pushing out the ribs and tugging slightly on the spine. Then he holds up the newly curved shape, taking care to hold it well at arm's length before taking out his lighter and giving it a flick...

The skeleton lantern catches light immediately, blue flames flaring up the bones and down into the inward-pointing ribs, creating a ghostly white blaze. Jack holds it carefully from the middle of the spine where the oil did not quite take. The flames, though bright, do not burn, and would snuff out entirely at the touch of human skin. Jack raises it to point the burning light out into the darkness of the neighborhood.

The lantern's beam reveals odd things as it cuts the darkness: streaks of color and movement that cannot entirely be a trick of the light. An undulating serpent form of green and purple pulls away as the light touches it. A patch of tiny, glowing blue mites coalesces into being before buzzing away in a firework swarm. Over everything lays a pale-yellow fog, so thin as to be almost invisible in the lantern light.

But Jack's are practiced eyes, well used to catching the surreptitious sneaking in the All Hallow's dark. He has seen fog like this before, in places where mortals sleep fitfully, locking their doors and windows as a matter of course, regarding visitors with distrust, and long, in their hearts, for an end to it all, whatever it all may be. It is a fog of vaporous, distilled despair. It is the stuff that mortals breathe when calamity has come and gone, and the future is unforeseen.

Jack follows the fog, pausing at each house as he goes. As he does so, he removes something from his pocket—something small, pale white, and irregularly shaped—and places it right at the edge of the house's perimeter.

He breathes the fog deep, past such things as despair or dread, a thing fully of the hollow night. As he breathes it, however, he can taste the impressions of dread on his tongue: bitter, bilious notes of sweet sickness and rot. He does not hear the voices that accompany it but feels their echoes in his bones.

Not again...

Please... no more...

Bring her back, please, God...

I'll kill us, I swear I'll kill us both...

Maybe it's over, oh God let it be over...

And on and on. Jack hears it all bone-deep, the unwhispered prayers of the community, the sour air that stands in memoriam to the victim's past of the thing called Trick'r.

Jack makes his way down, leaving his gift to each and every house, following the call of the fog. He marks the pattern by the lantern light, the places where the fog is thickest, and the desperation wails its most. Once he has marked his destination, he takes his time to finish his work in the rest of the neighborhood, planting the seeds at each property line. Those planted earlier are already stirring, green shoots slowly wriggling out of the earth and budding their first fruit.

When he has done all that he can for everywhere else, Jack heads down the final street, into a less well-maintained part of the neighborhood, where the houses flake paint and the grass is overgrown. Even here he finds the trappings of the holiday: paper skeletons and bats in the windows, Styrofoam tombstones and plastic spiders along the untrimmed hedges. The fog is thickest here.

He finds its source as he turns the corner down a badly lit cul-de-sac, sees the fire blazing lazily at its house in the lantern light. Pink flames, slowly lapping out the windows and roof like a sluggish tide, the color of oozing blood and juices from a fresh cut of meat. In place of smoke comes the yellow fog that has so thoroughly stained its neighbors.

At first Jack thinks he has found the only house in the neighborhood without Halloween decorations. But as he approaches, he sees something hanging from the front door: a mask, probably handmade, of sacking died bright orange with a thin, black hood. Its face includes a jagged grin and dark, ovular eyes, in shape similar to a Jack o' lantern but somehow more predatory.

Jack squeezes the lantern, causing it to immediately snuff out and dissolve into a thin white ash that drifts away into the night. He shakes the remains off of his hands. Then he takes the mask and bangs his fist against the door. Through the cracks he can see a light turn on.

In the set aside times, mortals respond to Jack as they would in a dream, aware but following an assumed nonsensical logic and unable to truly help themselves. This phenomenon occurs to all, from the recently woken to the already nocturnal, such as the officers Jack encountered earlier. And now...

A click, and the door opens slowly to reveal an old, beaten-looking man, hunched and thin with sagging, slightly jaundice-shaded skin and a skull cap of sweaty gray hair. His slight potbelly sags over filthy flannel night pants and his untrimmed toenails shine like beetle's shells.

"Yeah?" His voice is hoarsely feeble. He looks at Jack without suspicion or even particular unkindness, simply the elderly's resignation to whatever their considerable time upon the earth has thus far failed to throw to them.

"Evening, sir," Jack says. "I'm so sorry to bother you so late. My car's broken down and I need to call a tow truck. Is there any chance I could borrow your phone for a bit?"

The old man looks past him. Though there is clearly no car in sight the old man either does not care or is willing to take Jack at his word. "Don't have a phone," he says. "Got a battery you can use to jump it, though."

"Hey, that'd be great. Sure you don't mind?"

The old man shrugs, then leads Jack into the living room, where a well-worn recliner sits across from a small loveseat that looks catalog-new. "Have a seat and I'll get it for ya."

Jack waits for the old man to shuffle off a ways before retrieving the mask from inside his jacket. He runs his fingers over the eyes and mouth. Sniffs. Old sweat and damp, and the slightest bit of smoke, as much the scents of autumn as any scents can be. The face of Trick'r, hung like a warning or a protective talisman. Or a boast.

"It goes so much deeper than masks and candy," says Jack when the old man returns, lugging the battery in a shaky hand. "It used to be about the spirits of our departed loved ones, returned in the fall to receive their gifts. But then things got corrupted. Confused. Blame it on the Christians or...something else. Soon there were no more spirits, no more gifts. Just the mischief of wicked things and their particular hungers. Somebody always has to spoil the fun, it would seem."

Jack looks up suddenly, causing the old man to drop the battery, shaking and broken out in beads of sweat. He is staring at the mask as if he has never seen such a thing before, as if it might tear itself away from Jack and go for his neck.

"*Trick'r*, eh? It's a good name. You can even hear the apostrophe. How'd it go?"

The old man licks his lips, shakes his head. "I don't know what you're—"

"Come on. Horace. You can tell me." Jack lowers his voice, allowing a trace of the sepulchral tones of the long deceased to creep into his accent.

Horace trembles and stares at Jack with an expression of equal parts awe and fear, no doubt wondering what manner of being he has allowed into his home. He may think Jack the Devil, a mistake that has been repeated on more than one occasion. Jack, though resentful, has gotten out of the habit of correcting people on this point. At least the Devil had *choices* before the fall came, after all.

The old man stands silently as decades of secret-keeping fall away in his mind. Then he shuffles past Jack and settles into his old armchair.

"It was just gonna be one," he says. "Lorelai Cross, from down the street. Such a sweet little thing, all blond curls and rosy cheeks like you wouldn't... she'd smile at me, too, when nobody else was around. I'd be walking down to the liquor store and she'd be out in the yard, and she'd wave and smile at me. I knew...she never said a word to me, but I knew.

"Had to be careful. Her parents kept her on a short leash. I'd check the house when nobody was home, figured out where her room was. And when I'd have to...well. I finally found it."

There is color rising in the old man's cheeks, spittle collecting at the corners of his mouth. Jack just watches, listens. Smiles.

"Nobody even noticed when I was done. I dunno how her parents didn't hear us. They must have, but... maybe they wanted to keep it quiet. Even her funeral was so rushed, you know? Barely any mention in the obituary, let alone much of a turnout. That felt wrong. Lorelai deserved better. She didn't deserve to be swept under the rug like that. The cops barely even investigated. Never even came to talk to me. I dunno why...but it bothered the hell out of me.

"I knew what I'd done. I couldn't kid myself about it, not really. I know she hadn't wanted it. It was all me. But at least I could admit that to myself. The... the goddamn passivity of this place, these people... to just forget it all, forget *her*, and go on with their lives? That was worse by a mile. Worse than if they'd done the deed themselves. I might even have confessed except..."

Horace is staring at the mask again, this time with something closer to affection. Jack hands it over, watches the old man run his fingers over the cloth.

"It didn't have anything to do with Halloween at first," he whispers. "I just wanted to play with them, you know? The other pretty things, like Lorelai. And I wanted to scare them, the way I... so I made a new game. I'd send the cops a letter. A special letter. '*Season's greetings*,' the old man's voice goes croaked and coarse, a frog that's swallowed a waterlogged packet of cigarettes. "'*I've come for the treats. Each house without protection shall lose them tonight. Say goodbye to the sweet little things. Trick'r.*'"

The old man loses himself in the feel of his mask, stroking the cloth almost lovingly. "I took six of them in the end," he says. "For five years I played my little game. It took two for the cops to finally admit what was happening. They never published the letters, but word got out anyway. You should have seen the way they decked the houses. Graveyards and trees full of bats and ghosts, haunted houses and inflatable monsters. Jack o' lanterns as far as the eye could see.

"Of course, even then there were some that hadn't gone quite to the same level of effort." Trick'r laughs again in his throaty croak. "You'd think they'd get better locks at the very least, or send their children away, or even just get out of bed when they heard the table lamp fall over..."

He trails off again, staring into space and patting the mask like a loyal pet. Finally, Jack asks: "Six?"

Trick'r nods slowly. "Lorelai Cross. Samantha Woods. Bobby Bright. Tina Smalls. Jackson and Grace Boyd. After that I just...couldn't be bothered, I guess. Lost the steam for it." The old man sighs heavily and reclines in his chair. He looks very tired, head lolled to the side and sticky with sweat. The mask falls abruptly from his lap. He leaves it be, alone with his monstrous thoughts.

Jack considers. Then: "How would you like the steam back?"

The old man says nothing, his face still slack with exhaustion. His other face grins hungrily.

* * *

The old man makes a ritual of it, laying out his costume before proceeding. Jack watches him undress and don each piece of the outfit one by one: black underclothes, orange burlap trousers and shirt, belt of twine around his waist and neck, pale, clawed latex gloves. He kneels before Jack when it is time for the mask. Jack obliges him, setting it over his face.

Then Jack takes something from his pocket: a single severed goblin claw. He tests its point with his fingertip before bidding Trick'r to stick out his tongue. He does so and does not protest as Jack pricks it with the claw, drawing blood.

Trick'r swallows.

When it is done, and the goblin poison has wracked its changes on his body—his limbs lengthening, his back adopting an anthropoid hunch, the very air around him taking on a feverish sheen—Trick'r stands, sniggering at Jack like a jester to his king. And Jack, merry fire dancing in his eyes, leads the new goblin out the door and points him into the night.

Trick'r howls with delight as he scampers into the neighborhood, up the lane to his first house. He does not notice the new jack o' lantern sat beside the porch, or the others that blaze all around him: orange skin, yellow fire, hungry, happy, jagged grins putting shame to his own. He does not feel the breaking of the barrier as he crosses the property line. He does not feel anything then except the closing of Jack's fist around his throat, the booming laughter of the Hollow King in his ears, the tide of darkness closing in as he's pulled away into the Hallowed Realm.

COSTUMED HERO

DJ TYRER

"I CAN'T SAY I'M impressed with the quality of the costumes."
Sally sniffed as she observed the outfits her guests had chosen:
most of them wore tacky commercial costumes that predominated
between plastic bibs and capes and fangs for Draculas and
variations on animals, nuns and witches with loose morals. The
few homemade outfits were lamentably poor in terms of quality
and imagination. And, these were adults! A lame costume on a kid
could be just about endearing, but not on a grown man.

"We've had some right ones," John agreed. "There was this
one guy who came in his underpants. He was—"

"Yes, I think I can guess, and it's not amusing."

John chuckled at her annoyance. "It's just a bit of fun, nothing
more."

"Well, people could put in some effort. *I* spent hours designing
and making my costume." She saw the look on his face. "I'm
Queen Elizabeth Tudor."

"Oh, yes, I see it now."

"I mean, even your costume is streets ahead of this crowd. It might be rented, but you actually picked out a good-quality one, not some cheap tat. Let me guess... Hmm, the hand protruding from the pocket makes me think either Professor Frankenstein or Herbert West. Am I right?"

"Uh, yeah, Herbert West?" John had no idea who that was. Did he kidnap and kill those girls with his crazy wife? Maybe. The costume had just said 'Mad Scientist' on it.

She smiled and he felt good. He had fancied his neighbour ever since he moved in next door, despite being too scared to admit it to her, and was also happy when he pleased her. Which was the only reason he was here—as guest and aide—for he hated fancy dress parties.

"It's a shame."

"What is?" he asked.

"The way people treat Hallowe'en, so frivolous."

"It is?"

"Yes. Once the festival was the Celtic New Year and remembrance of the dead, a solemn day of celebration."

"Can you celebrate with solemnity?"

"Of course you can," she told him firmly. "You have a good time without making a fool of yourself, without getting rowdy and upsetting everyone."

"Like Eddie Smith?"

Sally winced. "Please, John, do *not* remind me of that man! I still cannot face a bowl of salad without feeling nauseous. But, yes, that is exactly the sort of awful behaviour to which I'm referring."

Just then, an unfamiliar figure stepped through the open front door. Most of the partygoers hadn't bothered with makeup or masks and most of the makeup that had been applied was a crude slathering of pallid grey-white or witchy green, while those who wore cheap plastic masks with their costumes were largely recognisable enough thanks to the lack of effort they had made with their costumes. But, this man, and Sally was fairly certain it was a man, *was* the part.

"Now, he *is* good," said John with a whistle, "I'll give you that."

The man approached, looming over then.

"Hello. I'm Sally; welcome to my party. I can't say I can tell who you are..."

A heavy eyebrow rose quizzically. "Bigfoot." The voice was deep, like an avalanche rumbling down a mountainside.

"Oh, yes. Ha-ha. I meant, I couldn't tell who it is *inside* the costume. I could tell you were the Yeti or something."

"Bigfoot."

"Well, I suppose I'll guess, eventually... Um, well, let me introduce you to John, he's my upstairs neighbour."

"Pleased to meet you," said John.

"And you," said Bigfoot, extending a huge, hairy hand in greeting.

John shook hands and winced in pain as his hand felt as if it were in a vice.

"Ow!" He shook his hand as soon as it was released. "That's quite a grip you've got there! You got some sort of gyros in that suit?"

"Well, I have been working out. I found an abandoned camp in the woods—well, I say abandoned; the hunter ran away as soon as he saw me—and amongst the usual tins of beans and junk, I found this doodad with springs that you can use to exercise your hands. You know the sort of thing, you give it a good squeeze, then relax. Makes a change from bench-pressing redwoods, you know?"

"I can imagine," said Sally with a flirty grin that annoyed John. For a huge, hairy beast, Bigfoot was far too suave for his tastes.

"I mean," the rumbling voice continued, "life can become quite tedious when you live out in the woods. Although, I must admit, things have improved since I got satellite TV and the internet. I had to get an especially adapted keyboard, of course."

"Of course."

"But, once I had that, it all kind of fell into place. I'm active online, Facebook, Twitter, that sort of thing. Not as myself, of course."

"Of course."

"But, one can be, well, *anyone* online and that allows me to just be myself." He laughed a loud, booming laugh. "It sounds silly, doesn't it, utilising a disguise to be myself? But, I'm sure you understand..."

"Oh, I do."

"It means I can order online—finally, I can buy the books I want without relying on what I can find in RVs and dumpsters. Also means I can book plane tickets, which is what brings me here – although I had a devil of a time actually getting *on* the flight!" He laughed again. "I'm staying with Jenny; we met online."

"Oh, you're a friend of Jenny?"

"Yes. She invited me along as her plus-one."

"How nice!" Her tone said she hoped they were more than just friends. So did John, for entirely personal reasons. "Well, I'm glad you came. I really do like your outfit. I must say you really are living the character. Amazing!"

"I'm just being myself," he told her, spreading his arms as if to display his costume. "Anyway, I ought to mingle and allow you to talk to your other guests."

Bigfoot lumbered off and they admired the costume as he went.

"It really is as if there are muscles rippling beneath the fur," marveled Sally.

"It must've cost a fortune!" John nodded, suddenly feeling incredibly underdressed. "I mean who wears such a thing to a fancy-dress party? Outside Hollywood, at least."

That was certainly the reaction of their fellow guests, who flocked around Bigfoot as if he were a celebrity in their midst. In a way, he was.

"He must be a successful man," commented Sally, "well-off and clearly a nice guy. Oh, I do hope he and Jenny make a go of it. They would be perfect together."

"Better than the last bloke she dated." That had been the infamous Eddie Smith.

"Please!" She winced again.

"Sorry. Hey, he's quite a mover, isn't he?"

John meant Bigfoot, who was dancing like a pro to some Daft Punk. He'd imagined the suit must be cumbersome, but Bigfoot was moving with grace and precision.

"Quite amazing," agreed Sally.

"He must have some sort of exoskeleton thingy under there, you know the sort of thing the military were developing. That costume must've cost millions!"

"Quite amazing," she repeated.

One of the partygoers, one of the men who thought a black plastic cape, some cheap plastic fangs and a tacky plastic bib printed with a shirt, waistcoat and cravat constituted a costume, came over to them and said, "Great party, Sally."

"Thanks." The man worked in the mailroom where she worked, but she could never remember his name, had only invited him because not doing so would have seemed rude.

"That Bigfoot is marvelous! A great costume and a fun guy. He told the most amazing joke—did he tell you? About the gargoyle and the lemming?"

"Gargoyle and lemming?" John repeated, bemused.

"Well, it *is* Hallowe'en... so, you haven't heard it?"

John attempted to redirect the question, but the man just rambled on regardless. Sally took the opportunity to quickly slip away.

"Well, there was this gargoyle on a church, right? And, every Hallowe'en it would come alive for one night. Now..."

John groaned.

Sally was glad to get out of earshot. The man was an absolute bore: even a truly brilliant joke would become tedious drivel when told by him. Besides, she told herself to still her guilt, she did need to circulate, didn't she?

"Hi, Sally—great party!"

"Love your costume, Sal!"

"Having fun? I know I am!"

"Have you seen that Yeti guy? Amazing!"

"—and the gargoyle sees a lemming—"

"Thanks for inviting us, Sally!"

"—and it jumps off the altar—"

The voices were all merging into a babble, and she was finding a smile and nod sufficient to play the part of the gracious hostess, when she spotted an anomaly. Normally, there was a casket on her mantle, made of gold and ebony, worth a fair bit in itself, which contained a vial that was said to contain, in turn, some of Rasputin's blood, taken at the autopsy which had failed to ascertain quite which of several fatal injuries had actually killed him. Her great-grandfather had been a diplomat to the Tsarist court with some peculiar interests. Tonight, however, there was a conspicuous space where the casket should have been and she knew that wasn't because she had removed it to somewhere safe. She should have, she knew, but then, hindsight always allowed perfect vision.

Looking around, she saw a woman poorly dressed as a witch carrying the casket out into the passage and towards the front door.

"Stop! Thief!" she cried, pushing her way through the revellers. Unfortunately, most of them didn't really catch what she was saying over the music and those who did looked around futilely, thinking she was pointing out a particularly fine costume.

"May I be of assistance?" boomed a voice from behind and above her.

Looking round at Bigfoot, she quickly gabbled out an explanation: "Casket—blood of Rasputin—stolen—witch—over there—stop her—please!"

"Sure thing," he told her, easily parting the crowd.

"Please, don't hurt her!" she called after him, remembering just how strong he had seemed.

"Oh, I don't hurt people," he called back, "I'm a vegetarian."

"But, Hitler was a vegetarian!" She paused. "I think."

"No," Bigfoot called back, "Hitler was a Nazi."

A few minutes later, Bigfoot was back, carrying the casket in one hand and the witch in the other.

"Here you go, one casket retrieved intact and one witch unharmed, more or less." He dropped the woman in a heap on the floor and handed the casket to Sally. "You know, if you wipe the green muck off her face, I think you'll discover this ersatz witch is, in fact, the famous media witch Juniper Sage."

"Juniper Sage?" exclaimed Sally, who recognised the name. "Doesn't she do tarot reading on some satellite channel?"

"Indeed, she does," Bigfoot nodded. "She is a leading figure in occult, oddball circles. Clearly, somehow, she heard about your vial of Rasputin's blood and came to steal it."

"And, I would've gotten away with it, too, if it wasn't for your pesky Sasquatch!"

"I prefer Bigfoot, personally."

"What's going on?" John called. Still being buttonholed by the joke reteller, he hadn't been able to tell what the rumpus was all about. His plea went unanswered as the man drone on, "—and then it said to the lemming—"

"Well, I'd better be going," said Bigfoot, "before any police or reporters show up. I absolutely detest getting my picture in the paper. Cheerio! Maybe I'll see you next Hallowe'en, eh?"

"Cheerio..." For some reason, Sally was beginning to wonder if she had had the genuine cryptozoological anomaly as a guest at her party.

"Because it's a Saturday!" finished the man retelling Bigfoot's joke, before collapsing in a fit of manic laughter.

"I feel very confused," said John, who'd failed to follow either the joke or whatever had just happened.

"Bye!" Bigfoot waved at him as he went past.

"Uh, bye," he replied. "Happy Hallowe'en."

"He's a real costumed hero," someone was saying as he wandered over towards Sally.

"A hero, definitely," said Sally, "and certainly real. But, I'm not too sure about the costume..."

THE AWFUL HORROR

JOE KOGUT

ALEX DREW A GRID ON the sidewalk with thick oversized pink chalk he swiped from his neighbor's yard. It made a glassy scratching sound as he hashed out the lines and labeled them as streets. Then he made boxes where certain premium houses we're located on the grid and labeled them. When he was satisfied, he sank back on his butt and detailed the plan to Joey and me.

"Okay. We're allowed to trick or treat on five streets in our neighborhood. The sun goes down around six thirty, so in order to get back to Mitch's house before dark to watch Hatchet Job Three: The Revenge, with the maximum amount of candy we have to do both sides of these streets, skipping the houses I marked in green because they never give out anything, and making sure we hit these houses." He pointed to the labeled squares with the tip of his chalk. "Because they give out whole candy bars and not the little bite sized ones."

"What's this house here?" Joey asked, pointing to a square with a rock stationed on it.

"The Patterson's. They give out pennies. That weighs us down too much."

We had to get back in time for Hatchet Job Three. It was on the Snipped Channel so all the gory parts would be cut out and our parents would let us watch it. We had watched Hatchet Job Two last year on Halloween but missed most of it because we hadn't been done trick or treating yet. So, this year we decided to let Alex come up with a strategy so we could have our candy and our movie. Only one thing stood in our way.

"What about the Rizchecks?" I asked, twirling a red maple leaf between my fingers by the stem.

"The Rizchecks have to be taken care of with a diversion. I've been thinking about this since last year. We cause a diversion, avoid the Rizchecks, get the candy and get back in time for the movie."

"What kind of a diversion?" Joey's face pinched up with the thought of last year's atomic wedgie delivered by Daniel Rizcheck still fresh in his head.

"You leave that up to me. We're twelve now. This is our last year trick or treating so we gotta make it count."

It was true. Once we turned thirteen, we could go to the Halloween dance at the Junior High. They called it a dance, but no one danced. The guys dressed up, ate cupcakes and stared at the girls on the other side of the gym. Still, it was a crossing over, from being a kid to something else. I suppose if we lived in a jungle there'd be some elaborate ritual where they smeared paint on our chests and sent us off on tasks of manhood. In our neighborhood, you got to go to the Halloween dance.

"Mitch, can you get your mom to make us some more of those pillowcase candy bags? Those were really sturdy."

"Sure," I said. "My mom loves to sew." And she did make sturdy candy bags, except when the Rizchecks tore them out of our hands and beat us with them. Good thing they were only a quarter full.

"Okay. And we all have our costumes, right?"

"I'm a firefighter." Joey's red hair ruffled up in the breeze and he unsuccessfully tried to tame it back down.

"You were a firefighter last year, Joey," Alex pointed out.

He shrugged. "My dad's a firefighter. I already got all the stuff."

Alex shook his head. "What about you, Mitch?"

I was pretty proud of my costume. "I'm going to be a space alien."

"Lame," Alex complained, and then asked, "What *kind* of space alien?"

"My mom made it. It's brown and green and she fixed it so that slime drips from the teeth." My mom's really crafty.

"Well, that sounds cooler. I thought you meant one of those stupid alien costumes with the little rubber masks that get all sweaty."

"Only babies wear those."

"I know, right? Good thing your mom knows how to make things."

"What are you going to be?" I asked. The maple leaf fell apart and the pieces blew off down the sidewalk.

"I'm going to a knight in shining armor."

I sniffed. "And you called me lame?"

"Just wait until you see it. It's so awesome. My mom got it online."

Alex Martinez was always just a little bit cooler than me or Joey. We were all twelve, in fact all of our birthdays were in September, something that our moms laughed about for some unknowable reason. But Alex was different. All the girls in our class liked him, and wrote his name on their hands, which was weird. He was a little bit taller, a little smarter; things just seemed to come to him quicker. Like his voice. It was already changing. Me and Joey just knew he'd be the first of us to shave because he was already really hairy.

It was almost dinnertime, so we all headed home, plan in place. We all lived on the same side of the same street, me and Joey next door to each other, Alex four houses down. This made things easier once we got dressed and had to get our pictures taken by our parents in our costumes. Then we'd go off trick or treating, they'd go back into our houses and hand out candy.

The Rizchecks lived over on the next street, the last house on the block. Their dad was a lawyer. His face was on the back of the phonebook. I asked my dad what kind of lawyer he was one time and he told me the kind that chases ambulances. That made sense since his kids were good at chasing things down too. There were six kids in their family. Five boys and one awful girl. Daniel was a year ahead of us, but he failed a grade, so even though he was thirteen this year, he couldn't go to the dance. Darlene was the next oldest, in our grade, with big curly blonde hair, and crooked teeth all hooked together with braces. The twins Bill and Phil were one grade lower than us. The other two were just babies so we didn't have to worry about them.

It was bad enough they bullied us at school all year long. Halloween held a special place in their hearts for torture of the rest of the neighborhood too. Last year they found us on Densmore Street, right off, and chased us all over until they managed to corner us behind the dry cleaners and beat us down with our own candy bags. We weren't hurt, but we lost most of our candy and wasted a lot of time making up our route. Plus, my mom's candy bags got ripped and she was mad. She called Mrs. Rizcheck, but I don't think it went well because she ended up hanging up on her. So this year we decided to come up with a plan to thwart the Rizchecks, get the candy, and see our movie. As we parted company on beggar's night, I was sure we could pull it off, because now we were prepared.

Joey and I were in the same 6th grade class, but Alex was in Miss Pachinski's across the hall. All day long we spent monitoring the movements of Darlene Rizcheck. With her sparkly braces and tumbleweed of blonde hair, she was our own personal Medusa. She sat the back table in our room surrounded by her friends, who thought she was so cool. I could hear them giggling, like girls do, and talking loudly about how next year they'd be at the dance and not trick or treating like babies.

We thought we might have caught a break because Darlene didn't come back to class after lunch. Also, we didn't have gym because it was decorated for the non-dancing dance that night and they didn't want us to rip the streamers they hung everywhere. At dismissal we met up with Alex and walked home together, confident that this year would be the best Halloween ever.

"I got these from my brother," Alex fished out three walkie-talkies from his book bag, passing one to Joey and me. "He uses them when they play paint ball. This way we can keep in touch if we get split up."

"Why don't we use our cellphones?" I asked, but Alex just glared, shoving it at me.

"Split up?" Joey asked.

"Yeah, last year Daniel yelled for us to stop, and we did, like dummies. This year we do not approach. We scatter and meet up later. Remember, maximize the candy, avoid the Rizchecks and get back to Mitch's house by eight o'clock sharp. Did everyone get a watch?"

We nodded. Alex was totally invested in this plan. The walkie-talkies and watches were cool, but really, we could've just used our cell phones.

"What's the diversion?" I stuffed my walkie-talkie into my backpack.

"You leave that to me. We have to consider that the Rizchecks might be scattered this year."

Last year they'd come out of the Rosenstein's back yard like a wolf pack. We ran, but they cornered us. We stuck together and shared a candy beating and several underwear ripping wedgies. Alex was right, we should have split up. The others must go on if one of us was caught. I just hoped it wasn't me.

Our parents were all serving an early dinner so we could get dressed and hit the candy trail. My mom had my costume in pieces all over out dining room table. My little sister Shannon was going to be a goldfish and she had her costume on when I got home. She was twirling around the living room in her glittering, scaly dress.

"Just let me know when you're ready and I'll sew you in."

"Sew me in?"

My mom put her hands on her hips. "I made that thing out of latex, foam and fabric. For it to stand up right I have to sew you in, so go to the bathroom first. Number two that is. Number one I think you could manage—"

"Mom!"

"Sorry. Just thinking out loud." My mom was always making something. She sewed; scrapbooked, painted, refinished, crafted and reused everything she could get her hands on. Most of her projects came out really nice. But some, like the suit she tried to sew for my dad, are better off bought in a store.

She loved Halloween. My sister and I never had a store-bought costume in our lives. She started putting up the decorations October first.

Mom went back into the kitchen to fix dinner while I scrabbled to do my homework, leaving the night free.

After dinner my mom sewed me into the costume, which felt like a thick foam wetsuit. It was cool how she had made the spikes stand up along the back and the way she shaped the head with its jaws open. "You put the can of silly slime in here." She opened a little compartment in the top headpiece. "I poked holes in the top of the can so the slime should come out slowly because it's so thick."

"You look cool," my sister said touching my latex claws.

"Move around, let's see you walk." My mother stood observing with her hands on her hips. I could walk, that was for sure, shuffle even, but running was out. I dreaded telling Alex I had limited my mobility.

"Excellent!" My mother handed me my candy sack. "We'll meet you down at Alex's house."

It was ten to six. I realized that once I was sewn into my costume I couldn't see my watch anymore. I shuffled down to Alex's, mouth dripping slime, big latex and foam feet bouncing up and down, sweating like a meatloaf.

Joey was already there. "Great costume!"

His firemen's outfit was cool too, except that it was six sizes too big for him and his dad's hat kept falling over his eyes. Last year his mom had gotten him a plastic fire helmet, but it got destroyed during the candy beating so his dad let him use the real thing.

Joey was standing out front in the driveway, his parents talking with Alex's. Alex's mom called into the house for him to come out. His mom always wore a lot of jewelry and had really big hair. Her name was Bonnie, but everyone called her Bonita because she owned a beauty shop. I heard my dad refer to her as Bonnie Boom-Boom once, but I don't think I was supposed to hear that.

Alex came out of the front door, striking a pose on the porch.

He was dressed like a knight in shining armor, with a shield and sword. The armor clinked as he moved, and the sword gleamed in the falling sun. His black hair was combed in place, the last of his dark summer tan was highlighted against the white of the ruffled shirt that peeked out from under the armor. He let us take it all in for a moment and then asked, "Well?"

"It's awesome," Joey breathed, pushing his hat out of his eyes.

"My little knight," Mrs. Martinez said, clasping her hands together. "Isn't he so handsome, like a little movie star."

"Maaaa," he complained, clanking down the steps. When he got closer I could see that the sword was plastic and the armor was some kind of thin, tinny shiny metal. My parents came walking up the drive with my little sister.

"I forgot to give you the other candy sacks." My mom passed out the other two. They were black with little orange bats on them with thick reinforced handles for maximum candy storage.

We posed for pictures, like we have every year since we were three, turning this way and that, smiling, not smiling and being goofy. Then Alex's watch started to beep and he announced, "We have to go, everybody."

"Be back at eight," my mom called.

"We will," I called back and Joey rang the Meyers' doorbell.

All went well that first street. We got candy from every house on our list and even from Mr. Prendergast who usually is in Arizona at Halloween, but he was home giving out Baby Ruth's. Not my favorite, but good when the other candy bars were gone.

The next street was Carlyle. We wove back and forth across the street, keeping watch for any sign of the Rizchecks. We knew from experience that they always started down on Densmore and worked their way forward. So far we had spotted no sign of them. We even went so far as to ask some of the other kids if they'd seen them, which was a risky move because if they heard we were looking for them they'd be sure to come and find us.

By street number three we thought we were in the clear. Halfway done with our trick or treating and no Rizchecks and it was seven fifteen according to Alex's watch. We were right on schedule.

Dundee Street was filled with kids. They were running up and down both sides, clogging the driveways. We were slowing down now due to the weight of our candy bags and our costumes. All my slime had dripped out. Joey could barely hold his bag and keep his hat up out of his eyes. We were ripe for the Rizchecks.

THE AWFUL HORROR

As we turned up the driveway to a big brick house known for giving out handfuls of candy, a bunch of giggling girls stopped us dead in our tracks. Sara Coggins, Amber Griffen, and Julia O'Leary were surrounding another girl, ignoring us. Sara and Amber were both dressed like cheerleaders while Julia was dressed like a mime.

The girls in our class were a mystery to me. They laughed at things that weren't funny. They made little hearts on their notebooks and put guys names in them. Some of them were pretty, kind of, in a weird friend sort of way. When we ran into them on the street my first instinct was to ignore them because they automatically started whispering and giggling. I was confused by them and their strange ways.

As we came up the driveway, they clammed up. They moved away from the fourth girl, who seemed to glide forward. She was dressed like a princess, with long, straight blonde hair past her shoulders, perfect white teeth, and pretty blue eyes. Her dress was lacy blue and low cut, revealing what would someday be a chest. She was beautiful.

Alex took a step forward, mesmerized just like I was until Joey yelled, "Darlene!"

It was Darlene Rizcheck. Somehow, she'd managed to straighten her hair and get her braces off all in one afternoon.

I snapped out of it and beat feet with Joey out of the yard. I was shuffling as fast as I could, while Joey tried not to trip over the edge of his jacket. We were halfway down the street when we saw that Alex wasn't with us. He was still in the yard gazing at Darlene. I grabbed my walkie-talkie and screamed into the mike, "Do not approach! Do not approach! Retreat!"

But from our vantage point in Mr. Hudson's yard we could see them drifting toward each other. The knight and the princess. I never saw such a look on Alex's face before. Surely the spell should have been broken once he realized it was a Rizcheck. But he was right up on her, talking to her, his eyes fixed on her and that was why he didn't see it coming.

Daniel Rizcheck jumped from the bushes and whacked him with a plastic axe from his lumberjack outfit. We could hear the metallic clank all the way down the street as it hit his chest plate. He pulled up his shield and cried into his walk talkie, "Go. This is the diversion!" He blocked another blow from Daniel and pushed him back. We loped off down the street just in time to see Alex holding off the twins with his sword.

"What do we do?" Joey asked desperately.

I looked back the way we came. "We go on. Get all the candy we can, for Alex. He sacrificed himself for us."

Joey's head hung a little. "We'll do it for Alex."

I nodded. "That's what he would've wanted."

We sprinted up and down the next and last street, hitting every house. Our bags were near bursting. Alex would've been proud

Then my alarm went off signaling ten to eight. Time to get back.

Joey and I were really overloaded, so we kept in the shadows, hugging the houses, making our way back to our street. We hadn't made it this far to get high jacked so close to home. As we scanned for the Rizchecks, we also kept an eye out for Alex, but there was no sign of any of them.

When I walked in my door at three minutes to eight my mom was setting up the popcorn in front of the TV. "Where's Alex?"

"He's coming," I said and plopped my candy sack down on the rug. It was full to the top. A couple of pieces of candy corn fell out and my dog ran over and scarfed them up. My sister lay passed out on the couch in a candy induced coma.

"Do you really think he's all right?" Joey asked hopefully when my mother went to get us some drinks. He'd taken his father's helmet off, his red hair plastered to his forehead with sweat.

"I don't know." I tried to pull my alien head off, but my mom had done a really good job sewing it on. It snapped back into place. I tried to get the feet off with even less success.

The opening credits just started when we heard the door open. Alex came in, candy bag gone, black hair tousled, his plastic sword busted. He sat down between us without a word and put some popcorn into his mouth.

"Jeez, Alex, what happened?" Joey asked.

"I fended them off," he said simply.

"Where's your candy?"

He shrugged. "You guys should have enough for all three of us. Now quiet, the movie's starting."

I looked carefully at his face. "What's that all over your lips?"

He wiped his mouth with the back of his sleeve. "Nothing."

Now Joey was examining him. "That's lipstick!"

"You're crazy."

"No. No. That's lipstick." Joey was bent forward, staring closely at his mouth. Then the realization spread over his face and he whispered: "You kissed the female Rizcheck."

"Her name's Darlene," Alex snapped.

Joey shrank back in horror.

My mouth dropped open and the last of the slime dripped out.

THE UPRIGHT

ERIK HANDY

"IS EVERYONE HERE?" Josh said. He dumped his bike in the pile with the others.

"Everyone who matters," Danny replied.

There were four of them and they came like they always did on Halloween evening. They stood on the far edge of town, lonely warehouses and abandoned semi-trailers to their backs, a growing dark of trees and bushes to their front. There used to be five runners, but two years ago, Johnny Weaver didn't arrive promptly at sundown. They never saw him again.

"Why do we do this?" Steph said, making sure her shoelaces were tight. "It's the same thing every year."

"Scared?" Ricky said, as he came around and slapped the teenage girl on the back.

Steph punched him in the arm harder than what was warranted.

Ricky grabbed his arm as if it was about to fall off. "Ouch."

THE UPRIGHT

"I'm sorry," Steph mockingly said.

"You guys ready?" Danny asked.

He was the first one there this year and like the others, he didn't see much point in the race. It was something they had always done. Sure, it brought them together for an hour, but what was one hour amid the years of their lives? How close could a group of kids get in that short time?

Simple answer: not too close. Not enough to form a forever bond. They didn't see each other outside of this one event. Danny assumed they went to the same school, but they never hung out with each other. He never saw them there or anywhere else in town. They never talked about school or life outside of the race.

"It's time," Josh announced.

The four teenagers lined up at the edge of the forest, where cracked pavement met wild grass.

The weather was strange this year. Instead of revealing their true selves, the leaves kept their green. Danny was about to mention it, but he assumed the others already noticed. It wasn't worth mentioning anyway. Small talk wasn't required.

"So do we all remember the rules?" Josh said.

"Yes," Ricky confirmed. "But would you like to list them like you do every year?"

"Okay," Josh said, ignoring Ricky's sarcasm. "We count down from three. Three, two, one, and then we go. Take any path you want. No physical contact with the other runners, Ricky."

Ricky flipped Josh off.

"First one to the piano and plays a note wins. Do we all know where the piano is?"

"Danny does," Ricky said. "Winner two years in a row."

Danny blushed. Yes, he was the first one to reach the piano in the woods two years in a row, but none of the kids were jealous. The only prize was another chance to win next year.

"But you all can follow me," Ricky continued.

"Shut up," Steph said.

"Are we ready then?" Josh said.

"Let's do this," Ricky said, winking at Steph.

"Three," they said in unison.

Danny's head buzzed with anticipation. Even though there was no prize and the winner's high was over in seconds, he felt the pull of the competition. It was magnetism on a whole other level. He started to feel truly alive.

"Two."

They all assumed deep runner's stances.

"One."

"Do we go?" Ricky said.

"Go!" Josh yelled, taking off first.

It didn't take long for the others to catch up.

The ground was uneven, but they jumped over exposed roots and maneuvered around trees, their muscle memory taking over.

Danny pushed himself hard from the get-go. The piano was only minutes inside the woods if one walked. The race rarely lasted longer than a minute and a half. There was one year when an early snow made for a frosty obstacle, but that only slowed them down a few seconds. This year the temperature was a bit warm, even in the evening. The oddity wasn't enough to slow any of them down.

He easily passed Steph, not giving her any advantage simply because she was a girl. She came in second to him the previous year, proving she could hold her own with the boys.

Not this time, Danny thought.

He lost track of Josh and Ricky. There were no shortcuts to speak of. He knew he didn't pass the boys. Had they pulled that far ahead? Danny was blasting through the woods. How fast were the other two going?

He was almost there when he heard the random, discordant notes of the piano ring out.

He slowed to a trot.

Ricky pumped his fist in victory.

Josh, second, didn't even touch the piano.

Danny touched the side of the instrument. Touching it signified a successful run. Danny guessed Josh didn't care. He was the last one to show up and Danny reckoned he wouldn't make it next year.

"Congratulations," Josh said.

"Yeah," Danny added. "Congrats."

Ricky was all smiles. "My first win in, what, six years? But who's counting?"

"Good run," Steph said.

"I dedicate my run to you," Ricky told her. "I couldn't get away from you fast enough."

Steph kicked up some dirt at him.

"Third place," Ricky said to Danny. "First to third. Man, you feeling okay?"

"I thought I was going as fast as I could."

"Maybe our hearts weren't in it this year," Josh vacantly said.

Danny knew then for sure that this was Josh's final race. He'd make sure to say goodbye to him when they parted.

Ricky hit some keys again. "Feels good!"

"Does it?" Steph said.

Ricky stopped to soak up the moment. "Oh yeah."

The old upright rested against a tree. Danny wondered how it came to be here and for how long. Maybe the people who created this tradition lugged it here, a suitable mysterious goal for a mysterious night. While costumed children went door to door asking for treats, some raced to the piano just to make a second's worth of noise. Danny didn't know who got the better deal, but he knew he wouldn't have traded these races for a million bags of sweets. The quick thrill was enough to keep him coming back year after year.

"So," Ricky said. "Who wants to race back to town?"

* * *

Erik Handy

"I can't believe we've lived our whole lives here," Suzy said, "and neither of us have done this."

Adrian made sure the flashlight worked. "Don't get your hopes up."

"I know." Suzy approached the upright. "Do we lift the lid?"

Adrian shrugged. "All I know is that for three days starting on Halloween, the dead will come to play on this piano."

Suzy lifted the lid. "I wonder if they'll play a song." She pressed a key and nothing happened. She pressed another and again nothing.

"Only the dead can play it," Adrian said. "Or so they say."

Suzy tried a few more keys before giving up.

Adrian rolled his eyes. "You do realize that we're wasting our time, right?"

Suzy started to pout. "You don't have to be mean about it."

"I'm not being mean, but come on. Ghosts don't exist. Some high school kids brought this out here in the fifties and started the legend. My parents said so."

"Maybe," Suzy said. "Have some faith, Adrian. It's Halloween. The walls between the living and the dead are at their thinnest."

"For the next three days."

"I thought there'd be more people here."

"All the locals know the story is bull. No one cares."

"I care." Suzy was quiet for a few moments before saying, "I just wanted to do something special tonight. Every Halloween we either stay home and watch movies or go to parties. I'm bored with all that."

Adrian put his arm around her. "I know. I am, too. It's this town. We've gotta get out of here."

"And watch movies somewhere else?"

Adrian let her go. "I don't know, Suzy. Halloween is pretty much a one-note holiday. Just like Thanksgiving and Christmas. You've lived through one, you've lived through them all."

"It should be special."

Adrian shone the flashlight the way they came.

"What's wrong?" Suzy said.

"I thought I heard something."

"Like?"

"Running."

Suzy got closer to Adrian. "I hear it." There was fear in her tone. Her hunger for enchantment was lost.

A breeze washed the sound clean out of the air. The tree branches rustled overhead. Somewhere above the canopy was a moon and stars. Below, just the two lovers, the piano, and strange noises.

When all was quiet again, Adrian said, "What time is it?"

Suzy checked her phone. "Almost eight."

"It's pretty dark for eight o'clock. Too dark."

"Don't scare me."

"I wasn't."

"You were about to. You were going to yell *Boo* or grab my side."

"No, I wasn't."

"Yes, you were."

Adrian grinned. "Yeah. I was."

"Jerk."

"How long are we gonna be out here?" Adrian asked. "You know Jay Number Two is having a party."

"Another party," Suzy said under her breath.

"We can stop by on the way home. If you want."

"I don't want. But if you want to, then we will."

"Damn, Suzy. We'll just stay out here until dawn with the deer and bugs."

"I haven't seen any deer."

Adrian paused. "Me neither. I haven't heard any birds either."

Suzy licked her dry upper lip. "Maybe –"

"BOO!" Adrian yelled as he grabbed her side.

Suzy slapped his shoulder. "Ass."

Adrian laughed. "I'm sorry."

"Ass!"

Once the moment passed, and it did rather quickly, Adrian said, "It says something about a place when this," he gestured to the piano, "is the only remotely interesting landmark."

"That we've never seen until now," Suzy added. "And we were raised here."

Suddenly, a perfect D-note from the upright spilled out into the night.

Adrian brought the flashlight around, catching Suzy's eyes with the light.

They were the only two people present and several feet separated them from the upright.

"Did you hear that?" Suzy said.

Adrian nodded, which Suzy didn't see so she repeated herself.

"I think so," Adrian said. And that was the truth. The sound was so abrupt—and impossible—that it could have just been the wind playing tricks again or a deer grunting in the distance. If it happened at all.

Then, a few more notes rang as if the piano was perfectly tuned.

Adrian rushed to the instrument and examined the front and back.

Suzy stood still, hugging herself.

Adrian pressed every key and was treated with just the clicking of each one.

"Do you believe now?" Suzy said.

Adrian backed up toward her, keeping the piano in his line of sight. "There's no way—"

The piano sounded again.

This time, the lovers clearly saw the keys being pressed by invisible hands.

Suzy screamed and ran.

Adrian waited a split second before taking off after her.

He tried to keep the light steady, but the ground was too rife with exposed roots and occasional depressions. Suzy was just ahead of him. He could hear her heavy breathing and heavier footsteps.

His left foot landed in one of those depressions, something dug by a forest critter. He lost his balance and desperately tried to correct his fall.

The side of his head slammed into a thick root which refused to stay buried.

He held onto the flashlight though.

"Suzy," he yelled.

She kept running.

Adrian rolled to his knees. The fall jammed his neck real good. He felt for his phone but couldn't find it.

Getting to his feet was easy. He was surprised that staying there was just as effortless considering the tumble he took.

"Suzy," he yelled.

She was too far gone to hear him.

"Suzy."

Adrian stepped over the hole which toppled him. He didn't have far to go. Just a few more holes to avoid. He knew these woods by heart now. He didn't even need the flashlight, but he kept it on just the same. Its harsh white light comforted him like Suzy did and his mother before her.

He firmly held the light and followed the beam back to the piano. No one was around to hear him play a few notes from a song he learned as a child.

THE OTHER KIDS

PATRICK MOODY

FROM *THE NICHOLS POST*, dated October 28, 1994: "*For a whopping tenth year in a row, Trumbull's Hilltop Circle has been named the best place to trick or treat in the entire state by **Better Homes and Gardens**. Locals attribute this to the close knit community, which bands together every Halloween to decorate their houses to the fullest extreme, offer (you guessed it) FULL size candy bars, and provide a safe, kid-friendly route for the hundreds of little ghouls, goblins, and witches to roam on the spookiest night of the year!*"

Dispatch,Trumbull Police Department. 10-31-1994. 11:30 pm: "*All Units, report to the neighborhood of Hilltop Circle. Backup needed. Officer down. Civilians down. Repeat, all officers respond. Swat requested. Threat unknown.*"

From the journal of Pete Wilson, age 37, dated October 30th, 2020.

THE OTHER KIDS

Well, you told me to keep a journal, doc, so here it is. My first entry. Said it would help me overcome my trauma, help me get past this. I hope you're right. I'm a writer, after all. A novelist, so it should be a breeze to write this all out, right? We'll see about that. Crazy that it's been 26 years. I remember it like it was yesterday. Still dream about it. Can close my eyes and see it. Them. The Other Kids. Well, here goes:

The streets were filled with monsters. They skipped and stumbled and sprinted down leaf-covered streets, their plastic and rubber masks glinting in the lights of the seemingly endless rows of grinning jack 'o lanterns, their bags, baskets, and buckets brimming with candy bars sure to warrant a late night tooth brushing, lest the Cavity Fairy pays a visit come early November.

These were the littlest kids in the neighborhood, from one to seven, trailed by talkative flocks of their parents who waited on the sidewalk while the little ones waddled up to doors in their ill-fitting costumes, singing out that ancient greeting of "TRICK OR TREAT!", their plastic pumpkins and glitter-covered pails at the ready.

The little ones always led the charge. It was five o'clock on the dot.

Halloween night was officially on.

* * *

"Best to start at the bottom," Preston Mayer said behind his blue Power Rangers mask. "That way we can go all the way up, then come all the way back. Double the candy! Here." He produced a wrinkled, hand drawn map from the pocket of his polyester jumpsuit. It had every single house listed on it, even though we'd grown up on Hilltop and knew it by heart, with a route drawn in thick red marker.

Brett Bachlekner flipped his skateboard up with one stomp of his Frankenstein boot, catching it and folding it under the arm of his scissor-mangled thrift store jacket. "Good. We should start early. You know the cars and buses come to drop off the out of town kids as soon as the sun goes down."

The rest of us nodded gravely, a solemn assortment of myself as a Ninja Turtle (Michaelangelo, of course. Cowabunga), Samantha Novak as Sailor Moon, Tiffany Kuwolski as a pink Power Ranger, and Jamal London as Raiden from Mortal Kombat. We were the Crew. The Hilltop Crew. And those cars and buses dropping off kids from the other side of town to more than six towns over were our mortal enemies.

The *Other Kids*. And as far as we were concerned, this was our neighborhood, thank you very much, so go and get your candy somewhere else.

We left from my house, rolling our skateboards over crunching leaves and wind-blown silly string, the sun a low, burnt orange sinking beneath the skeletal trees of Ribberkenny woods.

The adults were out and about, checking their decorations and making sure everything that lit up, made noise, and moved was working. The Whitmeyers' yard had been transformed into a ghoul-infested graveyard. Mr. Whit had even gone as far as digging up half the lawn, filling the holes with animatronic creeps that moaned and waved their arms. His wife was standing in the front door, armed with two massive barrels shaped like pumpkins, brimming with super-sized Kit Kats.

Across the street, the Giamettis were checking their inflatable witch and ghost, each a towering twelve feet tall, lit from within by purple and orange strobe lights. They waved to us as we rode by.

"Got some good stuff!" Mr. Giametti called over, "Granola Bars and toothbrushes!" He laughed, clutching his rounded belly.

Everyone knew the Giamettis gave out s'mores, which Ed, now a big bad teenager, cooked up right on the spot. They made for good walking snacks.

We skated on, passing by little kids who wandered in the middle of the street like ducklings, narrowly avoiding them on our skateboards, while their parents told us to slow down.

But this was Halloween, and if there's one thing you learned about Halloween, it was the only night of the year a bunch of eleven-year-olds could ignore adults and get away with it.

We reached the bottom of the street, the small memorial library on one side, our brick-wall bus stop on the other. Already, cars were pulling in. We watched minivan doors slide, truck beds swing down, and car doors open, unleashing the swarms of Other Kids. They poured forth like an army of ravenous zombies, racing towards the houses on either side of the street. I saw more Power Rangers, Ninja Turtles, and Sailor Moons than I could count, suddenly bursting with anger, as if they'd somehow intentionally stole our costume ideas.

We stood on the lawn of the library among the straw-stuffed scarecrows and watched them charge up the street, tearing into the neighborhood as fast as their costumed feet could carry them.

It was a few moments later that the strange van approached.

It was black. But somehow *more* than black, like the paint itself sucked in all the light. The windows were completely tinted. I couldn't even tell if it *had* windows, really. The tires were barely visible, silent even as they drove over the leaves and twigs. It stopped and ran idle for what seemed like forever before the door slid open, and a group of six Other Kids emerged.

I heard Tiffany and Jamal suck in hissed breaths behind me. Preston tugged on my orange Michelangelo headband.

"Pete... what the fuck are those things?" Brent had only recently discovered the joys of swearing and used every opportunity to do so.

"I don't know," I answered, and suddenly found myself wishing that my foam nunchucks were the real deal.

The Other Kids didn't make a sound as they walked out under the streetlights. They stopped, blocking the next group behind them, and just stood there, heads moving from side to side.

"What are they even wearing?" Samantha asked. She sounded worried. Samantha was never worried.

I squinted, trying to make it out. Their body suits must have been real expensive, the kind you see at the mall that are for adults and go for like a few hundred bucks. They were about our height, but their legs and arms were skinny. Too skinny, and their stomachs were so distended they all looked, well, *pregnant*.

"Looks like those commercials on tv about starving kids," Jamal said. "You know, the ones in Africa? They have bellies like that. Short like them, too."

I nodded. But this seemed different. Wrong, somehow.

They're just costumes, I told myself.

The masks were the worst part. They were painted fish-belly white. Human masks, bald-headed with wide smiles filled with sharp, thin teeth. Smiles that were way too wide. Their eyes were black pinpricks, too small for their faces, and they didn't have noses.

They didn't even have pillowcases or pumpkin pales. Who went trick or treating empty handed?

One of them spotted us. It (I couldn't tell if it was a boy or girl under that disgusting makeup) took a few steps forward, walking strangely on those shriveled legs, and waved. Its grossly long fingers flitted in the distance, the nails long and awful sharp looking.

I gave a small, nervous wave back. "What movie is that from, Brent? Can you tell?" Brent and I were the only ones whose parents let us rent horror stuff from Blockbuster.

"No frickin' clue. But those things are creepy as hell, dude."

"Agreed," Sam said. She readied her skateboard. "Come on. Let's hit the Cardells' before they get there."

"First run of the night!" Jamal said, fixing his black Power Ranger mask back on.

The Cardells' was a success. They greeted the door as a pair of Godzillas with chef's hats, both wearing aprons. Mr's said "*Kiss the monster cook*", Mrs' said "*I' add the flavor*". They dumped heaping amounts of Three Musketeers into our pillowcases, and we made off up the street. I tested my case, judging how much more it could fit before we made a pit stop at my house to dump our stash and set out fresh.

We left, making for the Windam's across the street, and I saw the Other Kids move towards the Cardell's. They walked in these strange, loping strides, all single file, silent with those huge toothy grins. I shuddered, trying to keep up with the Crew.

Four more stops brought us to the Kuwolski's. Tiffany's dad was in the driveway with the other a few other Hilltop dads, setting up the "Rad Dad Wagon", Tiffany's little brothers Red Rider that they converted every year into a mobile bar. It was a "Rad Dad" tradition.

"Hey dudes and dudettes!" Mr. Kuwolski called out. He was dressed, as he was every Halloween, as a cop. It was an easy costume, since he was one, and always made sure to take his favorite night of the year off.

"Sup!" Said Mr. Mulaney, already pumping the small keg into his red plastic cup.

We watched in fascination. We couldn't wait to drink. That was cool adult stuff. One time, Brent snuck a bottle of his mom's brandy out behind the library and we each took sips. All of us spit it out, and we decided that we should probably wait a while.

"You guys look awesome!" Mr. Novak said. "Killer Sailor Moon, kid!" Samantha rolled her eyes at her dad.

"Now don't mind us," Mr. Kowalski told us, "We'll be walking around, but don't let us cramp your style. Heck, if you pass by us, just pretend you don't know us!"

We all nodded, deciding long before that that's exactly what we'd do. They were pretty embarrassing, no matter how rad they claimed to be.

"Here," Sam's dad tossed us each a Milky Way. "That should tide you over. We got the good stuff for later, when all the other kids scram."

We dropped the bars into our bags and said goodbye, watching as the Rad Dads made their way to the opposite side of the street, their boom box playing "Are You Ready for Freddy" by the Fat Boys.

A faint scream echoed from behind us.

"Where'd that come from?"

There were only six houses at the bottom of the street. I looked at each yard, each front door.

The Cardell's front porch lights blinked on, off, on...

The Other Kids marched from their yard. Still empty handed.

"Must've been a trick," Brent said. "Since they can't carry any treats."

The Cardell's light blinked off. I waited, but it never came back on.

"Let's make sure we stay ahead of them," Samantha said.

"Yeah. It's creep central down there," Tiffany agreed.

We picked up the pace.

By the time we got to the midpoint of the street, we were shoulder to shoulder with the regular Other Kids, who swarmed up and down the sidewalks, careening into the yards to gawk at the decorations. Every Ninja Turtle I spotted made me angrier.

"Why can't they just go to their own neighborhoods?" Jamal asked.

"My mom said that some places are dangerous, or a lot of kids live off main roads. Too many speeding cars." Samantha said.

"Still, Sam. Can't they just... I dunno..."

"Find somewhere else?" Preston asked. "I wish."

We hit six more houses, our pillowcases close to bursting.

* * *

The Pitchers had turned their lawn into a haunted castle. Mr. Pitcher had built the entire thing himself out of plywood. He'd started work on it in the summer and had just finished in time for the big night. The thing was massive, sporting three gothic towers complete with foam-rubber gargoyles. You could actually walk inside, where Mr. Pitcher, dressed in a full fledged suit of armor (he was a history professor at Yale), was waiting.

"Halt, you miscreants of the night! You have entered the haunted castle, HA HA HA!"

"Oh, jeeze." Tiffany lifted up her mask and pinched the bridge of her nose.

"And what do we have here?" He thrust a wooden sword in my direction. "Some sort of ogre? I'll have you know, foul creature, that I have slain many in my day!"

"I'm a Ninja Turtle," I said.

The knight cocked his head to the side, metal helmet creaking. "A turtle? Very well, good sir. I hereby decree that ye honorable folk may partake in the feast. All of you!"

We left Castle Pitcher with Hershey Bars and Ring Pops on each finger. As we approached the Ribberkennys', I turned back once more.

The grinning, pot-bellied Other Kids were marching into the castle.

"Wait, weren't they still at the bottom of the street?" Tiffany asked.

"I saw them down there. I swear."

"Must move fast. We need to hurry before they pass us."

"Yeah," I said absently, and watched as one of them stopped outside the castle entrance and turned back to the street, its head looking from one side to the other.

Mr. Ribberkenny was a retired teacher. Since his retirement, he played the same joke every Halloween. He'd dress up in a hockey mask from the *Friday the 13th* movies and sit on a rocking chair next to his front door. He'd stay perfectly still while his wife gave out the treats, and only when you made your way down the front steps would be burst forth, plastic machete in hand. It scared me the first year. By the ninth, it just made me laugh. For an old guy he was quick as hell.

"Happy Halloween, Jason!" Preston said to him.

Mr. Ribberkenny stayed still as a statue.

We'd covered one third of the neighborhood.

* * *

I rang the Glazer's doorbell. Their lawn was lit by green lights. A gigantic papier-mache flying saucer was resting on top of their roof.

Mrs. Glazer opened the door. Her eyes were red and puffy.

"Oh, don't you guys look good," she said, forcing a smile.

"What's wrong?" Tiffany asked.

"Oh, it's just Scottie. He was in the yard, dressed in his little E.T. costume. I went out to check on him just a few minutes ago and... and I can't find him."

Scottie was a mean little sucker, but very cute. And I knew for a fact that he never left the yard. Every time I rode by the Glazer house he would run alongside and bark viciously, flashing his little teeth. I'd usually wave to him and smile, knowing full well all he wanted was to gnaw my legs like a chicken bone. But the little sucker never, and I mean never, left his yard. They didn't even have an invisible fence.

"We'll keep an eye out for him," I told her. "He couldn't have gone far."

"Oh, thank you, Pete. Tell your mom I said hi, yeah?"

"I will."

"Weird," Samantha said as we reached the edge of the yard.

"He probably just got excited," Jamal said. "Maybe one of the Other Kids was dressed up like a cat or something."

* * *

By the time we reached my house, our pillowcases were overflowing.

We opened my garage, the floor marked off with our individual spaces, and upended the sacks, mountains of candy spilling out onto the concrete.

"Score!" Brent said. "Dude, I'll be so sugar wired. Might even stay up all night and finally beat Sonic! Sega all night, baby!"

* * *

The trees and bushes in the Feinstein's yard were strung with violet and orange lights. They'd covered them in silly string, making menacing looking spiderwebs. They'd even tp'd their own yard, which gave it a very ghostly look.

We got our candy and moved on. Preston checked them off his map, then circled the Salard house. We cut across the London's yard, avoiding the teeming masses. As we moved around Jamal's trampoline, he held out a hand to stop us.

"How did they beat us?"

The Salard's house was set far back from the street, most of it hidden by a long gravel drive. The Crew knew to use the side door, since the front yard was the site of Mrs. Salard's prize winning garden. Most kids skipped it, even though they decorated the drive with cardboard cutouts of all the Universal Monsters, the gravel littered with plastic bones and fake, ripped-off rubber arms and legs complete with fake blood.

The spooky group of grinning Other Kids was gathered at the door.

"Come on," Preston whispered. "Let's take a closer look. I wanna see what the heck these weirdos get up to. Don't you guys?"

We snuck through Jamal's yard, crouching at the row of bushes that separated it from the Salard's driveway.

The Other Kids stood stock still and silent. Still empty handed.

The door creaked open, and Mr. Salard walked onto the porch in his mummy costume, which he made every year from Ace Bandages from Walgreens. His smile faded when he looked down at the gathered horrors that grinned up at him.

"Well," he managed, letting out a small, nervous laugh, "aren't you all... *something*. Here you go."

He held out a handful of Snickers.

One of the Other Kids walked up the steps, long skinny arms dangling at its sides.

"Don't you guys have any—"

The wide mouth snapped down onto Mr. Salard's wrist. Even from behind the bushes, we could hear a crunch, then a disgusting slurping sound. It happened so fast that it took a few moments for Mr. Salard to register what had happened. Then he screamed. The Other Kid turned around, a ring of chocolate and blood smeared around its much-too-wide mouth. The rest walked up, stepping over Mr. Salard, who was now trying to crawl, clutching the bleeding stump of his arm. His candy was piled on a wooden crate. The Other Kids opened their mouths in unison and pounced on it. Chomping and slurping. Clawing and hissing at each other, fighting over the chocolate as the one who took Mr. Salard's hand stood guard.

"Guys," Samantha whispered.

"Let's get the fuck out of here!" Brent cried. He sprinted to the street.

"Brent, no!" I dove, trying to grab him, but he slipped right through my gloved fingers.

The one Other Kid's head whipped around at the sound. It broke into a terrifying run. I watched in horror as it moved on all four of its emaciated legs.

"Jesus," Jamal said. "He's gonna get him!"

We stayed hidden. I know we should have gone after Brent, but we were frozen in place, unable to register what we'd seen. We could only listen as Brent cried out, his voice shrill and hoarse, and suddenly cut silent.

A few trick or treaters paused on the street, looking over to the Salard's driveway before walking on.

"We need to get him help," Tiffany said. "My dad!"

The Rad Dads must've been close by. They'd left soon before us, taking the other side of the street. Mr. Kuwolski was a cop. He'd know what to do.

We ran back into Jamal's yard and onto the street, nearly bowling over a group of X-Men and Disney Princesses.

We peered over the heads of the Other Kids, the *regular* Other Kids, searching for four dads and a red wagon.

"You see 'em?" Preston asked.

"No," Jamal said, standing on his tiptoes. He was taller than all of us by a good three inches.

"Maybe they passed us," Tiffany said. "They're not stopping at each house like we've been."

I pictured the rest of the street in my mind. Two houses past the Salards, it forked into Hilltop Place and Hilltop Road. There were about ten houses on each. I thought of the smiling, cannibal Other Kids. How many houses had they done that too, already? Had anybody noticed besides us?

"Let's go," I said.

"But that's where *they* are," Jamal said worriedly.

"They didn't see us," I told him. "We'll just blend in with the rest of the crowd."

We turned and walked up the small hill, eyeing every house, looking for the Rad Dads. And the Other Kids.

The last street on Hilltop Circle was the Helfridge's. Authentic iron cauldrons smoked and bubbled around the yard.

We slowed, cautiously studying our surroundings. A group of Power Rangers strolled around the cauldrons and up to the door. They knocked, calling out "TRICK OR TREAT" at the top of their lungs. No answer. One of them rang the doorbell. They waited for a good minute.

"What the hell?" Samantha said. "Where's Mr. Helfridge?"

The goofy lawyer was always dressed like a witch, with a long rubber nose covered in plastic warts. He thought it was the funniest thing in the world.

"Aw, man!" one of the Rangers moaned. The group walked away, dejected.

"Should we look inside?" Jamal asked.

"I think we have to," I said. "If they've been here..." I didn't want to say anymore. I could see Preston starting to shake. He lifted up his Red Ranger mask and took a long hit off his inhaler.

I led the Crew across the yard. The house was lit up, almost every window. I could hear "Monster Mash" playing loudly from the living room.

Samantha gasped behind me.

I spun and found her staring down into one of the cauldrons.

Inside, Mr. Helfridge's head bobbed among plastic bats and rubber spiders.

"Guys. Guys!"

It took a long time for me to look away. Mr. Helfrige's face was horrible, the skin bubbling in the hot water. His eyes were wide and terrified, looking up at me as if pleading for help.

I tore my gaze away, pulse hammering in my throat. Tiffany was pointing two houses up, down Hilltop Place. The Other Kids were waiting on the Santilli's front porch.

"There's only two of them," Preston said, his voice shaking.

"Screw this," I said, thinking of a safe place. "Let's go to Tiffany's. We'll lock the door and shut off all the lights. Wait this out until her dad comes home." It was the best I could come up with.

The crew nodded vigorously, hefting their pillowcases as they followed me back down the street.

The crowd had grown a lot smaller. I looked at my watch. It was 8:30. This should have been prime time. Maybe the rest of the out of towners were just then being dropped off at the bottom of the street, hitting up the Cardells for those king sized Three Musketeers.

We passed by the Salards. You wouldn't have noticed anything amiss. The side door was closed. Mr. Salard must've gotten himself inside, where I hoped he was calling the police. No sign of Brent, either. My heart went from jumping in my throat to sinking. We'd all wanted to save him, to stop him. But if we did, we might all be dead.

And there'd be nobody to warn Hilltop of the Other Kids.

We were walking fast, trying not to draw attention, but quick enough to get help in time. We'd ditched the skateboards at Jamal's. Samantha ran across the street to her house, checking to make sure everyone was ok.

"Oh, shit." Jamal had stopped. He was pointing to the Findley's place. Two Other Kids were just leaving, closing the front door behind them. Their faces were smeared in chocolate.

"Just keep moving," I said, and quickened my pace.

I saw the next one at the Glazer's. It was sitting on the yard, its face buried in a large bucket with Dracula's face printed on the side. It lifted its head, pin prick black eyes staring at me, and licked the sugary mess from its lips.

It wasn't until we reached the Pitcher's castle that we decided to stop. We'd seen ten more of them along the way. Which was impossible, since we'd only counted six when they'd arrived in that weird, black van.

"What are these things doing?" Samantha asked, "multiplying?"

"Let's go," I said, pointing to the castle. "Maybe Mr. Pitcher has seen them."

"Or maybe he's dead," Tiffany muttered softly.

"He can't be," Jamal told her. "Dude was wearing a full suit of armor. They wouldn't mess with him."

He was wrong.

The street was close to empty as we crossed over into the yard.

Castle Pitcher was covered in blood and smeared with brown globs of chocolate. The mix oozed down the spray-painted plywood, filling the castle with a sickening stench.

We found Mr. Pitcher, piece by piece. They'd chewed him in his armor, leaving nothing but piles flesh encased in crumpled metal.

Jamal puked all over his costume. It took Preston and me to stop Samantha from screaming.

"There!" I said when we got outside, "he can help!"

We raced over to Mr. Ribberkenny, still sitting in the rocking chair with his machete and hockey mask. I ripped off my own and shook him by the shoulder.

"Mr. Ribberkenny! It's me, Pete! Look, you have to call the police! You have to-"

Mr. Ribberkenny's head tumbled off his shoulders in a slimy squelch, rolling across the porch and into the lawn.

We couldn't stop Sam from screaming that time.

Across the street, eight Other Kids watched us, smiling.

We cut into the Ribberkenny's backyard and into the woods. What we called "Ribberkenny woods", ran far back and cut through all of the backyards of Hilltop. Now that they'd noticed us, we didn't have a choice.

We ran as fast as we could, stumbling over roots and rocks, our costumes snared by branches and tearing the further we pushed on.

I took the lead, leaving my mask behind. I looked to my left, watching as the houses passed by one by one. Screams echoed in the Whitmeyer's pool house. A window smashed at the Holmvik's. The beams of a few of the remaining trick or treater's flashlights swung around wildly.

"Pete! Stop!" Tiffany screamed.

I slid, tripping and bashing my shins on a large root, sending waves of pain ricocheting up my legs.

When I looked up, one of *them* was blocking my path. I managed to pick myself off the ground, gripping onto my stuffed pillowcase. If it came near me, when it came near me, I'd swing. It wouldn't do much, but it might buy me time to pick up a good sized rock to bash it's disgusting head in.

It made a strange chittering sound as it approached. The mouth opened wide. I could see skin tearing at the edges of its lips, forcing the smile wider until it seemed to wrap around the whole of its face. Its belly was so distended I was shocked it could stand up straight. It must have been poking out a good two feet, completely round. Round, and chock full of candy and human flesh. I readied the pillowcase, slowly swinging it to gain some momentum. Its head. I had to go for its head.

As I was about to swing, I heard someone yell behind me, and two full pillowcases of candy came sailing over my head, landing at the Other Kid's feet. It looked down, smile widening even more, somehow, and dove in. I threw mine over as well. It seemed to forget all about us, so fixated on the sugar.

We didn't stick around to watch the feast. Tiffany's was only two houses down, and we needed to make it before the Other Kid finished.

Tiffany grabbed the key from under the mat and opened the back door. The house was dark and quiet. Her mom was a nurse, and worked the evening shift. No sign of the Rad Dads, either.

"You know where he keeps his gun?" I asked.

"Are you crazy?" Preston asked. "You know we're not supposed to play with guns."

"This isn't playing," I told him. "Those things bit off Mr. Salard's hand. They killed Helfridge, and Pitcher and Ribberkenny. Shit, man, they probably killed everyone from the Cardells all the way up to Hilltop Road!"

Preston looked away, reaching for his inhaler.

"In the safe in the bedroom," Tiffany said. "I know where he hides the key."

"Show me."

* * *

Mr. Kuwolski sure liked his guns. The big safe held two pistols, a shotgun, and a few hunting rifles. The Crew watched as I loaded each of them.

"Where'd you learn that?" Jamal asked.

"My dad's a hunter," I told him. "I hate it, but he brings me every time I go to visit." My dad lived in Wyoming and was a complete jerk, but at least he taught me something worthwhile.

I handed the guns out. Pistols for Sam and Tiff, the shotgun for Preston, and rifles for Jamal and me. We looked strange, armed in our torn and soiled costumes. Like something out of a weird Nintendo game.

We made our way downstairs, posting up at the front windows, making sure to keep low. A few trick or treaters sprinted by, making for the bottom of the street. One of them was bleeding, crying at the top of her lungs. Otherwise, the street was empty.

"So what are they?" Samantha asked. "Aliens?"

"Monsters," Jamal said. "They gotta be. Sure ain't human."

"But where the hell did they come from?"

"Someplace far, far away," Preston said, nervously clutching the shotgun. "You guys see the car they came in? I never seen anything like that. Looked like something from a comic book."

We watched in silence for a long while. What did they want? What was their weakness? I turned the questions over and over in my head. It was hard to think, being so scared.

It took a long time before I got it.

"Candy!"

The Crew all turned to stare at me.

"Think," I said. "When we first saw them, what did they go after first?"

"Salard's hand," Tiffany said. "We all saw."

"No," I said. "Salard's hand was just in the way. They went for the *candy*, first. When you guys threw yours at the one in the woods, it seemed to forget about us. It went right for it. I saw one at the Glazers doing the same thing. They eat it like they're starving dogs or something. They don't focus on anything else."

"Until they run out," Tiffany said. "And we've seen what they go after when that happens."

I closed my eyes, trying not to think about Mr. Heldfrige's head in the pot.

"We need candy," I said. "Lots of it."

"Well we're outta luck, there," Samantha said. "We lost it all in the woods."

"Not all of it," I said. "I know where there's a stash. A big stash."

I told them my plan.

We ditched our costumes in Tiffany's kitchen. She went to her room and brought down a pile of clothes, some hats, and paint. All black. We suited up. Jamal, Preston, and I couldn't care less if they were girl's clothes. We had bigger fish to fry. Tiffany went around with black beanie hats, I guess her dad had a lot of them from the police force, and fixed them on our heads. Next, she took black face paint and did our faces and hands. Before long, we were covered up head to toe. Before we left, Tiff grabbed the small basket of Butterfingers her dad had been saving for us.

We moved slow through the woods, careful to stay far back, where the streetlights and motion sensors in the backyards couldn't reach. The Other Kids had those small, beady eyes, and I figured they wouldn't be able to see too well pitch dark. All the while, we dropped the Butterfingers behind us. I figured if any saw and decided to follow, those might slow them up.

It took a long time, and even as far back as we were, I could see the chaos unfolding on Hilltop Circle. Bodies lay strewn in the streets, hung over fences, hanging out of smashed windows and draped over mailboxes and Halloween decorations. Some of them even looked like decorations, until you saw the too-real looking blood.

My house was just around the bend. We crawled to the edge of the woods, stopping at the treeline where my yard started. The street was visible from there, and we stayed perfectly still as a troop of Other Kids, some fifteen or sixteen, made their way silently to the Fletcher's house across the street.

"Okay," I said. "Let's move."

We tore around my house, going for the garage, when we heard a boombox playing from the street. I stopped, peering around the corner, and saw the Rad Dads staggering along, by now completely wasted, blaring their music as if they didn't have a care in the world.

"You gotta be kiddin' me," Jamal said. "We need to get them, quick." He gestured to the Halpin's, where the Other Kids had stopped on the lawn, staring at the Rad Dads.

"Shit. Shit, shit, *shit!*" Preston breathed.

"Alright. Tiffany, you're the fastest, try to get them. Then you run inside the garage. I'll be there holding it open."

Tiffany nodded, psyching herself up. I'll get them."

While she raced down my driveway, the rest of us made for the garage door. I swung it up, breathing a sigh of relief when I saw our mountain of candy laying on the floor.

"Okay, guys. You know what to do."

They all nodded and got to work.

Soon the Rad Dads came stumbling inside, drunk as hell and laughing their asses off.

"Oh hey! Iss Pete! And the kids!" Mr. Kuwolski burped, "Whas' gon' on? You guys 'kay?"

"Wow!" Mr. Novak said, elbowing Mr. Mulaney. "Check out those guns! Man, they make 'em look so *real* nowadays!"

Tiffany pushed them back to the other side of the garage. They were in no shape to help, now.

I stepped outside into the driveway, rifle in the crook of my arm. More Other Kids had joined the group on the Fletcher's lawn. They were staring at me, grinning those sharp-toothed grins.

I took out a Hershey bar from my pocket and chucked it as far as I could. It landed in the grass just in front of them. One looked down, bent forward, and was brutally slashed by the one next to it. Three more joined in the fight until one came out victorious, slurping it down its gullet.

"More over here!" I called. "Much as you want!"

They regarded me for a moment. Twenty, maybe thirty pairs of eyes fixed on me, until the one who'd one the Hershey bar led the charge.

I ran back inside, jumping over the barricade Jamal and Samantha had made with my bikes, spare tires, and the old motorcycle my dad left behind. They'd moved everything to the far end of the garage, giving us a long, wide firing space. We took up position behind it, guns cocked, aimed, and ready. Tiffany had settled the dads as far back as she could. But not before she took her dad's walkie and got a hold of the dispatcher.

The first wave loped their way into the garage, pausing at the absurd amount of candy.

They hissed, the sound so alien and off putting that I started shaking worse than Preston. They sounded like cobras.

They pounced on the candy. Teeth gnashed, claws swiped. Fists and elbows and knees flew. Six of them were down and bleeding out within twenty seconds of the feeding frenzy as each one tried asserting its dominance, laying claim to as much chocolate as it could. The rest filed in. I counted twenty before I pushed our new eclectic garage door opener. They didn't notice it shut behind them.

"Ready?" I asked.

The candy was almost gone. Several of them were now looking at us. Hissing. Fangs dripping and filthy.

"Ready," everyone said.

"Ready?" Mr. Kuwolski asked, slumped against the back wall with the rest of the dads. "Ready for what? I sure am hungry. What about you guys?"

They came at us fast. I could smell the chocolate and blood.

"You killed our neighbors," I said, aiming the rifle. "Trick or treat."

The hail of bullets smacked them back against the garage door, filling the place with a foul reek that made my eyes water. We put plenty of bullet holes in the door, some a little too big, and I could see more gathering outside.

We kept firing. I helped Preston reload the shotgun, shouted to Jamal to keep his shoulder steady. Tiff and Sam were doing great.

The Other Kids took a lot of bullets to drop, but once they were down, they stayed down.

The ones outside were banging on the door. I saw more and more gathering. An army of wide, hissing mouths.

We just had to hold them.

Halloween was almost over.

Faintly, very faintly, I could hear sirens wail in the distance, and something humming.

A helicopter.

I hoped it was.

* * *

And back to the present. There you go, doc. The way I remember it. Word for word. I know writing it all out is supposed to help. In a way, it did. I've written and sold a lot of horror stories in my short career, but this one is the scariest of all, because it's true. I know you won't believe me. You'll say the Other Kids are a figment of my imagination, the embodiment of deep seeded psychological pain. But I swear, they're real. I'd tell you to check the police records, but the Bureau came in and had them all shredded. I'd tell you to visit Brent Bachlekner's grave, or Edward Helfridge's. Phil Picker's and Ned Ribberkenny's, too. But they're all in some unmarked site upstate. Probably in a landfill, for all I know. You could ask the others. Tiff or Sam or Preston. Jamal passed last year. On Halloween. Make of that what you will, but we all received his note in the mail. I burned mine. Couldn't bear to even look at it, once I read what he'd had to say. Loved him like a brother.

*I don't know if it's getting to what you call the "root of my problem". You know, that boy at the 7-11. I saw him again tonight through my bedroom window. He just stands there, staring into the store next to the Redbox machine. Never goes in. I know you think I'm projecting, that I have an irrational fear of some child I don't even know. Maybe all children, for that matter. But maybe now you can understand a little better. Why I won't go near the place, or leave my apartment after sundown. Especially now. It's October 30th. Mischief night. Hey, maybe he **is** playing a prank on me. Why else would he wait until 2 am to remove his shirt, exposing his fish-belly white skin, and turn ever so slightly, just enough for me to make out his horridly distended stomach? He waves, sometimes, with those long fingers. Never turns his bald head, though. I think if he ever did, I'd scream. Christ, I might have a heart attack at 33. Cause I know what I'd see. Beady black pinpricks for eyes.*

And he'd be smiling. Smiling ear to ear.

You better believe it.

I'm afraid he will, you know. Tomorrow's Halloween, and he looks like he has a real hankering for candy.

DEAD MAN'S FINGERS

PATRICK WINTERS

THE FIVE YOUNG FRIENDS were walking along the wooded side of Dresden Lane—swinging their bags of candy on their way to the rich folks' homes out in Winston Plains—when the ever-rascally Jake Dunn spoke up from the back of the group.

"You know, there are dead people buried out there."

It was a strange statement, made even stranger by how plainly Jake said it, as though he were sharing some well-known fact of life rather than something so random and macabre. If he'd said it with his usual bit of razz, his pals may have just blown him off and kept on walking, knowing full well that this was just another one of his devilish bits of fun. But putting that spin of certainty on it? That could pull them in. That could get them going along with the gag.

When they all stopped and turned to face him, Jake had to keep from grinning, because he knew his tact had worked, at least so far.

"What?" Jamie Howell mumbled. He pulled his Spider-Man mask up, revealing a sweaty (but curious) face.

Jake pointed off to the stretching forest of skeletal gray trees to their left, their branches bared in the chilled season. The whole of the tree-line was thick with brambles and brushwood, looking quite mysterious (and just a bit spooky) on this Halloween night, like something out of an old Grimms' fairy tale. A world unto itself, just off the side of the road. Insects chittered from deep inside the sanctum, but aside from that, the woods were perfectly still.

Jake gave a nod of absolute knowledge, his neon green clown's wig bobbing about as he repeated himself. "There are dead people buried out there. A whole bunch of them. Kids, too."

The insects' chirping seemed to get a little louder while Jake let his friends chew on the set-up.

Laura Danver's kitty-cat whiskers dipped down a tad as she frowned at him; Clay Oliver gave a casual chuckle and scratched away at his painted neck, having complained about his itchy Hulk muscle-suit all night long; and Bryan Michaels—ever the wiser to Jake's gags, always the toughest of them to con—just stood there, looking unimpressed in his Frankenstein getup, a bag of candy in one hand and his plastic monster mask in the other. But they were all paying attention to him, and if Jake could spin the story with just the right balance of wisdom and sensation, he could draw them right into the mischief. But first, he needed the return volley, and Bryan (bless his haughty heart) finally supplied it.

"You're full of it, Jake."

"It's true. Swear to God."

"Cut the crap, man," Clay grumbled. He fidgeted with the edges of his muscle suit. "Let's finish up with the next neighborhood so I can get out of this damn thing already."

He started to turn back around, the others following suit—except for Jamie, who still looked a tad uncertain.

"Haven't you guys ever heard of Lennie Duvall?" Jake called to them. And that made them stop in their tracks.

They all turned back around. The previous disgust on Laura's and Clay's faces had been replaced by glances of nervous recognition. And even though Bryan still looked far from biting as easily as the rest, his eyebrows were furrowed in just the slightest way, and his ears were perked for the listening.

"Who's Lennie Duvall?" Jamie asked. Jake had expected as much; Jamie was still the 'new guy' in their group, having moved to Marsden just over a year ago. He wouldn't have expected Jamie to know the story that he was fully prepared to tell.

"He was a serial killer—"

"*Supposedly*," Bryan cut in.

"—who lived in town back in the 1970s."

Jamie glanced around at everybody, his face gone slack. Then he looked back to Jake. "No way..."

"Yep. *Way.*" And then Jake went right on into it, selling it as best as he could.

"Lennie Duvall used to live right around here, long before all the rich people moved in and set up Winston Plains. Back then there were only some farmhouses out here. Old man Duvall lived in one of them. People say he was a mean old dude—the meanest around. A real a-hole. Kept to himself and hated just about everybody he ever saw. People said he'd rather spit at you than say hello. He tried buying up the land from all the other farmers out here—but not so he could work it himself. He just wanted to be left alone. *All alone.* But nobody would ever sell to him. And then, after years of trying, old man Duvall started to get real lucky. People began to disappear around here—a bunch of the other farmers. One by one, just gone, nobody knowing where they went. But there were stories—"

"*Stupid* stories," Bryan cut in again. But Jake didn't let it stop him.

"People started wondering if old man Duvall had something to do with all the disappearances—especially when the missing people's land went up for sale, and Duvall started buying it. People called him a murderer behind his back, but nobody—not even the cops—could ever prove that he'd killed anyone. Without evidence—without *bodies*—they couldn't do anything to him. Not even when the kids started to disappear, too."

Jake paused for dramatic effect, and good old Jamie picked up the tantalizing thread. "Wha—what kids?"

Jake widened his eyes, shooting for a creepy stare. "The kids that came out on Halloween night. The trick 'r treaters that headed out this way—*just like we're doing*—to visit the houses out here. Old man Duvall had bought up most of the land around here by then, but not all of it. There were still a few nice families around that probably had some treats for kids like us, but old man Duvall...he just had some nasty tricks. *Real* nasty."

"It's all just an urban legend," Clay grumbled, although he still looked a bit uncertain. "My brother's been telling me that crap to try and scare me for years."

"But it's not!" Jake shook his head. "There are records. Newspaper articles and stuff like that, even in the public library. I've seen them myself! At least five kids, and then three farmers before that, all vanished between 1970 and 1977. And all the kids went missing on Halloween night, and they were all supposed to be heading out this way when it happened. And they were never seen again"

Bryan sighed and shook his head. "I've heard better bull around campfires. Just stop it already, Jake."

But poor, shaking-in-his-Spider-boots Jamie wasn't about to let it go, no matter how pale he was starting to look. "What ever happened to old man Duvall? He's not... still around here, is he?"

And now, Jake couldn't help but smile. "Maybe."

"What do you mean?"

"Well, *officially*—and sort of ironically—old man Duvall ended up disappearing, too. On Halloween night of 1978, along with another kid. And just like all the other missing people, they never really found out what happened to them. But some say they're closer than anyone ever dared to think; some say they're in... there."

Jake pointed back to the trees, as still and ominous as before, the insects within playing their eerie tunes.

"The story goes that that's where Lennie Duvall buried all those people after he killed them. But maybe they didn't stay completely dead. Maybe on Halloween night of 1978, when he came back out here to bury another pesky trick 'r treater, they rose up from the graves he'd made for them, and they put him in the earth right beside them, angry and vengeful, even after death. And maybe—just maybe—that's where other people have wound up since then; because every now and then, someone else in Marsden has a habit of disappearing. Mostly kids. Mostly people who come up around these parts. And mostly on Halloween night."

This was it. Jake had cast the line, he'd gotten them to bite, and now if he could just reel them in...

"And if you don't believe me, I *dare* you to go walking around in there yourself. Because I bet you'll see their gross, dead fingers sticking up out of the dirt, clawing their way back into the land of the living so they can drag another victim down to join them!"

Bryan let out a big laugh. "Oh, jeez!"

Jake stuck his chin up, unwavering. "Davis Porter, the big football player from the high school? He was dared to go in there last Halloween by some friends, and he came running out of there yelling. He swore he saw hands coming up out of the dirt that night—that the stories are true, and all of Lennie Duvall's victims were rising up to get him. Even after all these years, they're still angry, still wanting others to join them."

"I remember hearing some older kids talking about that..." Clay said. His hand fell away from his itchy neck and his eyebrows dipped down in serious thought.

"I'd heard about it, too," Laura whispered, her eyes darting to the edge of the woods. "I just didn't realize this was where—"

"Oh, come on, guys!" Bryan huffed. He shifted his weight on his monster-sized boots and looked them all over with a disbelieving smile. "You don't actually believe all this crazy crap, do you? It's just a tall tale. Sure, maybe Lennie Duvall was a real jerk in his day, and *maybe a few* people have disappeared over the years, but really? I mean, people probably go missing from all over all the time. It doesn't mean murder's involved. And angry zombies from beyond the grave? Get real!"

"What about Davis Porter and the hands he saw?" Jake challenged.

"He's probably just as full of it as you are. Made it all up as a prank." There was a spark of realization on Bryan's face, and he positively lit up. "Or, even if he *did* see something, I bet it was just some kind of fungus growing out there. My dad and I saw it on one of those nature shows; there's a fungus that grows really weird and ends up looking like hands. They even call it dead man's fingers!"

"Thanks, Nat Geo," Laura mumbled. But the humor of it was lost as she stared glumly at her feet, avoiding the sight of the woods.

Jake brandished a grin. "Well then, if you think there's nothing but fungus in there, I guess you wouldn't mind going in and picking some for us, huh? Unless you think you could be wrong, or if you're just too...chicken."

Bryan sneered, but he didn't say a word.

"Come on, Frankenstein! Show us how big and tough you are!"

"Can't we just get out of here already?" Laura implored.

Clay nodded his agreement, and Jamie just stood there, looking like he was about to turn tail and skedaddle at any moment. But when Jake started to flap his arms and make chicken noises, Bryan stepped up to the challenge.

"Fine," he said, chin up and arms swinging as he went over to the tree-line. "I'm always up for proving you wrong. I'll get you your stupid fungus—and I'll make you eat it, too."

"Only if you make it out alive!"

Bryan spared a steamed look Jake's way, and then he turned back around, looking for a place to get through all the dense growth. When he found a decent gap, he stepped on in.

All it took was another four steps, and he was out of sight—hidden away by the woods.

*　*　*

The trees and the bushes didn't grow quite as close together past the tree-line, but it was still pretty tight in the woods. And it was dark, too; the moon peeked down on Bryan through all the scraggly branches twisting about overhead. He had to side-step it some and watch his footing along the pitted ground, but after making it a few yards in, things evened out a bit, and he had more room to move.

He set his eyes to the ground, scanning for some of that peculiar fungus and wondering (and not for the first time) why he and the others didn't just boot Jake out of their little group. He used to be a lot cooler back in grade school, but nowadays, he was turning into a top-notch dickwad. Being a class-clown was one thing; but when you were out of the class, it was just plain annoying. And if Bryan could wipe that smug smirk off that clown's face by proving him wrong—

A twig snapped from somewhere behind him, making his spine go straight. Bryan spun about, stopping mid-step.

"Guys?" he called.

A moment passed and no one answered, save the clicking and buzzing bugs.

"You out there, Jake?" He pushed onwards, but much more slowly, glancing back as he went. That superstitious flash of fear faded as quickly as it came; he could just picture that jerk creeping up on him, set to pounce and call him a chicken if he made him jump. The thought of it alone made Bryan's skin hot. "Might want to head back before the *zombies* get you, you twerp."

No answer. No movement.

Bryan gave a grumble and looked ahead again, narrowing his eyes in the growing darkness. He spied leaves, broken branches, the remains of a fallen nest—but no fungus. But there weren't any signs of shambling undead, either.

He kept at it, unsure of just how long he had been in here already. Could've been a couple minutes, could've been several; but he wasn't leaving until he found his fungus, or until he was certain there wasn't anything out here, which would be enough proof in itself, or so he figured. And he started to think that there *wasn't* anything out here, after all... until he caught sight of something.

Just ahead, away from all the trees and bushes, was a wide patch of dirt and dead grass. Something was sticking out of the ground there—five somethings, actually: thin and round and a little curled at their tips; four that were fairly long and one that was... stubby.

Bryan clenched his jaw and tightened his grip around his mask and candy bag. Then he inched forward, wondering if the night was actually getting darker around him, or if it was just in his head. He leaned forward, analyzing the little things poking out of the ground. They looked to have a bumpy and brittle texture under the moonlight, and they were colored gray, save for their tips, which were a straight white. It very well could've been the fungus he was hoping to find, or maybe...

Finger bones—sticking out of old, dead skin.

Bryan shoved the notion aside as he stepped onto the patch of grass and dirt. This wasn't a dead guy's hand, for Pete's sake; this was his great and wonderful proof.

He slid his Frankenstein mask into his bag and picked up some big stray leaves at his feet. Whatever those things were, he wasn't about to pick any of it up with his bare hands. Situating the crinkling leaves in his palm, he bent down and reached out to the five little things. He got a hold of the two biggest bits and squeezed down, pulling them away from the ground with a tiny *snap* that set his gut to tingling.

He stood straight again and loosened his fingers, sneaking a peek at what he'd found...

Something rustled off to Bryan's right. His head spun around and he stared into the dark; he couldn't see anything moving around—except for the bushes that'd gotten his attention, their wilted leaves and fragile twigs still shaking some. But what had made them do that in the first place?

A soft wind stirred, blowing against Bryan's sweaty face. There was a smell on it that set his nose to curling: a mix of soggy soil, aged wood, and something else.

Something spoiled. Rotted. Something that had to be dead.

There was another rustle in the bushes and shadows shifted against the trees, and that was when Bryan turned and bolted.

He ran as fast as his awkward boots would allow, his bag of candy rattling and smacking against his legs as he went. His breath huffed out of him like a locomotive building speed, and a blank wall of dread started to build itself up in his head, blocking out all other thought. And it kept on building—until he spied Dresden Lane through the trees, just up ahead.

With one last bit of effort, he launched himself though a gap in the woods and jumped out to the side of the road, coming to a stop on blacktop. He spun around, dreading to see what was after him—

Except nothing was. The woods had gone still again. There wasn't any creature running up to snatch him, from beyond the grave or otherwise; nothing came out except another breeze, and this one was just fine, no stink or nastiness to it at all.

When he was satisfied that he'd just scared himself and nothing more, Bryan hunched over, getting his wind back. He waited for Jake and the others to come rushing over to him, asking why he'd been running, wondering what had happened, and making declarations of being chicken after all.

"Found your dead people, Jake," he huffed out. "They said that next time, they'd like you to go in so they can give you the finger themselves..."

He turned around, holding out the prize in his hands and giving a safe, proud laugh. But Jake wasn't there. Neither was Laura, Jamie, or Clay. The road was empty.

Bryan turned and looked behind him, thinking maybe he'd popped out somewhere a little ahead of the group. But there was nobody that way, either.

"Guys?" he called. There was no answer.

"Come on guys, where the hell are you at?" he shouted. He looked back to the trees and called out for them again, thinking maybe they'd gone in to look for him after waiting for so long. Still, there was no response.

He looked back to the road, wondering if he might have been had after all—wondering if Jake had somehow convinced the others to pull a prank on him, getting him to go in there while they left and ran off towards the rich folks' homes without him. Then he saw something on the road, just laying there. It was fuzzy and could've been a bit of roadkill—if not for the neon green color of it.

Bryan jogged over to it, and sure enough, it was the clown wig to Jake's costume. And yes, it was lying right around where they'd stopped and listened to Jake's story. This is where they should've been waiting for him.

He let the stuff in his hand fall to the ground—the leaves, and what really were just some bits of fungus, after all. He picked up Jake's wig in their place and called out again.

"Guys! This isn't funny! Guys?"

Bryan stood there, shouting for them over and over. But it was no use. They never answered him, and they never would. All four of them had simply disappeared.

And, as the story goes, they were never seen again.

NEW WITCH IN TOWN

ROBERT ALLEN LUPTON

I SAT IN THE FRONT row of Mrs. McAlister's fourth grade class. The shiny apple on her desk slowly rotted into slurry. I glanced around. Janet Oberon, the suck-up who brought the apple, watched her gift decay. She gasped when the first worm poked its head through the browning red skin.

The apple was bright and new a few moments ago. I heard a soft snicker. The new girl, Mabel, spun her index finger in a small circle and mumbled under her breath. She caught me looking at her and winked. Janet shrieked when the apple's skin ruptured. Maggots and worms floated in putrid applesauce across the desk and dripped onto the floor.

It was great. Best day ever. Mrs. McAlister puked in the trash can. She sent Janet to the principal's office for bringing a rotten apple to class. I told my friends, Mark and Sammy, at lunch. They're in Mrs. Johnson's fourth grade class.

I said, "It was Mabel. She wiggled her finger and cast a spell on the apple."

"Ronnie, you're a moron. It's close to Halloween and you been watching way too many Harry Potter reruns. You think the new girl's a witch? Oooohhhhh."

I shoved Mark. "I saw what I saw. I'm gonna talk to her."

Sammy complained, "Not this week. Halloween's Friday. This is the last year we can trick or treat. We gotta make plans. Gotta payback Buddy Oberon and his friends."

Sammy had a point. Buddy and his two asshole buddies, Preston and Rich, were the town bullies. They were juniors in high school. They'd picked on us for years and stole our candy the last three Halloweens. Bastards.

"I know, but I'm still going to talk to Mabel."

"Go get her, lady-killer. When you're on the ground with a bloody nose and no Halloween candy, remember I told you so."

Mabel sat reading on the steps of the portable building we used for a classroom. I walked up and said, "You're new. I'm Ronnie. I know what you did to the apple."

"I don't know shit about no apple."

"Yes, you do. You wiggled your finger and said an enchantment or something."

"You mean like a spell. You think I'm a witch. How old are you? You're ten, maybe eleven, and you still believe in witches. Imagine that. Hang around a couple of months and Santa Clause will bring you some presents. I think I saw the Easter Bunny run under the building."

"Hey, I don't mean anything. I saw what I saw. I thought you might want a friend."

"Maybe, I do, Ronnie. Maybe, I do." She twitched her nose like the witch lady on television and I almost fell over myself backing away.

"Oh, Ronnie, don't make it so easy. Introduce me to your friends." She closed her book, stood up, and we went to find

Sammy and Mark. The bell rang right as I introduced them and we walked to class.

Sammy said, "We're going to work on our Halloween costumes at my house after school. You can come if you want."

"Thanks, I'll check with my mom."

Red-eyed Janet was back in class. She broke her pencil three times, her pen leaked all over her dress, and a fly landed on her face several times. Whenever I glanced at Mabel, she just smiled and winked.

Her mother consented and Mabel walked with me to Sammy's house. Mabel and I passed the signboard at the High School. It advertised the Halloween Ball this Friday night. I asked, "What's the deal with Janet?"

"Janet lives down the block from us. She's been really mean to me. Told the other girls not to play with me. She walks her stupid little dog and lets him poop in my yard."

"So I'm right and you made the apple rot. You are a witch."

Mabel looked around and said, "Not smart to piss off a witch. Ask Janet. I'm not a witch, not yet anyway. I'm more of a witch in training. If you tell anyone, my mama will turn you into a toad."

"Can she do that?"

"You wanna take a chance."

"No, what's a witch in training? Can I learn?"

"If you don't have the blood, you can study all you want, but your spells won't work. Until I'm a woman, my spells only work on inanimate objects and insects. Last week, I learned to control flies."

"Become a woman. You mean like sex?"

"Don't be gross. No, I mean when I mature enough that I'm not a child anymore."

"Oh, you mean when you have a period."

"I'm so not having this conversation."

I knocked at Sammy's and we went to his dad's basement workshop. Our work was laid out on the workbench. Mabel looked at the tattered and torn clothing. She picked up strips of cloth stained with red paint. "Zombies, you guys are going as zombies."

Mark answered, "Yes. Gloves and old shoes and makeup, lots of makeup. Makeup doesn't restrict your vision. We want to see everything. The big kids in this town will kick your ass and steal your candy if you aren't careful. That asshole, Buddy Oberon, is the worst. He blacked Sammy's eye last year. We're going to get him back. I'm thinking we'll put mousetraps in our candy sacks."

Sammy said, "That's stupid. It won't kill him and he'll know who did it. We gotta think of something better than that shit."

I had an idea I'd been saving. When Sammy said, "Shit," it appeared in my mind as clear as a vision of Christ himself, dressed in a gold sequined jumpsuit surfing down from the clouds on a sunbeam and singing *Onward Christian Soldiers*." I had the perfect plan.

"I got it. Laxatives. Laxatives and stool softeners. We'll fill the candy with laxatives and reseal the packaging with superglue. When Buddy and his pals eat the candy, they'll spend a week on the crapper."

Mark laughed, "What a shitty plan. I love it."

We worked on our costumes until dark. We made a fourth zombie outfit for Mabel. She was a wiz at makeup.

School was slow the next day. During the afternoon, a fly kept buzzing my ear. I gave Mabel a dirty look. She giggled and gestured for the fly to leave me alone. She guided it under Janet's dress. Janet shrieked and jumped on top of her desk. Mrs. McAlister sent her to the office. Another good day.

Buddy stopped his car in the street next to us that afternoon. "You little shits better be fast this Halloween. I got a date for the Halloween Ball and I don't have time to wait all night for you to fill your sacks. You could just bring the candy to the school parking lot. That might save you an ass-whipping, but I doubt it. Don't hold out on me. See you Friday."

Mabel and I bought plenty of candy. No one thinks twice about selling candy to kids. Mark and Sammy didn't do so well. People ask questions when a couple of ten year old boys want to buy twenty packages of chocolate-flavored laxative.

The pharmacist said, "You boys know this isn't candy. You don't want to eat this stuff."

Mark shook his head. "I told him my brother was in Africa and you can't buy good laxatives in Africa. He told me to bring a note from my mother."

"So you didn't get any?"

Mark pulled two boxes out of his pocket. "I stole these, but I don't think it's enough."

He unwrapped one of the packages and the chocolate had melted into sludge. He threw it in the trash. I said, "Well, my plan went to shit. Anybody else got anything?"

Mabel asked, "Buddy is Janet Oberon's big brother, isn't he?"

"Yes, he is."

"Then I'll help. I know a spell my mother uses to help people who can't poop. I can put the spell on the candy and people who eat it will crap like they drank a bottle of castor oil."

Mark and Sammy looked at me. "Yes, she's really a witch. Actually, she's a witch in training, but if she says she can do this, she can."

Mark said, "Prove it."

Mabel picked up a chocolate peanut cluster and smiled. "Okay eat this. Maybe, you'll be able to get off the toilet by Halloween. I dare you."

"Okay, if it doesn't work, we're no worse than we are now."

Mabel said, "I'll memorize the spell tonight and put it on the candy right before we start to trick or treat."

I walked Mabel home. We held hands.

On Halloween night, we added long coats to our costumes so people would think we only had one candy sack, but we each carried one for real candy and another for Buddy and his boys.

Mabel finished our makeup and piled all the candy on the work bench. She inscribed a chalk circle and pentagram around the candy. She lit red candles and placed them at the pentagram's points. She chanted for a few minutes and then pulled a sharp knife out of her pocket and pricked her finger. She squeezed a drop of blood into each candle's flames. The flames belched green smoke that smelled like an outhouse. Suddenly a breeze blew away the smoke. That wasn't good. There's no wind in a basement.

Mabel smiled and washed her hands. "Don't confuse which sack is which. It's almost dark. We going trick or treating or what?"

I shoveled the candy into four sacks and joined the other kids. It was a good night. Folks loved our costumes. We had quite a haul by nine o'clock. We hadn't seen Buddy. Mark suggest we hide our good candy and walk around until Buddy found us. We hid our bounty under the broken down car in Mr. Wilson's driveway.

It felt strange to walk around and wait for Buddy. I felt feathery touches on my neck and face. Shadows flitted just out of my vision. I slapped phantom fingers away from my face. Mark complained, 'Is it raining? Something keeps touching me."

Mabel said, "It's my fault. The spirits know I'm here. They know I cast a spell because they can smell it on me. The barriers between the spirit world and ours are weaker on Halloween. They won't hurt us, but they want to be near the action."

Sammy shivered and touched his neck. "You sure they won't hurt us?"

"Pretty sure, but it is Halloween, after all."

We had to jump out of the way when Buddy's car screamed to a stop. "Happy Halloween, you little shits. Trick or treat."

Preston and Rich jumped out the car and the three of them circled around us. They were dressed in slacks and sport coats. Preston said, "It's your lucky night. We don't want to mess up our clothes before we go to the Halloween Ball. Just put your candy sacks on the ground and back away."

Mark threw his sack on the street and ran. He stopped and yelled, "Kiss my ass."

Buddy said, "Little boy, that blows your free pass. I'll find you tomorrow."

I put my sack on the ground and so did Mabel. Sammy put his sack with ours. We moved away. Preston reached into a sack and pulled out a chocolate bar, ripped off the cover, and ate it. He tossed a bar to Buddy.

Buddy ate it and said, "Stolen candy tastes the best. Don't stay out too late."

They jumped in the car and drove toward the high school. I said, "We're gonna follow them. I got to see this."

Mabel asked me. "They won't let us in the gym. Only kids in high school can go to the dance."

Sammy smiled. "We've been sneaking into the gym to shoot hoops for years. We'll hide in the rafters and watch. You're not afraid, are you?"

"You mean because I'm a girl. You want me to turn you into a toad or just give you pimples? Your call."

The four of us climbed through a window in the janitor's closet. We taped the door latch so it wouldn't lock behind us and climbed into the rafters. There's a catwalk between the lights and cranks that raise and lower the basketball backboards. The backboards were raised high against the catwalk. We hid where we could peak over the backboards and people couldn't see us from below.

Buddy, Rich, and Preston came in with their dates. They dumped all the stolen candy into a bowl where the punch and other snacks were on display. Buddy's date ate a piece of chocolate.

"Holly shit. Everyone down there is going to eat the candy. There'll be more poop on the floor than in a pigsty. Mabel, you've got to cancel the spell."

"I don't know how, but even if I did, I'd need to draw a pentagram. I left the red candles in Mark's basement. Maybe my spell won't work."

Preston poured a bottle of pure grain alcohol in the punch. The high school kids danced, drank punch, and ate candy. Everyone ate candy and they seemed just fine. Maybe the spell didn't work.

It worked. Buddy was first. The cramps hit him in the middle of a slow dance. He ran for the men's room. Rich didn't make it off the floor. He bent over and poop ran down his legs. We could smell it in the rafters. Rich's date looked shocked and angry, but her anger vanished when the cramps hit her. I hope her parents didn't spend a lot on her dress.

Preston threw up and then ran for the bathroom. He slipped on his own vomit and liquefied shit stained his trousers. The carnage escalated.

"We gotta get out of here," whispered Sammy. Mark backed carefully down the catwalk, but the smell was too much for him. He gagged, held his hands over his mouth, and vomited on the crowd.

No one came after us. They were busy with their own problems. Mabel said, "I'll try to stop this." She waved her hands and began to chant. Spirits slowly congealed around her. They changed from misty apparitions to cold, half-solidified, gelatin forms floating through the rafters. They kept touching me and bestowed slimy caresses as they drifted around us.

Mabel said, "They're spirits. They won't hurt us. When I tried to cancel my spell, I accidently summoned them. They aren't demons, they're the spirits of my ancestors. I'll ask them to help us."

Sammy continued to crawl toward the ladder at the end of the catwalk. "I just want to go home."

The spirits continued to solidify. They looked like us. By us, I mean zombies. Their clothes were tattered and torn and their faces and hands looked like they had leprosy. One opened its mouth and I could see the ceiling lights through the holes in its head.

It hugged me. I froze and whispered, "Mabel, make it leave me alone. Can you make it leave me alone?"

She nodded and with a gesture summoned the spirit to her. "These three are my friends. Leave them be."

The creature extended its rotting hand. The hand dissolved into mist, drifted forward, and engulfed Mabel's face. She inhaled the evil smoke and her eyes rolled back. Her body quaked with a small seizure. Her eyes opened, she breathed out the smoke, and it reformed into a ghostly hand. Mabel said, "This spirit is my grandmother's grandmother's grandmother from a very long time ago. People hung her in a town called Salem. The spirits will stop the shitstorm. The people will stop vomiting and pooping. She says they won't clean up the mess. I don't blame her. The spirits require payment."

Mark reached in his pocket. "I've got eleven dollars."

"They don't want money. They want a servant. Someone has to go with them. It should be me. It's my fault we need their help."

I said, "Piss on that. If they want someone, give 'em Buddy. This is his fault."

I waved my arms and the spirits surrounded me. One reached for me, I slapped its slimy hand away, and pointed at Buddy. "Not me. Take him."

The spirits looked at Buddy and the reincarnated witches with rotting faces didn't just look happy, they seemed absolutely gleeful. They turned to Mabel for reassurance and she said, "Take him."

The spirits dove from the rafters and reverted to the consistency and stench of greasy smoke. The filthy wraiths flew above the floor. They didn't slow down when they came to the wretched partygoers; they flew right through them. The victims shivered at the brief moment of ghostly contact and passed out.

In moments, Buddy was the only one awake. He wiped his face and backed away from the zombie ghost witches solidifying around him. He slid down the wall. He tried to stand, but he was too weak and the floor was slippery.

Mabel's ancestor seemed to be in charge. The old woman zombie ghost witch shoved her hand into Buddy's mouth and her arm spun like small whirlwind. It vacuumed Buddy inside out. He deflated like a balloon. He disappeared feet first. His feet and legs vanished into his body. His hands and arms went next. It was gross and fascinating at the same time.

His head went last. The flesh flowed from his bones and the skull melted. His brain splashed on the slop–covered floor.

The witches faded into the mist and vanished. The other partygoers began to wake up. Some of them vomited again, but Mabel said that was because of the stench, not because of her enchantment.

We inched our way to the ladder. Mabel and I took one last look at the muck and mire splattered dance floor, the sewage stained dresses, and the lakes of human manure scattered across the hardwood floor. Buddy's brain grew smaller and smaller. It dissolved and mixed with the excrement and vomit. The sludge looked the same and I couldn't tell where the crap ended and Buddy's brains started.

Mabel said, "We have to go. Are you okay?"

I pointed at the last vestige of dissolving cerebellum. "I'm better than okay. Look. I always knew that Buddy had shit for brains."

DEALING WITH JACK

JACKIE FELLS

DANIEL SAT IN CLASS, his head slowly sinking as he doodled in his notebook and halfheartedly listened to the teacher drone on about the American Civil War. He had more important matters on his mind than seventh grade history. He scratched his pencil back and forth, watched the graphite color in the eye of his latest design. He sat back and looked at a page full of ideas staring back at him with goofy smiles and protruding teeth. They were all decent, but he still wasn't sure which would grace the face of his jack-o-lantern.

He looked to the clock hanging above the chalkboard. Only another half hour and then his mother would pick him up, whisk him away to the pumpkin patch so he could find the perfect specimen to carve up. Once that task was complete, he'd help his mother finish his costume, then he had figure out the best route through the streets on Halloween night. He wanted to maximize his haul and hit all the good houses before porch lights winked out to announce November.

Busy days lay ahead of him before Halloween. A lot of work—important work. Work that needed his attention more than history class. Daniel began a new design, this time giving the open maw a row of pointed teeth and twisting the corners of the eyes up so the face sported an angry scowl. He liked it, but it wasn't the face for his jack-o-lantern. Too scary for him. He told himself next year would be the year he finally put a frightening face on his pumpkin. He began to X the rejects out until he was left with the perfect one.

It was smiling face with triangle eyes and two large teeth, one from the top and one from the bottom of its happy mouth. A classic. Tried and true, but with his own little touch of eyebrows twisting up to match the corners of the mouth. It had a look about it that was deceptive, like something more sinister could be behind the happy mask. Daniel circled it and smiled to himself. The bell rang and without wasting a moment he pushed his notebook into his backpack and joined the bodies scrambling out of class.

The hall was loud with laughter and chatter. Daniel pushed through the crowd and turned toward his locker to see the last thing he'd wanted to see that day. Joey Brandt, a local hard-ass, dumb-ass, and all-around ass. He was few years older than Daniel and was blocking Daniel's locker, flanked by his two usual lackeys.

"Danny-boy!" Joey spread his arms out wide and smiled like he was expecting an embrace.

"I just want to get my stuff," Daniel said.

"Oh, come on, don't be like that, Little Dan-o. I'm not going to do nothing to you. Not *here*."

"What do you want then?" Daniel asked, trying to sound as tough as he could, but still feeling his voice waver in front of the older boys.

"Well," Joey said, "it's just, we know how excited you get for Halloween, and we just wanted you to know that before Halloween is over this year, any candy you get will be ours. Or... well, y'know how it goes."

Daniel stared at the boys, anger boiling in his veins, his palms clammy and his face flushed.

"You understand what I'm saying, Danny-boy? You get it, right? You're not going to make this hard on yourself, are you?"

Daniel opted to say nothing again and tried to push through the older boys to get to his locker. Joey grabbed him by the collar and shoved him into the waiting arms of one of the other boys. Daniel felt hands grab him around his arms and hold him in place. He was barely able to realize what was coming before Joey's fist rammed into his stomach and sent all the air from his lungs. He coughed, released a small whimper as Joey leaned down and talked with hot breath in his ear.

"I'm going to need to hear you say you understand, buddy," Joey said.

Anger and pain flashed across Daniel's face. "Fuck you, Joey."

Joey laughed as he slapped Daniel, hard. Pain flared across his face like he'd been hit with a frying pan. Daniel stared at the ground and watched stars dance in his vision. Joey was still laughing as the boy holding Daniel let go and he fell to the floor.

"That's fine too," Joey said, "it's always more fun when you fight back anyway. We'll see you soon, Danny-boy."

Daniel pushed himself to his feet as the three boys disappeared into the crowd of students laughing and talking about their Halloween plans. He opened his locker and grabbed his coat, pushed a hand to his cheek where the skin felt hot and tender. He could already feel the thin skin around his eye swelling.

He walked to the front of school where parents lined up to pick up their children, he hoped his mother had arrived early, gotten one of the front spots so that they could be on their way, get to the pumpkin patch while the sun was still up. He loved to watch the sun set over fields full of big pumpkins with corn stretching into the distance behind, a flatland of green rippled with shadow where only the occasional scarecrow jutted from the sea of stalks.

He stepped outside and scanned the cars near the front of the line but saw no sign of his mother. He walked towards the back of the line, scanned bored faces behind windshields as he passed. He began to feel doubt creep into his mind. He wanted to believe she wouldn't forget something so important to him, but somewhere deep down he was already telling himself to accept that she wasn't going to be there. He trudged back up the line of cars, watched the busses pull away from the back of the school, saw the one that would have taken him home if he'd known his mother wouldn't show. It pulled onto the small highway beside the school and rumbled off into the distance, stranding him.

Daniel plopped on the entryway to the school. He fought the feeling growing in his chest, a feeling that made him want to scream, cry out, and slam his fists into the ground to no avail. Instead, he put his chin in his hands watched other children vanish in droves as parents ferried them away. His mother never showed.

He felt sadness mostly, but there was a hollowness inside him that had replaced the excitement he'd been feeling only hours ago. He picked up his bag and slung it over his shoulder as he started his walk home. It wasn't too far, about four and a half miles by road, but he could cut an hour off the walk if he went through the woods that ran between the school and his neighborhood.

He'd done it with friends plenty of times, and he'd done it alone on the rare occasion that he had to. He didn't like to though, the woods were dense and dark even in the middle of the day, the canopy of leaves, even dead and beginning to fall as they were in October, blocked more light than they let in. He didn't like the idea of what could be out in the dense darkness. Watching him. Following him. Waiting for the perfect time to strike.

He weighed the options in his mind as he neared the trail leading to the edge of the woods. If he cut through, he *might* reach home with enough time that he could still convince his mother to take him to the patch. If he stayed on the road, she would already be half drunk and wouldn't be taking him anywhere. With a defiant step he turned towards the woods and quickened his pace.

The shadows were long from the setting sun, the sky was awash with pinks and reds, lighting puffy clouds overhead. He entered the woods and his footsteps crunched freshly fallen leaves to announce his arrival.

The sound of the highway faded as he worked deeper into the woods, a damp smell surrounded him, an aroma of dead leaves decomposing into soggy ground. His feet sank into the mush, mud gripped the sides of his shoes. He was picking his way through when he heard a branch snap somewhere behind him. He stopped and crouched, his heart beat fast as he turned and scanned the woods, craning an ear towards the sound of the unseen thing following him.

The setting sun cast the woods around him on fire, saturated with reds, oranges, and brilliant yellows dancing through the dark trunks. He squinted into the light, waiting to see any sign of movement. He heard something move to his left and he swung his head wildly in that direction. He saw something large and dark move through a thicket between the trees, only catching a glimpse of what he thought was an arm before the figure vanished. The hair on the back of his neck stood on end, his stomach felt like it was doing flips as fear crept up his throat.

"Dannny-boy!"

Daniel clenched his eyes shut hard and cursed to himself as Joey's voice rang out through the still woods. He still couldn't catch sight of them, but he was sure Joey had his two little lackeys with him. His mind flashed with the image of them holding him down while Joey beat the shit out of him.

"Oh, *Danny*, what're you doing out here all alone? That wasn't too smart of you, especially not after you insulted me the way you done. You best get to running, boy!"

DEALING WITH JACK

Daniel turned on his heels and sprinted into the woods. He heard heavy steps behind him. He pushed through branches and briars that grabbed at his clothes and backpack, the woods seemed to pull him back towards the boys wanting to harm him. He continued to run, his lungs screaming in protest, his thighs burning as he leapt and crawled. He fell down a steep slope, rolled until he landed in a shallow creek below. The water was cold and soaked through his clothes as he struggled in the mud to regain his footing and scrambled up the other side of the bank, he cast a glance back and saw two of the three boys hot on his trail.

He continued to run, having no idea where he was, having no idea which way home was at this point, all he wanted was to be safe from Joey and his goons. He followed the creek deeper into the woods as the sun continued to set, and the woods began to grow dark. The brilliant colors from before faded and twilight devoured the land. Daniel felt a briar grab at his cheek, tearing the flesh, releasing warm blood. He wiped at the pain, saw crimson on his hand. He heard voices behind him, but they were far off now. He slowed enough to turn back and see if he was getting away. He couldn't see anyone behind him anymore, all he saw were dark woods.

He slowed his pace and breathed heavy. Sweat poured down his face, stinging the cut along his cheek. He was wet all over, mud already drying along his pants and hands, crusting into a hard tack that clung to him as he pulled it off in large chunks. He looked around and realized he had no idea where he was. He knew if he walked to the east, he would eventually end up in some neighborhood that would lead him home, but he had no idea how long it would take. He felt the urge to cry grow in his chest as he realized there was no way he would be getting to go to the pumpkin patch. He wondered if his mother even realized, or cared, that he wasn't home yet. He had a sneaking suspicion that she hadn't, and didn't.

He walked on, continued to fight the urge to cry even as tears stung at the corners of his eyes. He noticed a break in the trees ahead, gray light broke through and gave him some hope he was at the edge of the woods. As he stepped through the break, he felt a combination of emotions ransack him. Disappointment first, as he realized it was not the edge of the woods, but only a glade in the deep woods he had never seen before. After the disappointment, he felt confusion and wonder intermingle and fill him as he realized what was in front of him. And finally, excitement welled in his chest, his eyes beamed as he studied the beautiful scene before him, a literal answer to his prayers.

At the center of the glade stood a single huge oak, taller than any trees around it, its branching leaves were a brilliant auburn even in the dim light. Fireflies danced on the air, hundreds of them milling about over the sweet treasure that coated the ground.

Pumpkins. More than Daniel could believe. All wild, still attached to the vines, resting on the ground in clumps and groups under leafy greens. Beautiful orange orbs just waiting for him to select one. It was his own personal pumpkin patch. He smiled, rushed into the glade, and dropped next to a huge pumpkin resting far from the ancient looking oak.

The pumpkin was beautiful, but about twenty pounds heavier than anything he could handle. He looked at the thick green vine stretching toward the other pumpkins resting in the glade. He followed the vine towards the oak, looking at each pumpkin individually. There were so many perfect ones that he wanted to take, but he was alone and exhausted. All the ones that caught his eye were too large, no way he could get them home once the twilight vanished and the woods were shrouded in true darkness. He followed the vine until he was under the reaching limbs of the old oak. There, resting near the base of the tree he saw a pumpkin that appeared to be the perfect size.

He kneeled next to it and realized he couldn't pull his eyes from it. It was almost as if the thing had a glow to it, an aurora that called to him, begged him to select that one. He glanced toward the sky and saw darkness beginning to win out against the twilight. He pulled his pocketknife out and flipped open the longest blade, still rather short and dull. He began to saw through the thick vine. The blade had a hard time biting through, but as he pushed and pulled, it began to shrink. He grabbed the vine on either side of the cut and began to twist, pulling in opposite directions, desperately trying to sever the tether before full dark set in. A satisfying snap sounded in the evening.

He picked up his new pumpkin, the perfect size and the perfect weight for him to get it home without having to roll it or break his back as he worked through the woods, gullies, and thickets that stood in his way. He hoisted his prize and set off into the dark woods, the fear inside him seeming to shrink, as if he felt that his new pumpkin would protect him from the hidden things lurking about.

* * *

When he finally exited the woods into a neighborhood he recognized, it was full dark. Streetlamps cast yellow cones of light, yellow cones of safety that he dashed between as he worked his way home. Yards were full of gravestones. Ghouls and ghosts hung from trees. Orange, green, and purple lights danced along eves and hid within cotton cobwebs spun across porches. He loved the streets leading up to Halloween, the decorations and the falling leaves, the cool air and brisk smell that announced winter beginning to peek around the corner.

As he scampered back home covered in mud, cold, holding his new pumpkin, he found himself cautiously looking around every corner. The closer to home he got, the surer he was that Joey would step out of a shadow and ruin everything yet again. He secretly wished something terrible would happen to Joey. He finally made it home safely. Covered in grime and freezing from a mixture of water and sweat that had chilled him to his bones, he opened the door slowly and stepped inside. He could hear the TV on in the living room, bright light from it bounced through the door into the hallway.

He slipped off his muddy shoes and walked down the hallway toward the kitchen where he set his pumpkin on the table and examined it in the light for the first time. It was even better than he could have believed. Perfect for carving. Perfect for the face he had planned for it. By the end of the night he was sure he was going to have the best-looking jack-o-lantern on the block.

He decided he'd go change into some dry clothes before he started carving. He peeked into the living room as he went back down the hallway towards the stairs. He saw why his mother hadn't come to check on him yet. She was sprawled across the couch, one leg hanging off the side, the other draped lazily over the back. A bottle of vodka sat on the coffee table in front of her and beside that was the little orange bottle, tipped over with long white pills spilling out on the table.

Daniel sighed, walked over to the coffee table, screwed the cap back onto the bottle of vodka and placed the pills back in their container. His mother's snores, soft and subtle, let him know she was fine, but he imagined she wouldn't be waking up anytime soon. He placed a blanket over her and headed back for the stairs, wondering if she'd had another hard day at work. That was usually what she said after he found her this way. She never explained what was hard about it, or what had happened that put her in such a mood, just said, *it was hard day, okay, Daniel,* and then never mentioned it again until the next hard day. They seemed to be getting closer together ever since his father had died almost a year before. Daniel wished he was still around, but wishes rarely come true, and Daniel knew that well.

He thought about his father often, and his resting place deep under the ground in the old cemetery just outside of town. His mother stopped going after about a week, the pain of it too much for her. She'd break down almost immediately and by the third time they went together, he saw her pulling from a flask she kept in her purse, a liquid courage to face the large stone in the ground that forced her to think about her dead husband.

Daniel quit going soon too. It stopped reminding him of the good times he'd had with his father. Instead, he found that all he could think about was the rotting corpse beneath his feet. The wooden casket surely deteriorated and broken now, worms and bugs crawling over a dirtied suit, once his father's nicest one, crawling over the shriveled husk of what had once been his face, in and out of the holes that had held caring and kind eyes. The thoughts became so persistent that even passing the graveyard filled his mind with horrible images of death and decay. He stopped going altogether, and just like that no one visited his father in the cemetery anymore.

After tucking his mother in, Daniel rushed upstairs and changed his clothes. He went back to the kitchen, spread old newspaper along the table before he started carving. He pulled out his notebook and consulted the faces he had drawn earlier in class. He sketched the winner out on the pumpkin with a Sharpie and then set to cleaning the pumpkin out. With each spoonful of seeds and gunk removed from the pumpkin he felt happier and happier, looking forward to the perfect jack-o-lantern taking shape. He saved the seeds in a bowl, hoping his mother would roast them for him tomorrow if she felt up to it. Once the cavity inside the gourd was cleaned, he began cutting out the eyes. With each piece removed, he leaned back and studied his work. They eyes were perfect before long and the only part left was the mouth. He looked back at the page full of designs in his notebook. While cutting the large, smiling, mouth, almost on a whim, he decided to use a feature from one of the discarded ideas. He gave the jack-o-lantern pointed teeth, big in the middle like a hellish creature's fangs, and smaller points near the upturned corners.

He leaned back and smiled. He loved it. It still felt happy with the triangle eyes and the large, sweeping, smile, but the pointed teeth gave it just a bit of extra scare factor that he wanted. He placed the top back on and cut out a small chimney. It was everything he had ever wanted from the pumpkin patch. An ending to the day that he had never expected only hours ago. He took a candle from a kitchen drawer, picked up his jack-o-lantern and went back up the stairs.

The window in his bedroom faced the street and he looked out at the decorations lining the darkness, saw jack-o-lanterns lighting many of the porches. He thought about how they all paled in comparison to his own while he set his jack-o-lantern in the window. He dropped the candle in and lit it up. The orange yellow glow of the face reflected back at him from the glass of his window and he felt happiness flow over his body.

He crawled in bed, glancing over to the jack-o-lantern occasionally, feeling content from a day full of hope, sorrow, fear, and excitement. He was emotionally drained, and sleep came for him without warning.

* * *

Daniel awoke abruptly. In his sleepy state, he thought he'd heard his mother call his name. He sat up, his limbs feeling numb and foreign after the deep sleep. He thought he heard his name again and looked toward his door. The clock on his dresser, bright red numbers cutting through the dark room, showed that it was three in the morning. He doubted his mother would be conscious yet.

"Daniel," the voice said again. It sounded deep, like a man's voice *in* his room. Daniel's heart began to beat fast. He rubbed the sleep from his eyes and looked toward the dark corners of the room.

"Who's there?"

"*Over here,*"

Daniel started to stand up but realized the voice may be under his bed at the last second and yanked his feet quickly back to safety.

"Over where?" Daniel asked. "Come out."

The deep voice laughed. "You have to turn me around."

Daniel caught a strange sight in the reflection on the window showing his jack-o-lanterns face. He saw the flesh of his masterpiece move in a subtle fashion as he watched. His mind refused to believe it. But his eyes kept observing the macabre dance in front of him. He felt his pulse quicken, felt a weight in his stomach like lead pulling him down. Fighting the fear inside him, he threw his legs over the bed and carefully took a step towards the jack-o-lantern facing the street.

The candle inside the jack-o-lantern cast strange light from within as the carved pumpkin moved its eyes somehow. They were still hollow, and Daniel could see into the cavity of the thing through the reflection. No brain. Nothing in there to allow life. And yet, the flesh of it moved again, causing the eyes to twist up towards the sound of his feet on the wood floor as he inched closer.

The thoughts running through his mind ventured on the edge of madness. Daniel slapped himself lightly in the face, tried to wake himself up if he was dreaming, tried to knock some sense into his head if he wasn't. His steps had become smaller as he walked toward the talking pumpkin, and the jack-o-lantern seemed to grow impatient.

"Daniel," it said, "taking your sweet time, aren't you."

Daniel stopped. He was a couple feet away, he leaned at the waist and reached with his arms, his fingertips just barely brushed the back of the jack-o-lantern. He yanked his hand back quickly, as if something had struck out at him. Nothing had and his hand felt fine. He had only touched a pumpkin that felt as it should, but in his mind, he was only steps away from death. He took another small step forward and reached out again. He left his fingertips resting on it this time, after a moment without anything happening, he spun the jack-o-lantern around so that its face looked upon him.

Daniel fell back against the bed, slipping to the floor with a heavy thud. The face on the jack-o-lantern moved again as it began to speak and Daniel felt the connections in his brain loosen, allowing the madness in front of him to seep in, convince him he wasn't crazy, convince him that what he was observing was true. Was possible. Somehow.

"Well," the jack-o-lantern said. "That took a little longer than expected, but here we are. It's nice to meet you."

Daniel opened his mouth, tried to speak, but all that fell out was a confused stammer. He wiped his eyes again, rubbed his temples, shut his eyes tight, and when he reopened them, he was still looking at a talking jack-o-lantern offering him a mischievous grin.

"What are you?" Daniel finally managed to say.

"I was a pumpkin living happily in the woods until you came along. You did give me a face though, and a fine one at that, so for now, I'm in your gratitude."

"How... how are you talking?"

"With my mouth."

"But how?"

"I don't know to tell you honest, but you find a strange pumpkin patch in twilight while running through wild woods, you take a pumpkin, you find an almost literal, and magical, answer to your prayers, and now you're confused there's a catch? There's always a price to be paid for things that seem too good to be true."

"How do you know all that?"

"Before I was picked, by you, I was kind of a part of everything. I felt your fear, your anger, the despise resting in your soul when you entered our glade. I knew all of it, and then I was vaguely aware of you leaning over me, severing my vine, carrying me home, but it's all foggy."

Daniel felt guilt tear at him, it wasn't as strong as the fear sitting in his belly, but it was close, and his whole body trembled with the emotions ripping through him.

"Did it hurt?" Daniel asked. "I didn't mean to hurt anyone."

"Not pain so much as shock. I didn't understand what was happening."

Daniel watched in fascination as the jack-o-lantern's face moved, wrinkled, and stretched as the thing carried on a conversation with him. He was still leaning against the bed, his legs feeling like they weighed a thousand pounds each, his mind was finally coming to terms with what was happening, but with each twist, grin, and look from the pumpkin the confusion began to build again.

"I still don't understand what's happening," Daniel said. "Do you have a name?"

"I never have before."

"What do I call you then?"

"I don't know. What's a good name?"

"How about Jack?"

"That seems fitting."

"Alright. Hello, Jack. I'm Daniel."

"Hello, Daniel."

Daniel pushed himself to his feet and sat on the edge of the bed, staring at Jack. Staring intently at the impossible thing happening in front of him. He regretted the pointed teeth now. Especially now that those sharp teeth were moving when Jack spoke. He was happy he went with gentle eyes and a large smile. Had he gone *too* scary with it, he thought he might have shit himself. At least Jack didn't seem able to move on his own.

"Why were you so afraid?" Jack asked. "When you ran into the glade, your fear, it was like a cloud that rolled over everything. Turbulent and violent. It was unlike anything I'd ever sensed."

"That must be nice," Daniel said. "I feel that way a lot. Especially after... after my dad passed away. He was always good at calming me down, good at keeping the fear at bay, you know?"

"What happened to him?"

"Drunk driver. You know what being drunk is?"

"Sure. A drunk hit him?"

Daniel hung his head. "No. He was the drunk. He fell asleep...drove off an overpass."

"Oh," Jack said. "I'm sorry, Daniel."

They sat in silence for a long while as Daniel's mind thought about the crash, thought about his father going splat when the jeep landed on the highway below. Thought about the closed casket at the funeral.

"Is that where it comes from?" Jack asked. "The fear?"

"Sometimes," Daniel said. "Sometimes it is, but most the time, it comes from this kid at school, this big kid, Joey. He's mean and nasty. Like's to beat on me for whatever reason. He was chasing me yesterday when I found the pumpkin patch."

Daniel felt sadness welling up in his chest. Talking about his father, about Joey, about the fear that seemed to consume him. Thinking about the pain that devoured his mother. It was a lot, a lot to think about at three in the morning. He was tired. As the fear of seeing his jack-o-lantern talk to him subsided and the sadness filled its space, he decided it was time to sleep. He crawled back to his bed, leaving Jack's face pointed at him, somehow finding it comforting that the thing was watching over him in some strange way.

"I'm sorry to hear that. I want you to know, I'll help you if I can."

"Thanks, Jack. I don't know how you could, but I appreciate you saying that."

Daniel pulled the quilt up to his chin and closed his eyes, feeling a tornado of emotions assaulting him as he drifted off to sleep.

DEALING WITH JACK

* * *

Daniel awoke Saturday morning to the smell of breakfast wafting up the stairs, sneaking under his door and filling his room. He sat up, saw early morning sunlight pouring through his window, dust dancing on the rays. He looked toward Jack. The pumpkin sat as he had left it the night before, its smiling mouth of pointed teeth watching over him as he slept. The candle inside had burned out and the flesh of Jack's face seemed static.

"Jack?" Daniel said hesitantly.

No answer.

Daniel swung his feet from his bed and walked toward the pumpkin, reached out with hesitation, touched the smooth surface, but there was no response. He laughed lightly to himself, realizing if he hadn't dreamed it, he had at least been so sleepy that he was borderline delirious last night. He vividly remembered his conversation with Jack the night before, but in the hard light of the morning he had to face reality.

Jack-o-lanterns don't come to life.

He grabbed the stem and pulled the top off Jack, reached down and removed the spent candle. He was placing the top back on when his door creaked open. His heart leapt in his chest and he nearly fell over backwards as he jumped at the sound. He turned, wide eyed, to see his mother peeking into the room. She pushed the door open further and stepped inside.

"I'm sorry," she said, "I didn't mean to scare you."

"It's okay," Daniel said, "I was just thinking."

"Danny," his mother said, "I'm so sorry about yesterday. I completely forgot about the pumpkin patch. I don't know how, it just slipped my mind. I'm truly so sorry, it was just that... I don't know, it was a—"

"I know, mom. I understand."

Tears appeared at the corners of his mother's eyes as she forced a sad looking smile to her lips. "I saw the seeds on the counter this morning, saw the pumpkin guts in the trash, and it all came back to me. I feel so guilty. I just forgot. I hope you can forgive me."

"Really, mom, it's okay."

"I made you breakfast, it's not necessarily an apology, but I hope it helps. And I have the pumpkin seeds roasting."

Daniel smiled, walked to his mother and hugged her. He looked up at her as a tear slipped down her cheek.

"It's perfect, mom. Really," Daniel said.

His mother grabbed his face with both hands, tilted his head back and examined the raised bruise beneath his eye, the cut on his cheek. Worry twirled across her face as she said, "my goodness, what happened to your face?"

"It was nothing, I just fell down yesterday. No big deal."

His mother looked at the pumpkin resting on the windowsill. "How did you get to the pumpkin patch, honey? Did you go with friends?"

"No," Daniel said, "believe it or not, I found that one while walking home through the woods yesterday. I went a new way and just kind of wandered into a wild pumpkin patch."

She looked down at him skeptically, "a wild pumpkin patch, really? I don't know how something like that could stay hidden, but that's exciting," she said smiling. "That makes this a very special pumpkin then, huh?"

"I think so," Daniel said, his gaze lingering on Jack, flashes of the conversation from the night before passing through his mind. "I think I was just lucky I stumbled into it."

"I'll say. I like the teeth, kind of spooky."

"Maybe *too* spooky."

His mother laughed, started to walk away, heading back downstairs. As she vanished into the hallway, she called back to him. "Come on down and grab some food while it's hot!"

Daniel got dressed and descended the stairs towards the kitchen, the delicious smell of pancakes and bacon surrounding him, pulling him forward. As he rounded the corner, he saw his mother's back at the coffee pot, a bottle of clear alcohol being tipped into her mug, giving her the start to the day he guessed she needed. He cleared his throat and sat at the table. His mother nearly dropped her bottle as she sat it on the counter and spun on her heels, trying to conceal her addition to the coffee.

"So," she said, "we're finishing up your costume today, right?"

"Yes ma'am."

"Anything else on the docket before the big night tomorrow?"

"I was thinking maybe we could watch a scary movie tonight? If you have the time."

She smiled as she prepared a plate for him and sat it on the table. "I would love that."

After the large meal, he felt full and satisfied. He helped his mother clean the kitchen, noticing a stumble here and there after her third cup of coffee with additives. Once the kitchen was clean, they moved to the living room where they set up the sewing machine and pulled out the half-finished costume. Daniel was going as a gunslinger, like something out of the old black and white westerns his dad used to stay up late watching with him. He wanted an exact replica of a costume he'd seen *Chuck Connors* wear while fighting desperados on *The Rifleman,* but his mother had squashed that idea. Too expensive, she said, and she promised she could make the exact same thing at home for half the price.

So far, she was half right. Right about the costume being too expensive. The one she was making for him did look good, but it also looked far from finished. She looked embarrassed about that, told Daniel he could go play, or do some homework, that she'd get it all finished for him. He declined and helped her as best he could. They worked late into the afternoon. Before noon, his mother switched from coffee to just pouring a bit of the strong drink into her coffee mug.

It worried Daniel to see. She usually started early with her drinks, and they'd been coming earlier and earlier as the anniversary of his father's death got closer, but it was getting to a point where he couldn't remember the last time he'd seen her sober after lunch. He wanted to say something, but he'd made that mistake before, and on this Saturday, the Saturday before Halloween, he didn't want to do anything that might jeopardize his costume getting finished. So, he just watched and worried, as the clear liquor disappeared throughout the afternoon.

They talked while they worked and before long his mother began to slur her speech, she became happier, but it was a fake happiness, like she was being forced to be happy. Her stitchwork became sloppy, she accidently sewed a button to the back of his black vest. That sent her into a fit of laughter, but it was short lived. Then she began cursing as she tore the button off and started over. Daniel took note of the amount left in the bottle. He wasn't surprised to see it empty as the sun set.

The costume was almost finished, and his mother instructed him to go to her closet to find his dad's old Stetson, the perfect finish to his western costume. He dashed upstairs and pulled the old, faded hat off the rack. He ran back down and as he turned the corner into the living room, he spied the little orange bottle of long pills, now on the coffee table. He hadn't seen her take one, but it hadn't been there when he left, so he could only assume.

He tried on the finished costume. His mother's eyelids drooped, and her smile sunk slightly to the left, giving her a goofy look as she applauded her own work and stumbled through a compliment about how wonderful he looked. He asked her if she still wanted to watch a movie with him, but all he received as an answer was a grunt and his mother tossing her head back to the side, eyelids shut, but fluttering as if a thousand thoughts were behind them, waiting to burst forth. He wondered what those thoughts were.

Daniel sighed and tossed a blanket over her. He knew she just missed his father, he missed him too, but he was worried. He kissed his mother on the forehead, said, "don't worry mom, it will all be alright," before he trudged up the stairs. He pushed open his door and nearly fell over as Jack greeted him.

"Well, howdy there, partner," Jack said. "All you're missing is the six-shooter."

Daniel slapped himself lightly in the face, rubbed at his eyes.

"Didn't we do all this last night?" Jack asked.

"I thought I must'a been dreaming," Daniel said. "Why weren't you doing this talking stuff this morning?"

"I was sleeping."

"You were sleeping?"

"I was."

"You gotta sleep?"

"Doesn't everything?"

"I guess." Daniel began to take off his costume, carefully folding it and setting it on top of his dresser. He pulled on his pajamas, but left the big Stetson on, enjoying the feel of it.

"Was the hat your dad's?" Jack asked.

Daniel nodded.

"How's your mom?"

Daniel looked at Jack quizzically, "Why would you ask that?"

Jack frowned, an emotion that was not easy to complete with his carved smile, but still, Daniel could tell there was frown beneath the moving gourd.

"You look sad," Jack said.

"My mom is sad."

"Because of your dad?"

Daniel nodded. They sat in silence for a while, just Daniel staring at the wall in pajamas and a Stetson, with a talking jack-o-lantern, named Jack. He wondered if he was insane. Figured he probably was.

"I been thinking on that," Jack said. "What if I had a way to take care of your problems?"

"What problems?" Daniel asked.

"Well, the two big ones I see, after only having known you this short time, would be a certain kid named Joey that beats on you. And then there's the constant pain and sadness filling this house. What if we could take care of both problems in one swift stroke?"

Daniel pulled the hat off and scooted to the edge of the bed, stared at the talking pumpkin on his windowsill. "How do you mean?"

"Well it's not easy. Not for you, I mean. You'll have to do something. It'll have to be tomorrow night, Halloween, only night it'll work, but I think we can make it happen."

"I'm listening," Daniel said.

* * *

Daniel slept fitfully that night, but come morning, Halloween morning, he felt well rested and certain of what he needed to do. He thought the decision may weigh on him later in life, but for now, he thought he had no other choice, and there were few times in one's life when they were presented with such an opportunity. Jack was once again a normal jack-o-lantern in the light of the day, sleeping as he put it, but the instructions had been clear and Daniel knew he'd come back once the sun set again.

He hopped out of bed and began making preparations for the night. He went downstairs and became concerned. There was no coffee or breakfast waiting. The pill bottle on the coffee table had shifted and there was new bottle of vodka open beside it. When he saw his mother on the couch, he knew she had started early in the morning, probably the moment she'd awaken from her stupor. She was on the couch, splayed out, legs and arms useless weights cast off in any which direction.

Daniel crept past and grabbed a bagel from the kitchen. He should have checked on her, he knew he should have, but he had a busy day, had to make sure everything went according to plan. He climbed the stairs quietly again, wondered if he was being a bad son, not making sure she was okay, but then again, he figured she was a grown up, knew how to take care of herself and all that, figured it wasn't his responsibility. His responsibility was getting dad back. And thanks to Jack, he had a plan about how to do that. If it worked, it would fix all of their problems.

* * *

As Halloween night began, he donned his costume, the fit perfect down to the too-large-for-him hat that occasionally fell over his eyes. He met up with friends as the sun fell behind the horizon, setting the autumn evening ablaze before disappearing altogether. The evening was cool, but not too cold, perfect for a long night of trick'r'treating. And other work.

He crossed paths with Joey only once as he made his way from house to house, holding open his pillowcase, watching the candy grow with each house visited. He darted down a dark side street when he saw Joey, not because he was afraid of losing his candy, there were bigger prizes at stake now. He hid because it wasn't time yet for Joey to see him. Wasn't according to the plan. And it was a plan he wanted to work out.

After the trick'r'treating, with a sack full of candy slung over one shoulder, he began to make his way back toward his house. As he walked, he watched the soft glow of the street lamps come and go, listened to the leaves scraping along the pavement, enjoyed the subtle notes of dampness on the air, a cleansing smell as the chilly air burnt through him with each breath.

He moved up his front walk, peeked in the window and saw his mother was still asleep on the couch, noticed that she'd barely moved throughout the day, her pill and vodka bottle, little soldiers in and unseen internal war, stood tall on the table in front of her, but she remained splayed out, sleeping off a big one, he guessed. He picked up Jack from the porch, where he'd left the pumpkin so that, even though Jack was a strange living thing, people could admire his work on such a great carving as they came up the stoop to collect candy from the bucket he'd left out. Jack hadn't been awake to put up a protest when he'd set him out, but now, as Daniel gathered the jack-o-lantern in his arms, he was back, and he was none too happy.

"Why'd you leave me out like that?" Jack asked.

"I wanted people to admire you."

Jack scowled as best his forced smile would allow.

"I meant no offense."

"Let's just get to it," Jack said impatiently. "Think it will work?"

"I think so. If Joey is where he usually is on Halloween night, then it should work perfectly."

"Good."

Daniel bound down the street in the creeping darkness, a talking jack-o-lantern in one hand, a bag of candy slung over the opposite shoulder. Most the trick'r'treaters had departed the streets. Porches stood lightless every few houses or so, the sign of Halloween night coming to an end. As they rounded a corner, Daniel saw Joey leaning against the fence down at the park. He was alone, his two lackeys off for the night, apparently. He had at least three bags of candy at his feet, but still he scoured the darkness around him, looking for another victim he could relieve of hard-earned candy, and doubt began to creep into Daniel's mind.

As if he was reading Daniel's thoughts, Jack piped up.

"Don't you chicken out on me now—remember, we're both getting something out of this. It has to work for me to work for you," Jack said.

"Can you hear my thoughts?" Daniel asked.

"No, but your steps have slowed to a snail's pace, and you're breathing harder with every step."

"I'm scared," Daniel said.

"I know that. But think of what you'll gain. And what do you have to lose?"

"I know." He took a deep breath. "I'm doing it."

Daniel stopped about a hundred feet from the park where Joey waited. He breathed deeply, enjoyed the cool air, closed his eyes and tried to calm himself.

"Hey!" he yelled towards Joey.

Joey looked up, squinted in the dim light. "Danny-boy, that you out there?"

"Sure is," Daniel called back. "You want your candy, fat ass? You'll have to come get it!"

There was no hesitation as Joey went from standing still to sprinting after Daniel in the night. Jack laughed as Daniel turned on his heels and ran into the dark woods along the edge of the neighborhood. The trail was impossible to follow, but he had an ace up his sleeve, he had Jack, and Jack led the way somehow, telling Daniel when to turn, when to go straight and when to watch out for unseen obstacles like ditches and fallen logs. Daniel cast glances over his shoulder, made sure Joey was following them, made sure Joey was walking into the trap. Thankfully, he was close behind, and it urged Daniel to pick up his pace.

Daniel stepped into the hidden pumpkin patch in the middle of the woods with heavy breath, ragged in his chest. A large moon lit the land, casting a magical scene in front of him. Moonlight and shadow flooded the glade lit by the occasional firefly floating through the darkness. Large orange gourds sat stagnant on the ground. Daniel raced through the glade to the single oak standing tall in the center. He placed Jack on the ground at the base of the old oak, just as instructed. Jack had no candle in him, but even in the dim light, Daniel could see the subtle movement, Jack's eyes searching the darkness for the devilish child that pursued them.

Joey crashed into the glade with a painful sounding grunt. He tripped over a vine and splayed out on the ground. He pushed himself up and wiped dirt and dead leaves from his shirt. He looked around the glade, his face contorted with confusion. He walked towards Daniel and Jack. Daniel looked toward Jack on the ground.

"Any time you're ready," Daniel said.

"Hold on," Jack replied. "He needs to be closer."

Joey was twenty feet from them then. He stopped after a few steps and began to laugh in the cool night. "Danny-boy, what you doing, man? Are you crazy? You come out here all alone, lead me into the woods, make me work for what's mine. I didn't know better, I'd think you're trying to piss me off."

Daniel said nothing, just waited for Jack to hold his end of the deal. Daniel had done his part, he'd brough Joey to the patch, the rest was up to his talking pumpkin friend.

"Come on," Joey said. "I already told you, you were going to get an ass beating. But now? Now that you've brought me all the way out here, I might as well fuckin' *kill* you. Nobody'd miss you, ain't no one gonna give a shit. Specially not your pilled-up mama."

Daniel stared at the boy across the glade. The anger in his eyes, the hatred living there, only confirmed to Daniel that he had made the correct choice. Now he just had to trust in Jack.

"Fuck you, Joey," Daniel said.

"Oh, boy. Some things never change," Joey said. He tried to take a step forward, but he nearly fell as something had crept up his leg. Joey looked down, saw a thick vine coiled around his calf, slowly inching higher. He started hitting at it, but the vine continued to advance, swallowing his knee and starting up his thigh as another vine crept around his other foot. Joey screamed out in the dark woods, fell forward on his hands. Tried to pull himself from the grasp of the vines until new ones began to engulf his fingers and slip up his arms. Tears spilled from his eyes as he begged mercy.

Daniel casually walked through the glade and knelt next to Joey. He was on his hands and knees, straining with everything he had to escape the vines coiling around him, pulling him closer to the damp earth. Daniel grabbed the back of Joey's head, wrapped his fingers in a handful of the boy's dirty hair, turned his face up towards his own. His cheeks were red with effort and glistening in the moonlight from the tears streaming down them.

"Hey, Joey," Daniel said, "Happy Halloween, you asshole."

"Daniel!" Joey cried. "Please, please stop whatever this is! I'm sorry! I'm sorry! Please don't do this." The last request came out a whimper as a vine reached and wrapped itself around Joey's neck. It pulled him flat to the ground, kept pulling, distorting his limbs as they popped out of sockets, caused his hands to look like they might pop as the vines pulled ever downwards, cutting off the boy's circulation. He grunted, screamed, and spasmed as the glade slowly swallowed him. Daniel turned away and walked back towards Jack under the large oak. He slid down the tree and looked over at the jack-o-lantern.

"Well, I held up my end of the bargain," Daniel said.

"You did," Jack said.

"And?"

"And I'll hold up my end. A life for a life. That was the deal. My glade will flourish with this nourishment, and your life will flourish with your new start. Go home, Daniel."

Daniel stood up, looked down at his jack-o-lantern. "Thanks, Jack," he said and turned to walk back through the dark woods, stepping over the squished corpse of Joey in the process.

* * *

He returned to his street to see not the orange and purple lights of Halloween decorations, but the flashing red and blue lights of emergency services. As he neared his house, he realized the cluster of police cars and ambulances sat outside his house. He walked faster, saw someone sitting on the porch that he never thought he'd see again. He dropped his candy and began to run, tears slipped from his eyes as he turned down the sidewalk and ran towards his father.

He jumped at him, arms wide, embracing his dad in a tight hug. He cried as he buried his face in the man's chest. His father hugged him back, shushed him, stroked his hair. Daniel looked up into his father's face. There were no worms or bugs crawling through his eye sockets, no scars or scrapes from his crash off the overpass. He was normal. The same father he'd lost nearly a year ago. Daniel couldn't believe it worked, couldn't believe that Jack had done it. He had no idea how, and he didn't care. He had his father back.

He looked into his father's face again and noticed sadness there. His father was crying, but not because he was holding Daniel again, no one seemed to be alarmed by the man that had been dead only hours ago sitting on his front porch, the EMTs and police walked by without a second glance. Daniel wondered if his father had ever been dead to these people. He hadn't asked Jack how it would work, only leapt at the chance, the prospect of it being possible.

"I've missed you." Daniel said as he hugged his father again. "Mom and I have both missed you more than you could ever imagine."

His father stroked his hair again. "Danny," he said, "it's..." He tried to say more, but his voice cracked and he looked away.

Daniel looked through the window and saw emergency personnel zipping a body into a body bag on the couch. A policeman was taking pictures of the open vodka and the bottle of pills on the coffee table. He looked back towards his father, saw again the deep pain residing there.

"Daniel, I'm so sorry. I should have been here."

Daniel fell into his father's arms, his chest rising and falling as he cried. Feeling a deep pain he'd never wanted to feel again. He thought of the unfairness of it all. He thought about he hadn't checked on her earlier that day, couldn't help but think it was somehow his fault she'd overdid it and died on the couch, full of booze and pills. He wondered if Jack had known, wondered if it was all some sort of sick joke played by his magical jack-o-lantern. He couldn't believe that though, if anything, Jack was the one thing he needed in his life right now.

If he brought one parent back from the dead, he could do it again.

He pulled away from his father, stopped and looked at him, still having a difficult time believing he was really there, then ran back towards the pumpkin patch. He ran as fast as he could, his labored breathing became the only sound he could hear as he entered the woods and stumbled his way back towards what he hoped would be the pumpkin patch. In the darkness of the woods, he could just make out a swath of moonlight ahead, it had to be the glade. He pushed harder and faster, fell to his knees as he tripped over a vine when he entered the glade.

He raised his head and saw the patch glowing in the night. He ran towards the old oak, hopping over Joey's body, now a puddle of red goo and ivory bones sticking up at odd angles. The stink of death rested in the glade like thick fog. He leaned down next to Jack and horror spread across his face. The pumpkin was beginning to rot. He looked around and saw that the whole glade was beginning to rot, taking Joey with it. Pumpkins sat at strange angles, their strong walls giving way as their insides turned to soup. Jack was a shriveled looking thing, the triangle eyes bowing from every side, the upturned smile tilting down at the edges, finally forming a true frown.

Daniel tried to pick Jack up, felt his hands nearly push through the spongy flesh of the pumpkin. He looked at his watch, saw that it read eleven fifty-eight, the last minutes of Halloween ticked away as he called out to Jack.

"What happened?" he yelled into the stinking fog rising in the glade. "Jack, what did you do!"

A voice began to form within the fog, Jack's voice, all around him. Laughing. The laugh faded with the rest of the magic in the glade, but as it drifted off into the night, he heard it clearly for a moment.

"Didn't I tell you, boy? There's always a catch."

FINAL HALLOWEEN

SCOTT MCGREGOR

ORCHID WOODS VIEW.

Simon stared at the sign as he chewed a bite-sized licorice, pondering whether he'd be able to visit a few more houses before the thunderstorm arrived. The alleyway formed by tall wooden fences the colour of eggshell led straight to the wealthiest neighbourhood within walking distance. He liked to think it homed the type of people who handed out full-sized candy bars on Halloween.

Since the age of four, Simon took immense pleasure in treat-or-treating on Halloween night. He loved candy in all its wonderful forms, so much so that when he turned seventeen—in spite of people telling he was too old—he still partook in the tradition of dressing up and scavenging houses for sweets. He promised himself seventeen would be the final year he'd go trick-or-treating, so he needed to make it worthwhile. Which is why for the past three hours dressed up as an eye-patch wearing pirate, he'd hit up every nearby neighbourhood and visited one house after another, filling up not one, but two pillowcases full of candy. The one location left to plunder for snacks belonged to a place he never feasted his eyes on: Orchid Woods View.

In previous years when his father accompanied him while trick-or-treating, they always skipped Orchid Woods View. *The Neighbourhood is filled with nothing but sleazy rich people who're too greedy to handout anything* he'd tell Simon. Reflecting on it over the years, Simon realized his father probably avoided the neighbourhood out of pride, not wanting to appear like a peasant pleading to the upper-class for something. But now, Simon stood in front of the path by himself, free to decide if he wanted to add another area to his collection of treats for his last Halloween venture. Unlike his father, scrounging to the rich didn't hurt Simon's self-esteem.

He whipped out his phone, only three percent of battery remaining. The time showed 10:10 PM, and according to the forecast, the downpour should commence in about twenty minutes. *Twenty minutes is surely enough time to visit a few more houses before it starts raining, and what my father doesn't know won't hurt him.*

So, he strolled down the path towards Orchid Woods View.

* * *

After five minutes of walking in the dark, he spotted a few streetlights past the wooden fences, as well as a ginormous oak tree shaped like a mushroom. The walk took longer than he expected, and a line of sweat ran down his face. Hauling forty pounds of candy for hours was the most exercise he'd engaged in all year. But, he put his back into it and continued onwards, for he felt it'd be worth it once he reached the wealthy suburb.

Finally, he reached the end of the path and entered a cul-de-sac formed by several houses. The kind of houses his father spoke of, estates richly decorated and possessing driveways large enough to fit a small community. At the center of the street, the massive oak tree overlooked the lavish neighbourhood, twice as high as any of the mansions. From across the street where Simon stood, he noticed another alleyway between two houses. And, down where the road led, he spotted the sign that read *Orchid Woods View*.

Of the eight mansions in the neighbourhood, seven kept their lights off. On Halloween, an absence of lights typically served as code for *we're not giving you candy, so get lost*. So, he dwelled not on the houses that shrouded themselves in darkness and focused solely on the one house welcoming trick-or-treaters. He heard it calling to him, saying *come get your candy, Simon*.

"Might as well," he said, and he headed toward the house.

As he walked, he got distracted by the faint taps on his head and shoulders. He extended his hand, feeling the raindrops dampen his palm. The storm must be starting sooner than the forecast issued, so he dashed across the street, hoping to get home before the rain drenched him.

He moved up the porch and saw five jack-o'-lanterns sitting atop a wooden stand, none lit. He paid no mind to the designs carved into the pumpkins and immediately rang the doorbell. The door opened, and a woman pushing forty stood in front of Simon. She wore a red and black dress—some kind of witch costume by Simon's guess—and a towel wrapped around her hair. Looking closely, Simon spotted faint specs of makeup along her neck that seemed washed away. When he noticed she held a silver bowl filled with full-sized candy bars, he knew he hit the jackpot.

"Trick or treat!" he said.

For a moment, the woman stared at Simon with one of her eyebrows raised, looking confused. "You again? Was one coffee crisp not enough?"

First, Simon paused, smile fading, then he said, "I don't know what you mean."

"Are you still lost? I could write down the directions if that's easier for you?"

"Um, no? I'm not lost, I'm just here trick-or-treating."

"Ah, so you are back for more. I see you fixed your costume. That was quite the tear you had, but now it looks brand new. Also, how did you dry off so fast? You were sopping wet."

During some of Simon's previous Halloweens, he witnessed his fair share of houses pulling pranks on whoever strolled up, most of which ended up being someone appearing from behind and screaming. Based on the woman's bizarre greeting, he figured this was such a house, so he looked over his shoulder and tried to spot if somebody attempted to sneak up on him, but he saw no one. When he looked back at her, he asked, "Is this some sort of Halloween skit?"

"Skit? You're the one who keeps showing up at my door."

"I don't know what you mean. This is my first time stepping foot into this neighbourhood."

"Enough with this. Do you need directions or not?"

"No. I'm here for candy like every other kid."

"You know what, here you go." She held out a full-sized Kit Kat. "I doubt I'm going to get more kids at my door, so you can have a second helping, but that's it. Please stop coming here."

"Thanks?" Simon said, reluctantly accepting the candy.

The woman gave Simon an irksome glare before she slammed the door. He stepped back onto the road, noticing the rain starting to hasten. The lights of the woman's house switched off, to which Simon took as her saying *leave me alone.*

"That was weird." He unwrapped the Kit Kat and left through the same way he entered, enjoying a late-night snack as the storm crept in.

* * *

The mild drizzle quickly shifted into a relentless shower as he walked back through the path. His skin shivered with each drop of rain, and his pirate costume which he spent four hours personally customizing was now ruined. Despite the added weight from his stuffed pillowcases, he jogged onward, eager to return home and out of the storm.

Was the path really this long before?

The thunder cracked above, frightening Simon. He recalled some of his friends telling him they found thunder scary, and he normally laughed at them for thinking so. Now, as he shivered in the rain while shrouded in darkness all alone, he understood where the fear stemmed from. If the battery to his phone hadn't died, he'd have called one of his parents to come meet him at the spot he entered the path from and pick him up, saving him from the eerie downpour.

After trotting down the path for what must've been ten minutes now, he saw what looked like another oak tree, along with some lights in the distance. He set free a heavy sigh, relieved to know he'd soon return to some form of civilization, and eventually, to his street guiding him home. But, when he carefully stared at the mushroom shaped tree, he couldn't help but notice it seemed awfully similar to the one in Orchid Woods View.

That can't possibly be the same tree? I've been walking straight for ten minutes.

The sudden strike of lightning startled Simon.

He fell backwards, feeling something in his costume stretch as he hit the ground. The thunder roared, and seconds later, he saw the oak tree collapse. A loud thud followed, and then what sounded like a woman screaming.

"Holy shit!" When he lifted himself off the ground, he saw the tear in his sleeve. "Great, just great."

Simon jumped, trying to spot where the tree landed, but the fences stood too tall for him to see. He darted forward, powering through the rainfall, wanting to see the aftermath of the lightning strike.

When he finally reached the end of the path, he dropped his candy bags and clasped onto his knees, heavily panting. Once he caught his breath, he saw in front of him a cul-de-sac formed by eight houses, with an enormous oak tree towering over the neighbourhood, and a sign down the street that read *Orchid Woods View*. After walking straight down the path he left from, he somehow ended up back in the neighbourhood.

He blinked a few times and wiped his eyes, making sure they weren't playing tricks on him. As he eyed the tree in Orchid Woods View, he thought back to the tree that collapsed from the lightning strike mere moments ago. *Must've been a different tree somewhere else, I suppose?*

Then, he noticed all eight of the houses within Orchid Woods View had their lights on, but why now and not earlier? If their lights were on, he figured they might be open for trick-or-treaters, and he debated whether he wanted to knock on a few more doors or not.

I can't, my costume is wrecked, and it's late, plus the rain...

The rain.

Simon had to pause and think about it for him to realize it wasn't raining anymore. Not only that, but the roads and driveways looked dry, as if a drop of water never touched the ground. He remembered the forecast stating the storm wouldn't let up until morning, so why had it suddenly stopped?

He began to fixate on the house he visited earlier, homed to the woman who handed him a Kit Kat, lights back on. Observing more closely, he noticed the dimly lit jack-o'-lanterns on her porch, each with a face more terrifying than the last. So, after he'd walked away from the woman's house, she turned off her lights, waited until he left the area, then switched them back on and lit her jack-o'-lanterns? Why? Did he really leave such an awful impression?

Standing in front of the house, he heard the woman's voice in his head: *Please stop coming here.* He still couldn't fathom what he'd done to upset her so much. But, Simon also remembered something else she'd said to him: *I could write down the directions if that's easier for you?* Although he didn't understand why she offered him directions in the first place, it seemed to fitting of an offer to pass up now. So, he walked up the steps and rang the doorbell once again.

The woman opened the door, wearing the same dress from earlier, but this time various coatings of black and white makeup canvased onto her face, truly capturing a witch's image. *She redid her makeup too? What's wrong with this woman?*

In silence, the two of them stared at each other for a few seconds, until she said, "Most people say trick or treat once the door opens."

"Sorry to barge in again, but I think I'm lost. I was wondering if I could get those directions you talked about before?"

The woman raised one eyebrow. "Pardon me?"

"After I walked away from your house, I tried leaving the cul-de-sac the same way I entered, but somehow I ended up back here."

"You were here before? No, couldn't have been, I'd remember someone dressed like you. That's quite the costume you've got. I like the idea of a pirate, but did you swim on your way over here? You're soaked. That's also quite a rip on your sleeve."

"Yeah, I fell on my way back here, plus I got drenched by the rain."

"Rain?"

"Yeah, from earlier? What about the lightning strike? That was something, huh?"

"Don't know what you mean. I don't recall any lightning and it hasn't rained all night. Not yet, anyway. It's supposed to start soon."

"I'm so confused."

"You and me both, kid."

"Do you seriously not remember me? I was here like fifteen minutes ago."

"Can't say I do. The last kid I handed out candy to was here an hour ago, and he was only half your height. I was just about to go wash up for the night until you showed up at my door. But, if you're lost, I can tell you how to get out of here."

"Yeah, sure, that'd be awesome." Simon didn't enjoy whatever sort of game the woman played, but the sooner he found his way out of the neighbourhood, the better.

"If you follow the road out of here, it should take you down to Barlow Street and then onto Hillcrest Drive."

"Perfect, that's where I live. Thank you."

"Oh, and here you go." She held out a coffee crisp.

"Another one? That's so kind of you."

"Not sure what you mean by that. Handing out candy is what you normally do on Halloween."

Simon didn't bother replying to her comment and snatched the coffee crisp.

"Have a nice night," she said, closing the door.

He proceeded down the road and left the cul-de-sac for the second time.

* * *

For ten minutes, he headed down the sidewalk at a slow pace, exhausted. He looked for any sign that read *Barlow Street*, but to no avail. Step after step, house after house, the road seemed endless. His grip around his candy bags loosened, hands sore after hours of carrying loads of snacks.

God I can't wait to get home.

He shut his eyes and lifted his head, taking long deep breaths. The rain running down his face helped calm his nerves. The rain helped rinse away his sweat. The rain...

He opened eyes and saw the rainfall, drenching his costume with a second wave. When did it return? And how hadn't he noticed?

By now, the rain likely seeped through his pillowcases, and he feared his candy might be watered-down, otherwise spoiling his favourite aspect of the holiday. The hairs on his skin began to rise from the cold, and a harsh swell of goosebumps crept along his skin. If he continued out in the storm for much longer, he risked catching hypothermia. Between the relentless shower, unfamiliar territory, and shear darkness of the night, he felt a surge of fright intensify, too fitting for Halloween.

Seriously, how much longer to the end of this street?

A few minutes later, he received his answer when he spotted a sign. His fear started to subside, and he power-walked down the street, eager to enter Barlow Street and for the night to conclude. However, when he moved closer, he soon realized the sign wasn't for Barlow Street.

It was for Orchid Woods View.

Once again, he arrived at the cul-de-sac, but this time, there was one significant difference that caught his eye immediately. The ginormous oak tree was knocked down, blocking a portion of the road, and a group of residents huddled around beneath their umbrellas to inspect the scene. Simon hesitated in entering the cul-de-sac, wanting nothing more than to return home and feast on his assemblage of sweats, but his curiosity overtook him, and he moved to the site of the tree.

When he moved close enough, Simon approached the closest person next to him, a greasy looking man dressed in a bowler's shirt. Simon tapped on his shoulder and asked, "Excuse me, what happened?"

"Oh man, craziest thing I've ever seen. A lightning strike knocked down the tree."

A lightning strike. "How long ago?"

"Fifteen, maybe twenty minutes?"

Simon tried to recall precisely when he saw the lightning from earlier, and fifteen to twenty minutes ago sounded about right. But it couldn't possibly have been the same lightning strike, for after it occurred, he saw the oak tree standing perfectly tall within Orchid Woods View himself. He figured it was possible for two different trees to have collapsed from two different lightning strikes in a single evening, as unlikely as it sounded.

Still confused, he scratched his head and said, "This is so crazy."

"It came out of nowhere," the man said. "Poor guy."

"Poor guy?"

"I thought dissecting frogs in high school was gross, but after seeing what the ambulance stretchered away, I'm going to have nightmares for years. I could've sworn he pointed right at me before it happened too."

"I'm sorry, I don't quite understand what you—"

"No!"

The shout—which caught the crowd and Simon's attention— came from a woman dressed in a bathrobe stained with red smears beneath the cotton. Not just any woman, but the same woman Simon interacted with two times already.

Her mouth hung open in a wide O, and her eyes fixated directly on Simon. She lifted her finger, pointed towards him, and said, "It's him. He's back. How can he possibly be back?!"

Everyone around began to stare at Simon, looking as confused as he was. He shrugged his shoulders and raised his hands, not entirely sure how to respond. "Is this a joke or something?"

The moment he spoke, the woman turned around and jolted back to her house, shutting the door and switching off the lights.

"What's her problem?" Simon asked the man.

"Oh she's just spooked is all," he replied. "Between you and me, she's always been a bit of a nut."

"Tell me about it. I talked to her before, and she gave me directions that led me back here. Speaking of which, you wouldn't happen to known a quick way to get to Hillcrest from here, would you?"

"Yeah, just take the path on your left over there."

Simon glanced over where the man pointed and spotted the second alleyway, the one path he had yet to leave from. "Ah, thank you. I've been walking around in circles for what feels like forever. Have a nice night."

As Simon walked away, the man replied, "I'll try. This'll be one Halloween to tell for years to come."

It sure will be.

For the third time, Simon left Orchid Woods View.

* * *

He hurried down the path with haste, feet sore and palms clammy. A part of him considered abandoning his bags of candy to make his trip home easier, but after everything he endured tonight, he deserved to treat himself to something. With all the wandering and exhaustion, he couldn't let his last Halloween be for nothing, so he kept his grip around his pillowcases tight and firm.

After five minutes of walking, Simon spotted another oak tree past the fences, and a swift rush of panic overtook him as he continued on. When he reached the end of the path, his fear confirmed itself when he saw the cul-de-sac in front of him. A cul-de-sac with a tall oak tree towering over the neighbourhood.

"What the hell? This has to be a different neighbourhood."

His assumption proved wrong the second he saw the sign that read *Orchid Woods View.*

"No. No, no, no," he repeated. He ran over to the tree, inspecting how it possibly stood again. He examined every corner, not a mark or crack in the base found. "This can't be happening? There's just no way."

Except it was happening, and the more he thought about it, there was only one logical explanation. It was a prank, a Halloween skit the neighbourhood played on him. And in the middle of the antic, the residence chopped down the tree, blamed the lightning when he asked, then somehow reattached it after he left. He didn't understand how they did it, but he knew a Halloween trick when he saw one.

"Alright, this has gone on long enough," Simon said, reverting his attention to the same house he received candy from twice. Even though the lights remained off, he trotted up the stairs of the woman's house, noticing the jack-o'-lanterns were unlit again. He knocked on the door with three heavy thuds.

The woman opened her door, this time dressed in a clean, white cotton bathrobe. She glared at Simon, sighed, then said, "Listen, kid, this is getting real old. Is this your way of pulling a prank on me, or are you pretending you're lost to keep getting all my candy bars?"

Simon clenched his fists. "I'm not the one pulling a prank, you are. All of you are, and I'm pretty tired of it. Pretending like you know me then don't know me, giving me directions that leads me back here, the huddle with your neighbours. It's an impressive act, and I'll admit I even fell for it at first. I'm not sure how you pulled that crap with the tree, but I'm not dealing with this Halloween skit anymore. The jig is up."

A vein on the woman's forehead throbbed, and her skin turned a ruby red. From her side, she grabbed her silver bowl and tossed a dozen candy bars below Simon's feet. "There, you win. I don't have anything left to give you. Now please, for the love of God, stop coming to my house!"

Simon dropped his bags of candy. He pointed his finger at the woman and said, "I'm done with this shit. You're going to tell me how to get back to Hillcrest right now, or you'll regret it."

The woman lifted her hands as if a gun was pointed at her. "Buddy, relax. I don't want any trouble."

"Oh, you've got it, that's for sure."

She attempted to shut the door, but Simon nudged his foot forward in the doorway to prevent her from doing so.

"I'm not leaving until you tell me how to get out of here," Simon said. "Enough with these games!"

The woman reached for something to her side, and a moment later, Simon saw she held onto an aluminum baseball bat. She swung downward, aiming for Simon's foot. He reeled backward, barely escaping in time. Then, she slammed the door and Simon heard her lock it. That didn't prevent him from knocking on the door loudly and swearing off the top of his lungs, demanding she'd direct him out of Orchid Woods View.

Lights from the other houses flickered on, and some of the residents opened their doors to inspect the commotion. And amongst the residence, Simon spotted the greasy looking, bowler shirt wearing man step onto his porch.

"Well well, look who's joined the show." Simon trudged down the stairs and positioned himself at the center of the street near the tree, watching all the eyes that fixated on him. He pointed his finger at the man he spoke to earlier. "Remember me? Of course you do. I'm the guy you've all been messing with for the past hour. My father was right to not visit here. You're all nothing but a bunch of greedy rich assholes who like to fuck with other people."

As Simon continued his rant, the woman emerged from her house and darted over to Simon, holding a cellphone in one hand and the aluminum baseball bat in the other. "This is bordering on harassment, buddy. I'm warning you, I will call the cops if you don't leave here immediately."

"Go for it. Let them come. I can't wait to tell them all the crap you've pull—"

The sudden strike of lightning shushed Simon's last words. From behind, he heard a loud crack, and when he turned around, he noticed the tree starting to shift in direction. The last thing Simon saw was the tree fall where he stood, too late to make a move.

Whatever remained of him splattered onto the woman's robe, thus concluding Simon's final Halloween.

THE HALLOWEEN MUMMY

DOUGLAS FORD

THIS TIME, WHEN CARTER once again wore the costume, he might finally wall up all the bad feelings inside a tomb where they belonged. You don't just forget about the kind of thing he went through, the humiliation. A process like that takes time.

This year, when he re-created his mummy costume, just as he did every Halloween, he would adorn himself in a far more realistic version of what he wore when the *bad thing* happened.

A stupid party, full of stupid kids, celebrating some stupid birthday that fell on the day of Halloween. That year, he watched all the mummy films in order for the first time, starting with the one featuring Boris Karloff and working his way through the final sequence with Lon Chaney, including his favorite, *The Mummy's Ghost*. Though the continuity between films didn't make a lot of sense, Carter fell under their spell, and his mother indulged him by helping him fashion the first version of the costume. It turned out that she had yards of old ace bandages, leftovers from when his grandmother used to wrap ice packs around her legs when her arthritis got bad. With a cigarette hanging out of her mouth, Carter's mother wrapped him round and round and round with the bandages.

"There," she said, exhaling cigarette smoke when he stood complete, the bandages covering his body from head to toe. "You look scary as hell."

But when Carter regarded himself in the mirror, he had doubts. For one thing, the beige color didn't look right, nothing at all like the dirty gray hue conveyed in the black and white films he watched. Nor did he feel sure about the way the bandages covered his face, not allowing for the exposure of withered flesh he saw in the cinematic incarnations of the mummy. Later, with yearly practice, he would fix all these problems, but this first time, he trusted his mother and went to the party in the form she prepared for him, barely able to walk thanks to the stiffness of the bandages. He knew the mummy walked a particular way, but nothing all like the stiff-legged gait he managed as he walked to the party.

At first, it felt good knowing he would show up as something different from all the others, something home-made that showed effort and stood out from all the store-bought costumes. Something creative, something that conveyed *soul* and *inspiration.*

But it didn't take long for it all to go wrong—the wrappings began unravelling almost as soon as he came through the door. That entrance occurred without much fanfare. Manny O'Brien's mom answered the door when he knocked and gave him dumbfounded look. She didn't get the costume at all. "You a car crash victim?" she said. "What're you wearing under that?" When he didn't answer—he could only mumble with the bandages covering his lips—she reached out and touched one of the safety pins that held the bandages in place, and Carter felt the first harbinger of doom, the shifting of the layers of bandages around his body. Manny's mom didn't mean to cause it, but no doubt just the placement of her finger started his unraveling.

Carter tried to hold off the inevitable for as long as possible, initially by not participating in any of the games, laying-low and sticking to the margins of whatever horseplay was taking place. As his unraveling became worse, he withdrew further, favoring the darkest corners and keeping quiet, anxious that no one would notice how the bandages continued to slip, first revealing his face, then eventually his bare chest.

But of course, they did notice. No one could miss it. And that point, no one needed to ask what he wore underneath the costume. It soon became apparent.

No such mistakes this year. He would present a *masterpiece* to the world outside the home he shared with his mother, though he no longer required her help.

Speaking of his mother, she no longer smoked, the stroke having robbed her of almost all her old habits. Now, she spent most of her time in her bed.

Carter stood in her doorway, allowing her to gaze for the first time on this year's mummy costume. He asked her what she thought.

Years before, he solved the problem of the face. No longer did bandages cover it. You could see features now, and he prided himself on how it went beyond even what the make-up artist Jack Pierce could devise in those old films, his features flaky, corpse-gray, and withered looking. This year he added a new effect for the eyes, and he wanted to see the impact of that effect on his mother.

The stroke had robbed her of control over the left side of her face, but he saw how her right eye widened at the sight of him. "You like it." He spoke for her because the stroke robbed her of speech, too, though he could tell by the way her lips moved that she wanted to tell him herself. "It's ok, don't try to talk. The eyes are new this year."

For the eye effect, he took his inspiration from Tom Tyler's incarnation of the mummy. When Tyler played the monster, the studio blacked out his eyes, making them look like hollow pits. Using a very crude but effective technique for the time, the filmmakers simply blacked out the actor's eyes on each frame of film. Carter couldn't understand why they didn't do that in subsequent films, too. Maybe it simply required a lot of work. For his own empty eye-pits, Carter added some realistic detail: streams of blood and ocular fluid.

He hoped that his mother didn't overexaggerate her reaction and that her expression of horror came from genuine sentiment. She couldn't tell him, of course, so he reminded himself that she would never lie to him. Exaggerate a little maybe, but never lie.

Before leaving the house, Carter took the time to move her to her wheelchair, and he rolled her onto the front porch. Hardly anyone ever came to the house anymore, not even on Halloween, almost as if it bore some invisible mark warning people away. To play it safe, Carter found the bowl filled with old candy, and he set it upon her lap, making sure that it wouldn't slip off. He looked into her drooping face to see if she understood what he'd done. He hoped that no one mistook her for some macabre Halloween decoration, but he also didn't want to disappoint any curiosity-seeker who got close enough to see her eye blink or her lip droop. With the bowl of candy on her lap, a trick-or-treater could help themselves and not retaliate with some kind of trick. It would devastate him if he returned home to find that his mother had fallen victim to something cruel.

From the bowl he took a bite-sized Snickers bar, unwrapped it and placed it in her mouth. "Chew," he said, but most of it slipped out of her mouth in a gooey mess. He sighed and kissed her on the cheek, careful not to get any of his blood on her. Taking a Snickers for himself, he set out upon the night's task.

THE HALLOWEEN MUMMY

The street appeared deserted, though orange lights and glowing pumpkins lit up several doorways. Carter reminded himself to keep faith, experience having taught him that he just needed to start walking and someone would show up in due time. People didn't go door-to-door the way they used to do, and that struck him as a damn shame, but he'd eventually come across someone. He always did. Starting forth, he used a gait resembling what he saw in the mummy films, dragging his left leg in a way that any smart observer would recognize as a sign of a fracture or perhaps severe paralysis from disuse over a long period of time. To the same observer, his left hand and arm would appear mangled from the way he held them molded against the tea-colored bandages of his chest. Not a safety-pin in sight either, though wisps of bandages hung from his body and occasionally blew behind him in the October wind, all held in place by the dried decay of the mummy's body.

He wouldn't unravel this time, not like the way he did at the birthday party.

Unravel down to a kid just wearing his underwear.

Didn't everyone have that nightmare at some point, the one where you showed up to school or somewhere else in public wearing just underwear?

In Carter's case, it actually happened. He went to a kid's birthday party wearing only a pair of thin, white underwear, covered solely by several yards of ace bandages that wouldn't stay in place and eventually fell off completely. He knew what the laughter most people only dreamed about sounded like in real life.

And the ridicule? Nothing at all like a bad dream. Far more painful.

He put that pain into his walk—drag, step, drag, step—not going up to any of those orange-lit houses, no trick-or-treating for him, just *prowling* until he found someone on their own. It needed to be someone alone. Just like him when he unraveled. All alone.

He came upon his quarry when the clouds overhead began to clear, and thanks to the emerging light of the moon he could make out some of the details in the kid's costume—some sort of Power Ranger, he guessed, though Carter didn't know what captivated the imaginations of kids these days. Times change, after all, and monsters go out of fashion, even mummies. The important thing was that no group accompanied him. Maybe he started out the evening trying to tag along with a group of older kids, only to get ditched at some point. That sort of thing happened, as Carter himself could attest. He knew what unmitigated cruelty felt like, and he felt something like pity as he began to follow the small figure, anticipating the special moment when his head turned and he saw Carter there behind him. Each year he needed someone to see him, and he could just imagine the kind of stories that resulted, the breathless accounts. *I did, I saw an actual mummy, no lie, I swear, right behind me. It was real, not a costume at all, no way, old, decayed, and dead, just appearing out of nowhere.* Carter wished he could follow this kid all the way home and listen, become a fly on the wall or something.

Speaking of flies, a group of them had formed around Carter, and maybe one of them buzzed by the kid's head, because he turned his head slightly. A glimpse of his features revealed something interesting. He looked like Manny O'Brien, the birthday boy himself. A little brother or cousin maybe?

That made everything even more perfect.

Even as his quarry picked up his pace, Carter hardly needed to break his stride to keep up, just drag, step, drag, step, the pads of his feet making no sound at all. He wanted the small figure to *sense* his presence, not hear him. Overhead, the sky cleared more, and a full moon filled the sky, illuminating all around him.

Without knowing for certain, Carter felt a cold suspicion that if he looked at an old calendar, he'd find that his costume accident occurred during a full moon cycle. The way things seemed to come together tonight filled him with a sense of cosmic awe and gratitude. His tea-colored bandages practically glowed, and he very much wanted his quarry to turn and regard him fully now. Judging by his quickening steps knew something pursued him now. He could feel Carter there behind him. The kid walked briskly, no doubt afraid to turn around, frightened of what he might see, and he didn't want to risk turning to any of the lit houses on the street. Carter didn't have to alter his pace to keep up. Even without running, the mummy always overtook his prey in the end, no matter how fast the prey ran.

And suddenly, the bag of candy swinging in his hand, the kid began to run. It didn't matter though. Just drag, step, drag, step, and Carter not only kept pace, but he began to close the distance. Closer, closer, until Carter could almost reach out and touch him with the parchment gray of his fingertips. The kid chose that moment to turn and look.

He screamed. He kept running, but how he screamed, still looking at Carter with wide eyes and open-mouth. No one else to witness this thing, this abomination behind him. Every time this happened, his quarry would drop whatever candy they carried, and Carter always made sure to claim it as his own, but he always wished for something more to happen.

This year, that finally happened.

This particular kid wouldn't stop looking over his shoulder at him, even as he kept on running. That combination—looking in one direction, running in another—would spell disaster in any scenario, but once the kid started across the busiest intersection in the neighborhood, the one that Carter knew all too well, it proved lethal.

Carter guessed that the car hit the kid at about fifty-five miles per hour, well over the designated speed limit. He heard the screech of brakes and watched the car leave a long smear of red on the road, the upper half of the body still attached to the front grille, the bottom half somewhere in the undercarriage. A beat of awful silence ensued when the car finally stopped several feet away. Then a lot of shouting and crying.

Carter picked up the bag of candy dropped by the kid. He looked inside the bag and withdrew a Milky Way, opening it as a pair of teenagers exited the car and began walking around in circles.

As he ate the candy, he thought of how the car that hit him all those years ago didn't even stop.

The kid who just got run over could at least rest easy with the fact that this car didn't drive away. At least this car's occupants actually bothered to climb out and look at their handiwork. Carter had to admit though that he bore some responsibility for the accident that took his own life—after all, he did trip over the few remaining bandages that clung to his body as he tried to run home—but he didn't know what excuse the driver had for the way he kept on going, not even looking back. After the car struck him, Cater just laid there in the road, a dead kid wearing only his underwear. The remaining bandages blew off into the wind and wound up hanging from the branches of a tree. They hung there for months, no one quite realizing their origin, nobody ever quite connecting the dots, though Carter knew that his mother saw them whenever she crossed the intersection. Finally, she couldn't stand it any longer, and one day she stopped the car in the middle of the road and began pulling down those bandages herself. She had to jump to reach them, but she managed to pull them all down, every single strand, finding a few remaining safety pins attached here and there. Unable to bring herself to throw them away, she stored the bundle of old bandages under his bed, the one he would never sleep in again. Not long her declining health resulted in the stroke, Carter came back and used those very same bandages for his new outing as the mummy. Each year after that, he improved upon his look little by little.

This year, he finally perfected it. Everything came full circle, like the full moon that shined down on him. Under its light he drag-stepped his way home, still carrying the bag of candy, his newest bounty.

Why didn't he feel great then? Something felt off. Traces of those bad feelings remained.

Maybe he sensed what he'd find when he arrived home, though it still came as a shock. He expected to see his mother still seated on the front porch, the candy perched on her lap where he left it. He planned to add the contents of the bag he now carried to the bowl, just as he did every Halloween. But now he found the wheelchair upended, the bowl upside down, and its contents scattered about. He wondered where she'd gone. Had someone taken her away from him?

In his worried state, as he picked up the candy and returned it to the bowl, he almost didn't notice the way the front door hung ajar. Still drag-stepping, he passed within, and if he could breathe, he would have done so with a sigh of relief when he found his mother on the floor. She could barely use her limbs anymore, but somehow, she managed to overturn her chair and drag herself inside. Carter reached for her with his free mummy hand, causing two maggots to fall of him and land on her back. You never saw maggots crawling on Lon Chaney's body, but plenty of them dug around on Carter. He turned his mother over, and she looked at him again with her wide, terrified eye. Her mouth hung open and drool trailed from his lip. He wiped it away carefully, avoiding any more maggots falling on her.

"It's ok," he said. "It's just me, remember. Just me under all these bandages." He pulled her wheelchair in after him and lifted her back into the seat. Then he narrated to her all that happened that evening as he wheeled her toward her bedroom. While he helped her into her bed, she continued to regard him with the open, terrified eye. He added the bag of candy he scavenged from the dead kid to the bowl and placed the bowl on the night-stand next to her bed. Opening another Snickers, he placed it inside her mouth. When it rolled out, he cleaned up the gooey mess it left behind with a tissue.

He still felt the rush of the evening's events, the magic of a holiday devoted to dead things like mummies, and he found himself starting the whole story again from the beginning. Her gaze remined on him the whole time, and she hardly blinked.

Carter didn't know yet what it meant, the confluence of the night's events and the way they lined up with what happened years ago. He didn't know if circumstances would allow him to don the costume again next year and carry out the same routine, but he hoped they would. Already he began thinking of ways he could improve upon his costume. The maggots looked good, but what about actual scarabs eating around the hole in his chest? What if he trailed not just bandages but entrails as well? What if on next year's outing he met someone like him, someone who would join him, someone with the imprint of a car's grille on the upper half of his body?

Some kids grew out of Halloween, but he hoped he never would. Some kids grew away from their mothers, and he certainly hoped he would never do that either.

But certain things remained outside of his control.

With his lipless mouth, he kissed his mother on the forehead, and after brushing away another maggot that had fallen there, he backed up so she could look at him fully one more time. You never know when you might see someone for the last time, he thought.

"I love you, Mom," he said to that wide, staring eye.

Then he began unraveling his bandages.

TRADITIONS LOST

CLARK ROBERTS

"DO YOU BELIEVE the story?"

Jim doesn't immediately answer. He frowns before glancing down at the girl stepping stride for stride with him. They should be back at the house and closing out the night, him inspecting candy wrappers for unexplained tears while the girl waits for her bounty. *That tradition is going to be gone someday,* he reminds himself. Instead of pillaging the homes of their neighborhood, today's kids are being indoctrinated into church put on "trunk-or-treats" and a sort of group celebration at the town's main park. It pains him to admit that such a delightful and nostalgic memory from his childhood is disappearing as easily as covering a marred wall with a paint stroke. Undeniably though, it's happening. And rightfully so, considering what had come to pass ten years prior this night.

Instead of answering her question Jim suggests, "Maybe you'd rather go to Center Park. We still have time. It sure sounds like fun."

Even at this later hour, the chilled dusk air carries the sharp and festive noises of ominous organ chords and children's squeals from the distance. It sounds every bit the celebration it should be for little demons and witches and cartoon characters taking place in the center of town. It saddens him that it can't be that way for the girl beside him.

"No, I want to continue to West Park" the girl answers. Her nonchalant tone indicating that particular notion has never been a slip in her mind.

Jim recalls his own annual childhood Halloween jaunts. Costumed like a pirate or a ghoul he'd paraded up and down neighborhood blocks, his mildly entertained parents in tow. On those nights he'd greedily cashed in on whatever delicious treats each house had dished out, and for the following week or two had gorged like a child's version of a king.

"You didn't answer my question," the girl states. "Do you think the story is really true?"

"Yes," Jim nods.

There is no point in trying to spin the conversation to another topic. It's the same ritual each Halloween, has been now for the last ten years. The girl plays the wide-eyed naivety card and he assumes the role of a knowing adult. Year after year she has tormented him with this game and he plays along with the enthusiasm of a father exhausted from being tugged to a play set tea party one too many times—*but I'm not her father.*

Yet to refuse to play would be harsh, and more than that he knows how persistent the girl will be about West Park if he tries to put his foot down.

"Is it true their faces were sliced off?" the girl asks.

"That's what it said on the news." Jim sighs a breath of disconcertment. He can't help but ponder how wrong this all is. This girl, bobbing ponytail and innocent mannered, should not be so fascinated with such a gruesome ghost story at her age, especially one so violent.

"Is it true they haunt West Park on Hallow's Eve?"

"That's the legend."

"Is it true *The Bad Man* scooped out their eyeballs?"

Jim seals his lips. It's too gruesome for him to focus on, so he turns and looks at the houses they walk past.

"It's okay, Mr. Jim," the girl says. "I haven't really forgotten. I just like to make sure you haven't forgotten."

Jim remains quiet, continues to study the neighborhood's homes.

The porch lights of the houses they pass by are now all dark. Whatever few people are left that still cling to the old autumn tradition of door-to-door trick or treating have given up the ghost at this point. Jim wonders if the occupants behind these closed doors think their efforts have been worthwhile or are they at this very moment having a discussion about whether or not to even bother with the carved pumpkins and the tacked up cobwebs next year. Are they so disheartened by the lack of knocks on their doors that they'll close up shop on Halloween for good?

The man and girl pass beneath the cone of light at the last street-crossing of the town. The fluorescent pink of the girl's costume absorbs the light, and when they are once again swallowed by the darkness the outlined bones of her costume momentarily glow.

One block up the road curves and there will be West Park, a drab effort at best from the city planners. It has always been nothing more than a stretch of grass with a corkscrew slide, one set of squealing swings, and planted tractor tires the poor kids crawl over or into to hide. It's as if the original municipal planners had set it down simply to give *"the wrong side of the tracks"* another thing to complain about and then they'd wiped their hands of it.

Off to the right a dog barks viciously.

Lost in his thoughts, the sudden and violent outburst startles Jim.

The large dog leaps to a two-footed stand, and its front paws rattle the chain link wall of its pen.

Then, the girl asks Jim the question he never wants to hear. "Do you think the brother and sister will ever get to move on to where it is the dead are supposed to go?"

"I hope so," he says, but his voice is hardly a whisper.

The beast of a dog is barking even more ferociously at them, and Jim can't help but wonder what would happen if it wasn't caged, how persistent the animal would be in its bloodlust. Would it chase after them, rip them down like prey? *It's an animal and isn't capable of reasoning out the futility of that type of violence.*

Why is it the same for some humans?

"I hope so too," the girl agrees.

Before Jim is even aware of what is about to pass over his lips, he suddenly asks, "Why me?" He's never voiced this question aloud, although many a nights he's sought answers in his own head while staring up at his bedroom ceiling. It feels a cruel question to ask the girl, but once it's out he can't stop. He kneels to her level, feels the sting of tears brimming. "Why was I chosen to be your guardian? Did *you* choose me? Was I handpicked by God? Why am I the one you haunt?"

"Is that all I am to you—a haunting?" The girl frowns and her eyes turn to the ground.

"I didn't mean it like that." Jim lifts her chin. "I just... I can't for the life of me see the thread. I'm not your parent, so I can't come to terms with why it's me you spend time with but the rules won't allow you to visit your parents."

"Why don't counting numbers never end?" The girl shrugs, as if returning with this double-negative question is actually a proper answer—and maybe it is.

"Is it the same for your brother? Does he have a guardian like me that he stays with the entire year?"

"No," the girl straightly states. "He has nobody."

"So where does he go after each Halloween?"

"He just stops."

"What does that even mean?"

"Just that—he stops being here." She glances over the ground, turns her gaze heavenward and scans the starry night sky.

Jim closes his eyes, shivers. *Does she understand the word, exist? Is that her truer meaning—that her brother becomes a void, a nothing?*

"I'm seventeen now," the girl says with mercurial nature.

Jim can't help but feel she has intentionally changed the subject to protect his sanity, but it isn't really helpful. Because, yes, he certainly does know the girl's age, as he's the one that brings a cake home to her each year—ten years since she has entered his life and not a single one of those days reflects on her face or ghostly body.

"Like you said though, I'm not your child, so I can't stay with you forever." The girl does an about face and skips ahead and her ponytail bounces. When West Park is in sight, she turns and yells, "Come on, let's race!"

Before he can answer, she shows the soles of her bare feet in an urgent sprint.

"Wait!" Jim yells. "It might not be safe!" but she is already lost to the dark, and he has no choice but to run in chase.

When Jim reaches the park, there is a second child waiting with the girl. This one is also dressed as a skeleton but with bleach-white bones rather than pink. Unlike the girl, the boy wears a plastic skull mask completing the costume.

"You remember my twin brother," the girl states.

"Hello again," Jim pants. He doubles over in an effort to catch his breath.

The boy kindly waves at Jim.

"My brother and me are going to play now, Mr. Jim," the girl says.

"Have your fun." Jim straightens, points off to the side, and continues, "I'll be over there."

For some time, the twins scamper about like reunited puppies.

They run and chase one another in circles. They pump their legs to see who can fly highest on the swings. They climb the rusty metal steps of the twisty slide and twirl downward. They start up their game of tag a second time and tumble into one another's arms and fall to the ground. They laugh, and it's music to Jim's soul.

And then—the boy magically produces a second skeleton mask and offers it to his sister.

The boy's voice drops low and far too serious for a seven-year-old. Behind his own glowing mask, he says, "It's almost *hide-and-seek* time."

This time on this night, unlike the previous years, on this the tenth anniversary the girl accepts the mask. She stretches the thin elastic cord over the back of her head and lets the mask snap gently into place. She momentarily plays with it as if to set it comfortably on her face. She scampers over to the side where Jim has stood and watched the siblings frolic like siblings should.

"I'm leaving you this time," the girl says. She tilts her head up so Jim is now face-to-face with a dollar-store skeleton.

The immediateness and bluntness of her announcement is a blow that winds him and his shoulders sag. He has always held onto hope that the girl might be more mature if this moment ever rolled into his life, that her voice would be weighted with sympathy, or that her words might have been more tactfully chosen in her farewell. It's an unfair expectation, because— seventeen years from her date of birth or not—the girl is still a child, hardly a fall or two past a toddler.

But she isn't *his* child. He's often thought of reaching out to the parents. He hadn't known them when the worst kind of parental tragedy touched their lives like lightning scorching a tree. He'd only seen them on television way back when, answering questions so openly that their innocence was obvious. Neglectful?—without doubt. But guilty?—certainly not. In those one or two local news interviews a self-imposed imprisonment as vastly far-reaching as outer space had been apparent behind their vacant eyes of misery. The parents had since moved out of state, probably an effort to escape the haunting past, but in the age of technology tracking them down wouldn't be difficult. It was the unknowing that prevented Jim from doing so, and quite honestly, it would seem the cruelest of all jokes. What can he say? *You're dead daughter sought me out and lives with me. I can't answer why I have the ability to see and hear her and you don't.*

What comfort could he provide them? Explaining their daughter seems destined to childhood purgatory here on Earth feels more like a punishment than anything else. Would they even believe him if he did reach out, or might they angrily cast accusations of Jim being a cruel attention whore? The truth is Jim has been singled out for reasons unknown to even him, like Job in the bible, and sometimes like Job, he feels like there is something about him God just doesn't like. If questioned by anyone on the issue, Jim would only be able to turn his hands in complete bafflement. So no, she isn't *his* child.

Still, he's grown to love the girl and yearns to know that emotion is in some way reciprocated.

"I thought you might leave me tonight," Jim says, solemnly. He crouches. The holes in her mask are now nothing but dark caverns with seeping blood. It's pure dread to look into those holes, but he is the adult here and she is a child, forever a child. He places his hands on her shoulders and feels how they are chillier than the night air. Yet her skin bears no goose bumps, and this revelation is enough to shudder a chill up his back.

"What's wrong?" The girl asks.

"Nothing, I just—"

"Should I take the mask off for our goodbye?"

"No." He hurries the reply, and it escapes in a rush, his voice as nervous as the rustling of fallen leaves. He knows it's rude, possibly even harsh, but he believes whatever magic has kept the darling girl with him for all these years is already traveling elsewhere. He fears that if she removes the mask, she will now be revealed to him in the true and everlasting state as her twin brother, a child with the face detached and the eyes scooped out into pits. He doesn't want to see that horror, doesn't want to be forced to accept that, because the weight of that burden might be too much for what languishing sanity he has left. When he arrives to home and tosses in his bed, he will struggle to hold onto the image of the girl's curly blonde locks, her sweet and innocent cheeks that plump when she smiles.

"You've done nothing wrong, Mr. Jim," the girl consoles. "It isn't your fault; it's just time for me to move on."

Jim nods, and in a way he's happy, and in another he still doesn't like it. After ten years he is tied to the girl with deep affection. He asks, "Why tonight do you leave for good?"

"Because *he's* coming back tonight," the girl whispers.

The hairs on the back of Jim's neck raise.

"The Bad Man!" the brother shouts, while leaning over the side guards atop the slide.

Jim looks up at the boy. For the past ten Halloweens, Jim has walked the girl down to this park so she can play with her brother, yet this year is the first the boy has ever acknowledged Jim's existence. There are so many questions about the boy. Why is he here only on Halloween night? Why each year, does he stubbornly refuse the offer to come stay at Jim's house? Does the boy simply vanish at midnight? It's all so cruel and absurd, it hurts Jim's mind to dwell on these things.

"The Bad Man comes tonight," the boy repeats, and then continues with the resolve of a natural leader, "and this time my sister and me will be ready for him."

Something frigid touches Jim's hand and he shivers. He looks down and instantly laments the momentary lack of self-control, for it's the girl who has reached out and gently touched him.

"It's okay," she says. "I know I'm cold. My brother is right, though, you need to go. It's only supposed to be me and my brother when he gets here. The Bad Man really is coming back tonight."

The Bad Man.

As if on cue, distantly Jim can make out a low drone in the night.

Jim knows the lay of the town, and once the drone morphs into a growl it's obvious the sound is fast approaching from the only road into town from the west.

"Leave or hide," the girl urges. She is shaking his hand with a tight grasp. "Thank you for everything, and—and—I love you, but this is about The Bad Man, my brother, and me. Not you."

"Hide!" the boy commands. He points to one of the big tractor tires that are quarter-buried into the ground. He turns to the noise of the fast approaching motorcycle. The boy speaks one last word. *"Revenge."*

The girl turns and quickly climbs the slide's stairs to join her brother.

Jim has no other clue of what to do next, so he simply obeys the boy's order. He scampers to the large tractor tire. He tucks himself in tight, like he's a player in a hide-and-seek game of life or death.

The volume of the motorcycle engine increases tenfold, like thunderclouds that have skated overhead, and Jim knows it has curved onto West Park's street. Then, its intensity winds down until it shuts off completely.

The night is suddenly filled with silence, and it's the loudest silence into which Jim has ever been tuned.

He waits, feels a cold sweat break on the back of his neck. Of utter instinct, a prayer passes over his lips, but he wouldn't be able to explain if it's for him or the ghost-children.

Footsteps approach—the sound of a heavyset man falling to his ass.

"Ten years I've lived with this," The Bad Man says in a growl as deep as the night is dark.

Jim hears The Bad Man swig from a bottle. There is a pause and then another longer swig.

"You shouldn't have been here that night." The Bad Man's voice cracks like something long-dwelled in his belly is crawling up and free. "I couldn't control what happened. The drugs in my system that night, they had me by the balls."

Jim affords himself a peek.

The Bad Man is a complete replica of what the mind draws when thinking of a hardened biker. He is seated with arms wrapped around his pulled up legs. He is decked out in leather—black boots, black jeans and chaps, black vest, black everything. He is bald on top but a genuine biker beard, ghostly grey and ending in tied forks hangs from his face.

"It's your parents' fault," The Bad Man sobbed. "Fuck them for letting you play out here alone so late on Halloween."

"No," a second and much younger voice returns. "Fuck you."

Jim's eyes flick to the slide's top.

Two shadows rise up like cobras.

In Jim's glance, he sees the girl latch onto the top bar and swing her body down the slide. She raises her hands high like a teenager on a roller coaster. At the bottom, she lands to the ground firmly on her feet.

The brother climbs over the side, scaling down the outside panels like King Kong in reverse.

The Bad Man launches the liquor bottle at the shadow crawling down the slide, but it misses and clangs away to no effect.

The boy finishes his descent, and together brother and sister face The Bad Man.

"I'm sorry," The Bad Man says, a blubbery confessional. Tears fall in wide tracks down his cheeks. "I can't explain why... or what took over me that night... or how I'd suppressed the urge to kill until then."

Skeleton masks stare forward, one a luminescent white and the other a glowing pink—both expressions of indifference.

The skeletons step forward in unison.

"That was the only time," The Bad Man cries, his voice raising octaves in pitch. He turns his palms at the children and shakes them as if to say *let's talk this out.* His eyes grow wide as white saucers as the immediacy of the moment cuts off his sobbing. "The only time, I swear. I haven't hurt a fly since. That has to count for something!"

Another step, and brother and sister reach to push their masks up and off to expose the fate to which The Bad Man has forever sentenced them.

Jim can't stand it to look. He shuts his eyes fiercely, squeezing out his own tears. Cowering like a child, Jim listens to the rest of the encounter.

There's a low and hungry growl, yet distinctly childlike. It's joined by a second, and then The Bad Man's screams fill the air.

The struggle lasts only minutes, but to Jim it might as well be the length of a decade. Despite knowing they've been earned, the pain-filled yowls and grunts emitted from The Bad Man will haunt Jim's nightmares for the *next* ten years to come.

Finally, complete silence.

Two words from the girl: "It's over."

Jim opens his eyes.

Brother and sister stand side-by-side, holding hands like teammates. They've discarded the masks. The flesh of their faces is back properly in place, but their lips are smeared in blood. The boy's mouth slowly moves up-down and side-to-side like a bovine chewing cud.

They turn, and still holding hands skip away like only children can.

Jim crawls from his hiding spot.

The Bad Man is supine and unmoving on the ground.

His face is hamburger. His eyes stare up, white stones in a mush of flesh and blood.

Halloween is over.

There is already a considerable distance between Jim and the children. Jim watches as they skip out of town and off into the night—off to whatever is next for them.

A Halloween tradition is forever lost.

THE PARADE

E. SENECA

THEY ALWAYS CAME OUT around this time of year.

Night was falling quicker than ever, and he hurried along the sidewalk, careful not to look too deeply into the encroaching darkness. There were shapes moving there, flickering lights where no-one lived; things that emerged from their holes and slithered out of their crannies to join the feast. If he strained his ears, he could even hear the lilting strains of unearthly music drifting on the bitter wind, music that plucked at his skin and made his blood sing in his veins.

He shuddered and huddled deeper into his coat, ducking his head away from the white face of the All Hallows' Eve moon looking coldly down upon the world. On the opposite side of the empty road, two costumed children had their hands held tightly by adults, being walked briskly out of the area, some instinct compelling the family inside.

It hadn't really been his intention to be caught outside so late into the evening on this particular day, but he hadn't expected the sun would set so soon either. The dying orange rays of the sun bled across the sky as the silvery light of the moon grew stronger, tinting the whole world in sickly purple-grey. The heavy clouds over the western edge only made things worse, and there was a deep chill in the air that hadn't been there yesterday. Chewing at his chapped lips, he pushed up his sleeve to glance at his watch, then slowed his steps to glance to and fro at the deserted streets.

The memories from the year previous were still fresh in his mind: all the eerie, horrible sights he'd witnessed from behind the safety of the shutters, watching through a crack. These images flashed through his mind as he hurried over the scattered gravel, unable as he'd been to wrench his gaze away from the countless eyes. The monsters, walking beneath the sky that was the deepest, darkest, richest blue he'd ever seen, their eyes glowing a sickly orange hue—laughing in their enormous parade, heading somewhere beyond human comprehension; laughing as they looked through that tiny gap in the shutters and saw him, turning his blood to ice in his veins.

There was nothing here on the street, he told himself firmly, it was just his imagination.

But anxiety rose up, a snake rearing its fanged head, ready to erupt into panic and sending cracks of fear seeping through his attempt at remaining calm. At this rate, it would take him well over forty-five minutes to get home, and dusk would fall in less than twenty. Worse, he didn't even know this area—and getting lost was a terrifying prospect he didn't want to spend too long entertaining.

One way or another, though, he was wasting precious daylight just standing on the spot. Shaking himself, he began to walk again—as quickly as he could without breaking into a run. The cold air chilled his lungs, making him shiver, and the wind tore a few dry leaves from their branches and scattered them over the cracked sidewalk before him.

In his periphery, just behind a fence, glowing orange eyes appeared out of the gloom, and when he looked over his shoulder, they were jack-o-lanterns, their faces carved into malicious grins—why hadn't he noticed them before? He pushed the thoughts away: there was no use fretting over pumpkins. But he glanced ahead once more, and somehow without his noticing more had appeared from the tangled underbrush—and he couldn't tell if they were pumpkins, or something more sinister.

He wanted to believe that they were benign, that there was nothing more substantial than candlelight to the gazes he felt on his back, but when he looked out into the encroaching gloom of the darkness surrounding him, there were too many shapes, and there was the music...

Distantly, the howl of a dog rang out, and he broke into a trot, the noise awakening some deeper instinct that would not be silenced. He couldn't tell where it came from, and maybe it was perfectly harmless, but how could he be sure? The frightening sense of being alone in the world pressed down on him heavily, the sensation that no matter how far he searched or how loud he screamed, there would be nobody there. He hadn't even seen anyone since he'd turned the corner—how long ago had that been? Surely it was only minutes, but it felt like hours. It couldn't have been, not with the light—it was just his mind playing tricks on him, that was all.

He tried not to look back anymore, to only look ahead: he had to focus if he ever hoped to get home. He had to keep going.

The long shadows of the hollow buildings fell across his path in strips of black, and he stepped over them as quickly as he could—it sounded like the music was getting louder, clearer, to the point where he could make out individual instruments: bells and flutes, the deep strains of a violin or a cello. The rhythm seemed to be rising, not quite as slow as before. He glanced over his shoulder but saw nothing, and stumbled over something—when he looked down, it was another pumpkin. Here? In the middle of the sidewalk? They hadn't been here before, had they? And lit, too?

Where were they coming from? Beyond the sound of the music, all was silent—no footsteps, no rustling: but the sensation of being watched, of some alien presence's eyes on him was undeniable. The unnatural weight on his shoulders, the cold sweat trickling down the back of his neck, the tightness in his chest. Of course—this was the day when all the barriers and walls were thinned, when all those things responsible for the music had crawled out of their holes to celebrate.

He shook his head and vehemently pushed the thought away. The music was growing louder: richer, more vibrant, deeper and thrumming with an unnatural tempo that made him want to sway. Not even the pounding in his ears could drown it out, not even the racing pulse that made his heart hammer in his throat. It was too clear, too bright, too vivid as the wind swept the notes along in its frigid embrace, scattered them like the dead leaves tumbling across his path.

The corner was but a few feet away. The music sang on, bright and sweet.

He took his first step off the curb—and froze as a new sound pierced through the enthralling song. It was a high-pitched wail, and his mind instantly placed it as the voice of a crying child. It was close, very close, perhaps even around the building just behind him. He couldn't move, rooted in his tracks and wracked by indecision. Should he go back? Keep going?

Time was of the essence, he couldn't linger outside if the monsters' parade was coming—but to leave a child outside—they would eat that child in a heartbeat, he just couldn't. It would only take a second, a moment, not long at all.

He stepped back onto the sidewalk and looked around, acutely aware of turning his back on the music. The child's voice warred against the music. He rounded the corner of the building and caught sight of a small, pale form, sobbing and sniffling. It was indeed a child, dressed in a costume made from fluttery cloth with their golden hair crowned by a wreath.

Cautiously, he took a step nearer, not wanting to waste time but also not wanting to startle them.

"Hey," he said gently, softly. "Hey, are you lost?"

The child's head jerked up, and she blinked two blue, watery eyes at him, shrinking a little. "I—I'm lost, yes..."

He couldn't just leave her there, not with the oncoming parade. "Come on," he coaxed, "it's not safe to be outside. Where do you live, do you remember? Is it that way?"

"I... I don't know."

There wasn't time to waste. The parade would be coming, and soon. He approached as slowly as he dared and held out his hand: "It's not safe right now. Come on, let's get inside and I'll try to get you home."

A little reluctantly, she took his fingers with five small, damp ones. He judged the girl to be maybe no older than six or seven. Too young to be out alone—where were her parents? How had she been left outside alone like this? It didn't matter right now, getting to safety was the important part.

His own home wasn't that far from here, they just had to get back to the intersection and begin going back—he looked around the corner of the building and his breath caught in his throat. The wind brought back the sound of music, and overhead, the moon blazed, silver shafts falling upon the road and opening a path, turning the black pavement into a shimmering surface like water, a long silver-white river.

He swallowed hard and turned away; he couldn't cross that pathway now. Effectively blocked off from heading home, the only option left was to seek shelter elsewhere, somewhere deeper in the town.

"This way," he said, and it only took a few steps before he realized the girl's short legs were going to slow them down far too much. He bent and carefully picked her up, and automatically the girl's arms wrapped around his neck. "Do you remember— remember which way you came from?"

"It was that way." She pointed down the street, and out of his periphery, he saw the silver river of moonlight seeping along the road, progressing onward with an inexorable force. He broke into a trot, for all it was worth, and felt her little warm hands clinging to his collar.

"Do you know your address, by any chance? Anything?" It was probably too far from them, though, so it didn't really matter. The first place they came across would be the one he'd choose, be it a gas station or a convenience store—anything that would allow them to get inside.

"I—I don't remember." She looked over his shoulder, and said, "Why are we in a hurry?"

The rustling of the leaves was louder and stronger than ever, and they cartwheeled and skittered across the road and the sidewalk, flickering from gold to white before they disappeared into the darkness, leaving trails of silver behind them. Distantly, there was the creaking of metal, the shrill shrieking of what was probably a fence being wrenched out of place or being scaled, and with it came the music, wild and free. Something sounded and the cadence of it was uncannily like raucous, throaty laughter.

"Don't look," he told the child, taking the first turn they came to. "Just don't look."

"But—"

"*Don't.*" He couldn't slow. Even the quickest glance over his shoulder showed that the river was spreading further and further. He took another turn, winding deeper and deeper, despite being an unfamiliar area. Lost in an urban environment would be better than lost near—or worse, caught in—the parade.

But there was little shelter: endless concrete walls with high-set windows, all of them dark and drawn. And on this night, if the lights were off, it was highly unlikely that anyone would open up.

Alarmingly, the noise of the parade sounded like it was getting louder, closer. He couldn't quite tell where it was coming from—it seemed to be everywhere, around every corner, the music traveling well beyond the source, drifting on a supernatural wind to saturate the atmosphere with its intoxicating melody.

He turned another corner and was brought up short by a dead end: a construction zone. Exhaling sharply, he returned the way they'd come, the sense of urgency growing heavier on his shoulders. It suddenly became painfully evident that he was indeed lost, and that he had no idea where he was going or what he was doing. Trying not to let his growing panic show, he took the last turn in the opposite direction. The vibrations of the countless feet drumming against the road were faintly palpable, and out of the corner of his eye beyond the buildings, the silver path glinted and shone, stronger than the yellow streetlights flickering to life overhead and casting garish light over the sidewalk.

He pressed on, hurrying past sinister-looking shrubs and towards the distant yellow glow of civilization. Past closed-down offices and businesses, through empty intersections and barren streets. He couldn't see the moonlight path anymore, but the wavering, unearthly music remained ever-present, making it impossible to tell whether or not he was getting nearer or farther away. It was somewhere close by, but also seemed to be everywhere—from behind him, from beside him, hanging in the very air and worming its way into his brain, chipping away at his sanity. Heart thudding painfully, he rounded another corner—and froze.

The demon parade. The sight of it rooted him in place, the gripping terror and morbid fascination keeping him riveted in a horrible trance.

Centipedes walking upright, carrying lanterns made of human skulls; green-skinned spiders with a plethora of eyes on bony legs tipped with claws, pumpkins dangling from their oversized maws and the lights within guttering from the slaver dripping down the orange exteriors onto the asphalt. Emaciated humanoids with necklaces of faces hanging around their necks and heads consisting of nothing but a cluster of feelers; red-stained skeletons merrily swinging baskets with sloshing contents; tall creatures with six arms and no legs and several mouths with flutes to their lips, piping the lilting, skirling music.

Hairy beasts with sweaty, leathery hands plucking at lutes; winged things with clusters of eyes and bulging stomachs whirling and bobbing drunkenly to the music. Sprightly glistening imps flitted from one monster to the next, offering brimming bone flagons of a crimson liquid that splashed and spattered everywhere. They laughed and sang in their own guttural language as the procession progressed, following the winding silver pathway, onward and onward to wherever it led.

He backed away from the procession, slowly, trying not to draw attention to them—the monsters were fairly engaged, it was possible they could escape sight unseen—and he was almost back to the shadows when he felt the girl squirm in his arms, heard her tiny gasp, and the entire flow of the parade skipped, juddered. Although he was already turning on his heel, fleeing into the maze of buildings. He could feel the countless eyes settling on them like a torrent of icy water crashing down his spine; heard the shout, the cry of excitement that went up through that whole section of the parade—and the sound of myriad feet and paws pelting after them.

He ran, ran faster than he knew he could run. His breath rasped in his throat and burned in his lungs, but he barely felt the pain when above the wild pounding of his heart, all he could hear was the snarling, the sound of claws scraping against concrete. He zigzagged in a frantic attempt to lose them—and then he saw it: a church.

Its dark walls were a smudge of solid, reliable darkness, the thickness of its graceful arched windows and double doors promising safety and sanctuary. He put on a desperate burst of speed and sprinted towards it and across the grounds to the side door, skidding to a halt and seizing hold of the old knob, jiggling it frantically. It rattled in the lock, metal clacking against metal and grinding—the parade's hunters getting nearer and nearer, leaping over the sidewalk—then suddenly the catch gave and the door swung inward, allowing them to tumble inside.

He set down the girl and slammed the door, throwing the bolt and chain and leaning all his weight against it as something crashed into it from the outside. The knob and hinges juddered dangerously, but it held—for the time being. Panting, cold sweat trickling down the back of his neck, he stood fast as the slam was followed by another whump, and then another, something snuffling around the edges of the door and snarling, clawing at the old metal-enforced wood and setting it quivering beneath his hands. He wanted to continue believing that the demons couldn't enter here, but he didn't know for sure and the heavy doubt felt deadly and certain.

But whatever was making the noises moved away, and in his periphery, a cluster of shadows and bobbing lights moved beyond one of the windows beneath the pulpit. Tentatively he released the door, and when it didn't implode, sighed and lowered his arms. He turned back to the girl while keeping an eye on the shapes on the other side of the glass.

"Looks like we're alright for now," he said gently. "Are you okay?"

She nodded, but even in the dimness, her blue eyes were glassy, and her pinched lips and balled-up hands were trembling. Unsure how to comfort her, he got down on his knees and opened his arms, and she tottered into his embrace, sniffling into his neck and clutching at his shirt.

"'m scared," she whispered.

That made two of them. "It's gonna be okay," he said, rubbing her back and smoothing her hair. "Everything's gonna be okay." Some part of him ached making such empty promises, but he didn't have much idea of what else to say. She could probably feel that he was shaky, feel that his own heart was racing.

She sniffed, and he mustered up his strength again to pick her up and carry her away from the door to somewhere safer. It was dark in the church, the only illumination coming from the streetlamp outside muted by the frosted and stained windows, leaving the interior a murky, unwelcome gloom. He could make out the shapes of the pews and some of the floor, but the far ends of the room were fuzzy and woolly with darkness. Where could they go away from the windows? There had to be a back room or a supply room: the demons had begun to press their ghastly faces up against the glass, fogging it with their breath, and some of them definitely had to be strong enough to break it.

Passing under their gazes was nerve-wracking, particularly as the child's grip on him tightened to the point of pain. Her hands had moved up around his neck, making him halt and sway.

"What's wrong?"

She had gone still and stiff in his arms, staring wildly at the clamoring, fighting shadows outside, her eyes wide and round as saucers. She inhaled sharply, and her voice was barely audible: "My—my mommy's out there."

"What? No, honey, no, she's not. You're seeing things." He hastened to take her away from the window, but her tiny nails bit into his neck, small but sharp, and made his steps falter.

"She is!" She squirmed violently in his arms, and he hastily put her down and she rushed to the window. She had to stand on her toes to press her fingers to the glass, staring out frantically while the things outside scratched at the panels, claws screeching horribly against the glass. He ran after her and picked her up again despite her writhing and protesting—"Lemme go! She's there, I saw her!"

"I'm sorry, but we need to find a safe place in case the glass breaks." Where, he didn't know, but there seemed to be a short corridor on the other side of the room, a door at the end—maybe a closet. "It's not safe to be out here."

She kept squirming, and he tightened his grip, making his voice firmer. "I'm sorry, but your mother isn't there. The only things out there are monsters."

She went limp, still in his arms, her fingers gripping his arms tightly. For one moment, silence reigned, heavy as the darkness and the weight of the night outside.

Then she turned her head and looked up at him with huge, glossy bulging eyes, devoid of pupils and leaking slowly out of their sockets.

"Who said my mommy was human?" she rasped through two mouths full of dripping teeth.

On pure terrified instinct he hurled the child—hurled *it*—away from him, and rather than tumble helplessly to the floor, it caught itself on one of the pews. Its human disguise began to melt away to reveal scaly green skin and a reptilian face, but he didn't wait to see more. He dove for the corridor, ducking as he heard the pew clatter. The monster lunged and missed his back by inches, hissing, its claws scraping the wall.

He lunged for the knob of the door and yanked it open, falling inside and jerking it shut just in time to hear something slam into it. Long, thin claws scrabbled under the gap at him, making him flinch back, but there was barely any room to move, his elbows colliding with the corners and his heels with the walls. As the door rattled, he spotted a metal bar set into the jamb, and with brimming panic he slapped it into place. A quick glance downward showed that there was a second one, and this bolt too he shot, flinching back against the wall as the door shook again.

The monster on the other side snarled, tapering off into a whine that almost sounded sad. He swallowed hard, mind racing over whether or not it would be able to break inside if it was determined enough, or if it would seek other prey. He had nowhere to go, nowhere left to run. The closet was empty but tiny, with nothing so much as a broom to use as defense if it broke down the door. The only thing he could do was hope and pray.

He slowly sank to his knees in the furthest corner, trying to breathe slowly but unable to slow his speeding pulse as the dust in the air made his throat itch. He could still hear the monster outside, prowling back and forth, scraping at the door at random intervals and making him tense up further. The ones that had chased him into the church howled outside, their unearthly voices turning his blood to ice.

He waited, the seconds dragging by, hanging in that horrible limbo of uncertainty, absolutely positive that at any moment the wood would splinter, and the monster would be upon him. At any moment death would touch him, and there would be nothing he could do to stop it. One moment of foolishness, one instant of wanting to do good, and it would cost him his life.

All went silent. Still, he didn't dare even think of emerging until morning. He remained huddled in the corner, heedless of the aches the position created when adrenaline still sang in his blood, when fear still clawed the inside of his chest. He would continue to wait.

Daylight dawned cold and bright. Pale white rays seeped unimpeded through the crack beneath the door, and with stiff limbs and aching muscles and a heart thudding wildly under his clavicle, he clambered to his feet and reached for the knob. It took him a moment to turn it, fingers stayed by cold dread, and half-formed plans raced through his mind should the young demon still be there. Still, there was nothing for it—sooner or later he had to come out.

He pushed the door open with a slight creak, and nothing jumped on him to tear his throat out. The church was empty, early morning daylight streaming in through the windows upon the dusty floor and the rows of pews, tinted green and red from the glass. The air was still and all was silent, and despite his fear, there was no sensation of being watched. Tentatively he crept out, and saw that the side door through which they'd entered hung ajar, allowing sun to pour inside.

He stood by the pulpit, gazing numbly at the gleaming windows for a few moments, before he finally shook himself and went to the door, stepping out into the warmth of the sun and the sweet air.

His foot collided with something hard and he flinched back— but it was only a jack-o-lantern, rolling in the grass and showing its ugly carved face. Its yellow edges were curling, the innards already beginning to rot. It was well and truly over.

The demon parade was gone, not to return for another year.

GRANDPA GEORGE'S DEAL

PATRICK MEEGAN

MIKE MADE AN OBLIGATORY pass through the gymnasium, greeting the teachers and chaperones, before finding a quiet spot by the bleachers where he could keep an eye on Maddy without interfering with her friend-time. He watched her try to toss a glow ring over a traffic cone made to look like a witch's hat.

The grammar school gym had been decorated as a "Safe Trick or Treat Night" party for the grade schoolers, replete with party games, sugar infused everything, and kids in costume running wild. Polyester cobwebbing hung off anything with an edge, accenting the giant spider dangling from the ceiling. Mike grimaced around a cup of way-too-sweet punch.

Amanda had arrived that evening and stood at his side. Mike had hoped she would, but wondered if it would have been better if she hadn't. For everyone.

"I love her costume," she said.

"She wanted to be a princess, so I went all out."

"You did great." Amanda leaned into him with her shoulder as they watched the kids. "And you make a very handsome king."

Mike made a show of smoothing his blue velvet tunic. "Thank you. I held back on the crown, but couldn't resist the ruby cape."

Amanda smiled. "And you found a look for that ridiculous beard you've grown."

"You should show more respect for the king."

"I just miss his handsome face."

Mike noticed her check the clock. "What is it?"

"Nothing." She shook her head.

Maddy had looped the glowing ring around a cone and one of the parents—dressed as a witch—handed her a prize: a plush bat. Maddy laughed, showing it to her friends.

"It's so nice to see her happy," Amanda said. "I'm glad she wanted to come tonight."

"She's come a long way. Her friends have helped out a lot; they're really sweet kids."

"I think you've done a pretty great job too."

Mike took her hand, wishing things could be as simple as they used to be.

Amanda pushed his hand back down to his side. "Careful."

He snorted. "With all the chaos in here? I don't think anyone will notice."

Amanda looked past him, her eyes widening. "Oh my god."

"Hi, Mike."

Rachel, mother of Maddy's friend Kate—and Amanda's former bestie—came up behind him.

"You look great," Rachel said.

"That costume is sooo not appropriate," Amanda said, under her breath.

Rachel had dressed like a devil: her curly hair parted by glittered horns, her red dress cut a little too high above the knee and a little too low up top.

"I don't think devils put glitter on their boobs," Amanda said.

Mike tried not to glance at the splash of sparkle across Rachel's chest. "Hi Rachel, so do you."

Rachel smiled. "And you're a king to your little Princess Madeline. I love it." She reached out, squeezed Mike's forearm and stepped a little closer, her voice softening. "I'm so glad you two made it. Really. I can only imagine how tough this night must be for you both."

"It's getting better," Mike said. "And thanks... for everything."

Rachel made a dismissive gesture with her hands. "Please."

"No, you've been a big help. Taking Maddy in on all those sleepovers. It's really meant a lot. I think she's finally starting to adjust. Thank you."

"Don't be silly. I love having Maddy over. Besides, since the divorce, it's just me and Kate in that big house. I enjoy the extra company, even if it is just another seven-year-old in there with me."

"I know what you mean," Mike said.

Rachel grabbed Mike's arm again. "Hey, if you're up for it, a couple of the other parents are coming by my place after for some grown-up time. We can let the kids sugar binge in the rec room while we actually have some adult interaction."

Amanda gasped.

Mike took a small sidestep to block Amanda's view. "That sounds great Rachel, but... I think we're just gonna head home after this."

"I understand," Rachel said, taking her hand from his arm. "Maybe another time?"

"Sure," Mike said, "that would be great."

"Great. I'll be in touch," Rachel said. "I really am glad to see you out again." She turned and walked back across the crowded gym.

Mike kept his eyes front as Amanda walked around to his side, trying not to acknowledge her shocked expression. He took a sip of awful punch and set it down on a folding table beside him.

"Sure, that would be great." Amanda mimicked.

"She's very nice," Mike said. Trying not to smile.

Amanda huffed, looking after Rachel. "You mean her ass?"

"She's been really kind to Maddy, and she... *was*... your best friend."

Amanda put on a pout. "Some friend. I die and she wants to take my husband."

The levity in this exchange, that old feeling of lightness and love Mike felt when Amanda teased him about something, it all fell away, leaving him hollow. Amanda showed it too. As soon as she said the words, the bright mischief in her eyes went out and they just stood there. One living. One dead. Both alone.

"I'm sorry," Mike said.

"It's okay. Now stop talking to no one. People will think you're nuts."

Amanda wrapped her arm through his. Her touch chilled him, but he would never tell her.

"I miss this," she said.

"Me too."

They stood like that a while, together, watching their daughter. Mike didn't have any more jokes to help pretend that this—seeing his dead wife on the anniversary of her death—should be normal. Last year, when Amanda first appeared, he assumed he had lost his mind. Now... he still didn't know for sure.

Maddy and her friends laughed as a bald man in a cape performed close-up magic for them. Mike felt guilty about keeping this to himself, not letting her know about her mother's ghost.

Amanda refused when he mentioned showing herself to Maddy, saying it would only cause more harm. He knew it broke her heart.

Amanda cut the silence between them. "I'm the one who should be sorry. I never should have shown myself to you. You need to move on with your life here, and I need to go on to something else."

She unwound her arm from his and stepped away, brushing at his shirt sleeve as if trying to remove any trace of herself. "You should be dating my best friend."

He started to speak, thought to tell her no, but couldn't. He didn't want this to end, but knew it had to. That it happened at all seemed wrong, unfair to both of them.

Amanda's eyes went to the wall clock again and she bit her lower lip. It's what she did when she didn't want to tell him something.

"What is it?"

Amanda put her thumb to her mouth and worried at the nail. "Nothing important."

"Okay. This is all crazy enough. What aren't you telling me?"

Amanda sighed, folding her arms. It's what she did when she had bad news. "Last year, before I appeared to you, I spoke with my mother. I found her here."

It made sense, finding dead relatives in the afterlife. Mike just never gave it any thought.

"Uhm, how is she?"

"The same," she said. "Anyway, she told me to watch over you and Maddy on Halloween. Apparently, it's the only time we're able to cross back over to this side." She made spooky jazz hands. "On All Hallows Eve, from dusk till midnight, we roam the earth." She dropped her hands. "It's all very B-movieish, I know, but that's how it works. My dying on the same night makes it kinda weird, I guess."

That made it weird... yeah.

"Isn't that something the, uhm, dead do?" Mike said. "Watch over the living."

"No. We try to stay away, mostly. It's not good to dwell on your past life. Mom wouldn't tell me why, and I just did it because she wanted it—you know how she gets. But it felt so good to see you both..." She shook her head. "I never should have shown myself, Mike. Trust me, my mother still can't stop bringing it up."

"I'm glad you did."

She wrapped her arms around him. "Me too."

Mike stood there, careful to keep his arms at his sides, wanting only to hug her freezing body closer, and finding it easy to forget why this shouldn't be.

"There's more," Amanda said. "My mother told me a little this year, but not everything. You know how she keeps me in the dark about anything important."

Mike nodded.

"Two years ago, today, I died in my sleep."

Mike winced.

"And a year before that, on the same day, my mother died in her sleep... a horrible coincidence."

Mike didn't want to relive any of this.

"But it wasn't."

"What?"

"We were murdered, Michael."

Mike had never considered it. No one had. Not the police, not the doctors. "How..."

"It's something here, in this place, where I am now. Something that used this night to get to us. It murdered my mother, and then it murdered me. I don't know much more, but my mother thinks Maddy might be in danger. That's why I'm here now, and why I came last year."

"What?"

He had to fight the impulse to sprint across the gym. Forget about being noticed, maybe he needed to be. Maybe he *had* lost his mind, maybe someone should know that he talks to dead people. He began losing control, breathing heavily, wringing his hands, standing alone in a crowded gymnasium and losing control.

"Take it easy," Amanda said.

"Take it easy?" Mike asked. "I'm not even sure you're real."

"Of course I am."

He never doubted it before. When she first came to him, it took only a moment to believe, and less time to dismiss any bad ideas about what it might mean to see her again.

On the other side of the gym, Maddy sat on a bench with two other girls, hugging the plush bat in one arm while one of the girls tied a black and orange friendship bracelet around her wrist.

Doubt would only make things worse right now. He couldn't risk losing Maddy too.

"The party is almost over," Amanda said. "We'll meet my mother at home. Just try to stay calm and don't let Maddy know anything is wrong."

Mike looked at his dead wife. Sure... calm. Just another normal day.

* * *

Mike held the door of their SUV open while Maddy climbed in and pulled the seatbelt over herself.

"Did you have fun?" Mike asked, scanning the parking lot.

"Yes," Maddy said, settling into the seat. "I think Mommy would have liked our costumes."

Amanda stood beside Mike. "Oh, I do honey." She stepped back, bringing her hands to her face. Mike heard her sniffle as she turned away.

"Me too," Mike said. He took his smartphone from his pocket, tapped the screen and offered it to Maddy. "Angry Birds?"

Maddy smiled, "Yeah," and took the phone from him.

Mike went around the back of the SUV where Amanda stood, wiping her eyes.

"Are we in danger?"

"Not sure," she said. "I told you, my mother is very secretive when it comes to family stuff."

"What do you mean: family stuff."

Amanda froze, biting at her lip.

"Amanda?"

She folded her arms. "I think this involves my grandfather."

Mike brought his fists up in front of him and opened his mouth in a silent scream.

"I don't know for sure."

"Grandpa George!" he said, stage whispering. "That's just great!"

"He's not that bad, Mike."

"Grandpa George? The guy who spent half his life in and out of prison for nickel and dime hustles?"

"It may not involve him."

"The Grandpa George who only showed up at our wedding to borrow money? The Grandpa George who got shot over a bet? That Grandpa George?"

"All right!"

Mike put his hands to his face, rubbing his temples. "Of course this has something to do with him."

"Okay, yes." Amanda said. "I'm sure it does."

"I need to speak to your mother. Why isn't she here?"

"I think she went to get Grandma."

Mike lowered his hands to his mouth, staring over them at Amanda. "She's not coming, is she?"

The streetlight above them blinked out. Mike looked up. "She must be here."

"Don't be mean."

Two more pole lights near them blinked out.

"What's happening?"

"I don't know. Get in the car, Mike. Get Maddy home."

Mike dashed to the driver's side and fell into the seat.

"Who were you talking to?" Maddy said.

"No one. Just thinking out loud." He pulled the seatbelt over his shoulder and started fumbling with his keys. He dropped them into the center console. "Dammit."

"What's wrong, Daddy?"

A cold hand slid over his shoulder, squeezing. "Calm down, Mike." Amanda had taken the back seat. "Maddy can't know about this."

"Nothing, sweetheart. Just clumsy." Mike retrieved his keys and got the SUV running. "How's your game going."

"Okay."

A dark shape darted over the hood of the SUV. Mike froze. It had been something big—the size of a person big... and flying.

"I saw it too," Amanda said. "Just drive."

Mike put the SUV in gear and proceeded thorough the parking lot, stopping at the main road. When he turned to check for traffic, he saw it: a shadow figure perched like a vulture on the large sign bearing the school's name. The thing's face lay shadowed in the folds of a hood, a long black cloak hanging lifeless around it.

Mike's hands tightened on the wheel and his knuckles turned white. He looked up into the rear-view mirror and saw Amanda looking back at him.

"It's a wraith," she said. "It can't interact with us. They just watch."

"How you doing, Maddy?" he asked.

"She can't see them," Amanda said.

"Fine. Level three," Maddy said.

Mike looked back to the mirror. "So, why can I?"

"Why can you what, Daddy?"

"I don't know," Amanda said, "but there will be more. They must be following us."

"Daddy?"

The wraith stared, pinpricks of light watching him from within the dark folds.

"Nothing, Sweetheart. Just thinking out loud again."

"You're acting silly."

"Yeah, silly," Mike said. He pulled out onto the road, checked his mirror and saw the wraith fly off into the darkness.

He drove the rest of the short trip home as fast as he dared without risking an accident or alarming Maddy. The wraiths followed. He would catch them in the corners of his eyes, sweeping past the SUV and flashing away into the darkness.

"You're doing great," Amanda said.

Mike pressed the garage door remote while they were still a half-block from their house and the light shone from inside as he pulled in. He hit the remote again, checking his mirrors as the door began to close.

"They won't follow us inside," Amanda said. "They don't like the light."

Mike thought of the lights that had blinked out at the school parking lot, but the garage remained bright. He got out of the SUV and went to get Maddy inside.

The little girl still had her head down to the phone as Mike leaned in, undid her seatbelt and scooped up her things. "Let's go, Princess." Maddy slid out of the seat and went to the door. Amanda stood beside it.

Mike got the door open and Maddy went down the hall to the living room.

"What now?"

"We wait for my mother," Amanda said.

"No. I need to do something now. Whatever... killed you, I'm not waiting for your mother, or Grandpa George to fix it."

"I'm not even sure what it is."

Mike seethed. Needing to know, needing to act.

"We just have to wait."

Amanda went off down the hall after Maddy.

Mike watched her go, trying to form a plan without even knowing what he had to plan for. Man, did he hate Amanda's family.

When he entered the living room, he found Maddy sunk into the overstuffed couch working on her game. Amanda stood in the middle of the room, glaring at a chair. She turned to Mike, her face hard with anger.

Mike raised his eyebrows, lifting his hands in a silent question.

Amanda turned back to the armchair. "Show him," she said.

Mike couldn't explain how it happened. He didn't materialize slowly, he just appeared, sitting in the chair: Grandpa George.

"Hi, Mike," he said, smiling his car salesman smile. "I can't believe how big Maddy has grown. She's doing great, and you're doing great for her. You know, I always said, Amanda got lucky with you."

Mike wondered if he could choke a ghost.

"What did you do?" Amanda said.

"Do?" George changed his look to shocked. "What do you mean, I haven't done—"

"I spoke to my mother. What little she would tell me includes you being involved in her death and mine."

"Now, sweetie, I would never intentionally do anything that would hurt you, or your mother. I'm sure whatever she told you isn't accurate, you know how stories go."

"Have you seen her?"

"Your mother?" George said. "She doesn't need to know I'm here. I just wanted to check in on you. See how the family has been adjusting. It's so tragic how the last few years have gone. And can I say again, Michael, what a great job—"

"She's meeting me here."

George sputtered for a moment. "Well... hey... that's great. Your mother, coming here. Like a little reunion. Uhm... when is she arriving?"

"Soon," Amanda said. "She went to see Grandma."

Grandpa George froze. "She's not coming, is she?"

Mike realized he had been standing in the middle of the living room—and as far as Maddy could tell—staring at the wall. Being unable to shout at George, he gave him the angriest look he could and took a seat at the other end of the couch. He picked up his tablet from the end table and pretended to browse through it while following his dead wife's conversation with her dead grandfather.

They both stopped talking and turned. Mike looked back and saw only the door.

"Hi, Mom," Amanda said.

"Susan," George said. "I hoped you would come."

Amanda continued staring at the door. "He knows; he can see us both." She paused, closed her eyes and sighed. "I know I wasn't supposed to, but I did. Can we just get past it?" Another pause. "Well, I think it would be easier for all of us if you just appeared to him."

And, just like George, Mike's mother-in-law appeared. Not as he remembered her, but as a proper-looking woman in a pantsuit that would have been trendy—and a bit rebellious—in the 1970's. "Hello, Michael," she said. "Don't get up."

Susan strode to the couch and stood over Maddy. "She's so beautiful. Thank you for taking such good care of her, Michael." She tilted her head, watching Maddy play her game. "Of course, maybe not so much of this video game nonsense. It'll rot her brain."

Michael stared up at her, offering a tight smile, suddenly glad he couldn't speak.

"And let me just say," Susan continued, "how sorry I am that my family has gotten you involved in all this." She turned to George. "Aren't we, Daddy."

George went back to his shocked expression and stood from the chair. "Susan, I... I don't know what you're talking about. I simply came here to—"

"Enough," she said, stopping him. Susan put her hands on her hips and stared him down. "I spoke to Mother."

It surprised Mike to see a ghost turn pale.

Susan pointed her finger. "And she told me about some deal you made on this side that went bad."

"Wait, what deal?" Amanda asked.

"I'm not sure, exactly," Susan said. "Your grandmother likes to keep me in the dark when it comes to family matters."

"It's nothing, really," George said. "She's not coming, is she?"

"What deal?" Mike said.

The ghosts all turned to him. Susan raised her eyebrows, indicating Maddy.

Maddy didn't seem to notice.

"What deal?" Amanda said.

Susan crossed her arms. "As far as I know, one of his usual schemes involving the sort of people—or whatever they are—that you don't get involved with in the afterlife."

"It's not like that," George said.

"Not like what?" Susan said. "Not like the sort of thing that gets your daughter killed, then your granddaughter and now—" Susan stopped herself.

"Oh no, Grandpa George, no," Amanda said. "Please, not Maddy."

Mike's hands balled into fists.

George dropped his hands to his sides and his shoulders sagged. "I didn't think it would be like this."

"I knew it," Susan said.

George put his hands over his face. "I'm so sorry."

"Tell us," Susan said.

George took his hands from his face. "It's not my fault though, honest." He looked at them as if hoping for some help. "Michael, I…" He put his hand to his mouth. "I'm sorry you had to go through this. I've ruined your life, I know." He looked to Susan and Amanda. "And you're both… because of me."

"What did you do." Susan demanded.

George started to answer but Amanda interrupted. "What about Maddy?"

"No, no," George said, "I worked it all out last year. That's why nothing happened to Maddy. See?" He held his hand out toward the girl. "She's fine."

"Then why are you here?"

"I... it's... it *technically* wasn't *totally* worked out last year. But it'll be fine, I swear."

Mike stood up, ready to demand an answer and stopped himself before he began shouting at an empty room in front of Maddy. Instead, he ran his hand through his hair in frustration, clenching it in his fist and squeezing his eyes shut.

"Look at what this is doing to poor Michael," Susan said. "You never should have shown yourself, Amanda."

"Enough, Mom."

Mike walked to the front door, trying to calm himself.

"Everything's going to be fine," George said. "I promise."

Mike stared out through the window beside the door. Not wanting to look at him.

"Fine?" Susan shouted. "We're dead because of you!"

The streets were quiet. After eleven o'clock, everyone but a few delinquents had ended their night. Bright lights burned on porches and walkways to deter the pranksters, but Mike's front yard lay in darkness. The lamp post at the end of his walkway had gone out. A wraith stood beside it in the gloom, watching him. Mike pulled himself back from the window.

Behind him, the arguing continued.

"It'll all be fine," George said. "I just came by tonight to make sure there were no... misunderstandings."

Amanda had her hands out at her sides, exasperated. "Misunderstandings?"

"Don't worry. I found Ned here, he's taking care of—"

Susan cut him off. "Ned? Your lifelong co-defendant?"

"Oh, Grandpa," Amanda moaned.

Mike couldn't stand it anymore. "Okay, Kiddo," he said, walking to the couch. "Let's head upstairs for bed. It's really late."

The others paused.

"If you're going for a world record, maybe we can pause it for a bit and continue upstairs. You can keep playing while Daddy takes care of a few things."

Maddy didn't respond.

"Maddy?" Mike put a hand on her shoulder but she didn't move. "Maddy!" Mike dropped to his knees and pushed his little girl's body upright. She leaned back into the cushions, her head lolling sideways, eyes closed. The phone slipped from her hands and fell to the floor.

"Oh, no, no, no." Amanda rushed to Mike's side, putting her hands to her daughter's face. "I can't feel anything. Michael, help me!"

Mike put his hands to Maddy's neck, then over her heart. "She's alive," he said.

Mike could hear George rambling. "No... It's not right... I settled it."

"Enough!" Mike said. "You caused nothing but problems in life, old man, and everyone let you. But you're gonna start telling me something right now."

"Michael," Susan started, "this is a family matter."

"Shut up, Susan."

Susan gasped.

"George. Tell me what I need to know."

George took a step back, looking to Susan and Amanda for help. The women remained quiet.

"I..." George said, "It wasn't my fault."

"Liar." The voice made them all stop. The room chilled.

Grandma Dorothy had arrived.

Unlike Susan, Dorothy appeared exactly as Michael remembered her: wearing the same black dress, gloves and pillbox hat she wore to George's funeral.

George's voice became small. "Hi, hun."

Dorothy ignored her husband and went straight to the couch.

"Poor little princess," she said.

"Grandma," Amanda said. "What's happening to her?"

Dorothy's face showed no emotion, her dark eyes shone from within the creases of her face. She took Amanda's hand and patted it. "She's fine, Darling. Just sleeping while I make this right." She gave Michael a curt nod and turned to George, her hands folded in front of her.

"I should have known. Even in death, you would find a way to hurt your family."

George put his head down, scratching at his neck, avoiding Dorothy's eyes. "It's not like that," he said softly. "honest."

"Don't you use that word," she hissed. "Those filthy wraiths are outside right now watching us. Fortunately for you, I know who they're working for."

"Mother, what's going on?" Susan said.

Amanda stood from the floor, her hands out at her sides. "What did he do!"

George fidgeted like a child under Dorothy's gaze. "Hun, please. I can sort this out."

"No, George. You can't. But having wasted my life with you, I know better than to leave our family's fate in your hands. I've made a deal of my own."

"What?"

"Dorothy!" Mike said.

She turned to him and he felt the room go even colder.

"I need to protect Maddy," he said. "All this,"—he waved a hand to indicate the others— "all this family drama. I'm done with it. You tell me what's going on. Now."

Amanda put her hand to her mouth.

"Oh, dear," Susan said.

Dorothy stared Michael down.

"Well," she said. "Good for you, Michael."

Susan's mouth opened. Amanda's eyes went wide.

"And you're right," Dorothy said. "I'm sorry."

Amanda and Susan gasped.

"I've been far too busy this evening, cleaning up after my"—she paused, sighed—"husband, to be conscious of anything other than him. I should have told you first. George made a deal with—"

The house trembled, lights flickered, pictures fell from the walls.

Mike ran to Maddy, shielding her with his body.

Dorothy remained in the center of the room. Her hands folded in front of her.

"This has been settled," she said. "I suggest you go back to your master."

The shaking stopped and something moved within the ceiling. A few flecks of plaster fell down onto the shoulder of Dorothy's dress. She swept the dust from the black fabric with a gloved hand.

A small hole opened in the ceiling directly above her. Cracks spiderwebbed around it.

"Don't you dare," Dorothy said.

Something poked through, shiny and slick like a worm, wiggling as the ceiling began to darken and sag around it.

"No!" George rushed to Dorothy and pulled her from beneath the hole as part of the ceiling gave way. Mike grabbed Maddy from the couch and retreated to the nearest corner of the room. Amanda got in front of them with her arms out wide in a defensive stance.

Something oozed through the ceiling.

It reminded Mike of an octopus's body. A purpled mass of rubbery flesh drooping through the hole. It had no features. A dark, viscous oil dripped from it in globs as greasy tentacles squeezed out from around it and reached into the room.

Dorothy brushed George's hands away and marched up to the hanging mass of pulsing flesh.

Tentacles surrounded her.

"Get those disgusting things away from me," she said.

One of the tentacles separated itself from the others and drew up in front of her.

Dorothy's eyes narrowed, her voice lowered. "What a little coward you must be, to have to appear as something so vile." She paused a moment. "Speak to me so we can settle this."

George slinked up behind Dorothy. "Hun. This isn't a good idea."

"Quiet, George."

The tentacle drew closer and Dorothy swatted at it. "I told you. This nonsense does not frighten me. I—"

The tentacle struck Dorothy, sending her across the room and into a wall where she crashed to the floor in a heap of black dress.

A dripping tentacle lashed out and wound itself around George's neck, pulling him off the ground.

"Ned," George rasped. "Go see—"

The tentacle squeezed as George beat at the slimy appendage, his eyeballs bulged. The creature slammed him to the ground.

A deep voice came from all around them, "I've come for what you owe us."

George got to his knees, gasping. "I told you. Just go see Ned."

More tentacles slid into the room, creeping toward Maddy and Mike. Susan joined Amanda in blocking their way.

The voice came again. "We will deal with that. But first, the girl."

The tentacles moved toward Mike and Maddy. Amanda swatted at one as Susan grabbed another. Mike put Maddy against the wall and got in front of her, kicking at a tentacle that slithered across the floor.

"No!" George screamed.

Susan fell to the floor, still holding onto a dripping tentacle as another wrapped itself around her waist and pulled her away. Tentacles crawled up around Amanda's legs and she beat at them as another slipped by and latched onto Mike's wrist.

"You owe us," the voice said. "One death for every year you fail to deliver the item. Last year you tricked us. We are due one death."

"No! I didn't want that to happen. It wasn't a trick, I swear. It's just been hard to get it. We can only do it when we're here, and there's a narrow window. I promise. We have it this year!"

Mike fought to hold on to Maddy. He felt the tentacles tighten, pulling him back. Another made it past and crept up to Maddy's neck.

"Stop!" Mike screamed, being dragged away from the only thing he had left in the world.

The tentacles continued to wrap around Maddy.

"Please!"

The creature did not reply.

Mike stopped pulling against the tentacles and went with them. He charged the oozing creature, jumped up and grabbed hold around the base of two tentacles.

"Take Me!" he screamed. Pulling at the creature. "Not her, take me!"

Amanda had run up, trying to pull Michael back. Susan beat at the slimy arms wrapping around Maddy. Tentacles wrapped around Mike's arms, both his legs, and started to pull. Mike felt his joints pop, tendons stretching, his flesh drawing taught. He screamed.

"That's enough."

The purple blob yelped. Like a small dog being stepped on. The tentacles released their holds and Mike fell to the floor beside Amanda.

A man stood near the door. Middle-aged, handsome, his dark hair slicked back. He adjusted a cuff on his fine suit, barely acknowledging the room. A ruby stone flashed on a pinky ring.

"The deal is done. You may go."

The tentacles retracted through the ceiling and the creature vanished with a wet popping sound. Bits of plaster fell over Mike.

Dorothy stirred. The man went to her and helped her to her feet. As she stood, she changed. The black dress and pillbox hat fading with the years on her face. She now appeared as a young woman, her long hair falling to her shoulder over an evening gown.

"Wow," Amanda said.

"My apologies," the man said. "I hope you're unharmed."

"Fine," Dorothy said. "But I would think someone like yourself would have better control of the help."

The man bowed his head. "The strains of management can lead to oversights."

Dorothy pushed an errant lock of hair behind her ear. "I suppose it must be difficult doing so much alone."

"Yes," the man said. "Though I'm considering a new partnership."

"Just be sure you make the right offer," Dorothy said.

"Uhm..." George had crept back into the middle of the room. "Hun?"

Dorothy turned to him, dark eyes blazing. "Don't call me that." "But..."

"We're through."

"What?"

Dorothy put a hand on the man's forearm. "Please excuse me a moment."

"Of course."

She turned back on George. "I told you I made a deal. It took me three years, but I found your creditor and settled in one night what you couldn't." She turned to the man, smiling. "He turned out to be quite a gentleman, really." She looked back to George and the smile evaporated. "And after dragging Ned to him, we reached an agreement."

George stared blankly.

"It's over, George. This curse you've brought on our family, and this relationship I never should have been in."

"Hey!" Mike had managed to get to his knees, his limbs still in their sockets. "Someone is going to tell me what's going on."

The man looked to Dorothy, raised an eyebrow.

"I didn't know he had it in him," she said.

Dorothy went to Mike, held out her hand.

He stood without her help.

"It would take more time than we have to explain," Dorothy said. "And, sadly, what has been done, cannot be undone. But you can be sure Madeline is safe now. She'll wake up once we've gone. And thank you, Michael. I do feel better knowing she has you with her."

She didn't wait for him to reply.

"Girls," she said to Susan and Amanda, "I'll see you after midnight. We should talk. And George,"—she turned to him—"Never let me see you again."

"But..."

Dorothy went to the door and the man joined her. He offered her his arm and she slipped her hand through as they disappeared.

Mike stared at the door for a moment. Rubbed a shoulder that he thought had been dislocated. It seemed okay. He looked up to the ceiling, saw only the floorboards of the second floor.

"Mike?"

What the hell had just happened?

"Mike?" Amanda calling for him.

Maddy. Mike got up and went to her. Amanda had the girl in her arms.

"She's okay," Amanda said. "She'll wake up once I've gone." She wiped at a tear.

"It's almost time," Susan said.

"Well," George said, "Looks like everything turned out—"

The three of them turned on him, glaring.

George vanished without another word.

Susan exhaled a long breath, then looked to Mike. "I really am sorry for you, Michael, and I meant what I said about you taking such good care of Madeline." She bent down and touched Maddy's face. "So sweet," she said.

Susan strode to the door, "Don't be late, Amanda," and disappeared.

Mike sat there with his dead wife, holding their daughter.

"Soooo," Mike said.

"Yeah," Amanda said. "I guess it's over."

Amanda leaned her head into his shoulder. "This is the part I wish wouldn't end."

"It's okay," Mike said. "It couldn't be forever."

"I know."

Mike took her hand, pulling it to his heart, not knowing what to say, so he said the only thing he knew. "I love you, I always will."

"I know," Amanda said. She leaned back from his shoulder. "And I love you both so much." She pushed his hair back. "Please go on with your life and be happy." She touched Maddy's face, sighed. "Goodbye, Michael." She leaned in and Mike met her halfway. Their lips touched. Hers were cold and he didn't mind.

Their time ran out in that kiss. Mike opened his eyes and Amanda had gone. Dead again.

At his side, Maddy stirred. Mike picked her up from the floor and tried to leave the wrecked living room before she could see it, but she leaned back and yawned, opening her eyes and blinking in surprise.

"What happened, Daddy?" Her voice came thick with sleep.

"You fell asleep, honey."

She leaned back from his shoulder. "No," she said, "what happened to our house."

Mike looked over the wreckage, trying to decide what a seven-year-old might believe. "I think a pipe burst in the ceiling while we were out." He checked her expression. She seemed to accept that. "Good thing we weren't home, huh."

Maddy looked up at the hole in the ceiling. "Is it safe, now?"

Mike looked up too. "Yeah, Maddy. It is."

A BATTY TURN OF EVENTS

R.C. MULHARE

"DYANTHE, WHATEVER ARE you wearing?" Farnsworth Mingott-Bracknell, formerly the scion of a floundering New York shipping magnate, now the nominal Earl of Barsetshire, said to his lady wife, the Countess of Barsetshire, as she preened before her dressing room mirror.

She turned toward him, posing dramatically in her black velvet gown, a sleeveless number cut down from the voluminous folds of a far more conservative gown culled from her mother's clothes press. Rather than adopt her foremothers' stodgier formal attire, Dyanthe kept at the riding edge of fashion, if she had not already honed that edge with her narrower skirts and revealing contours, even for the costumes she designed for her fancy dress engagements. For this All Hallows' Eve, when the spirits walked abroad and all good people should wear their disguises to confound the ghoulies and ghosties and long-leggedgy beasties, she had donned, over a black velvet evening gown, a hood-like visage made of a piece with her gown, leaving her lower face uncovered. Surmounting the hood, where many ladies would wear a plume, perched a taxidermy bat with wings outspread and jaws agape, as if it would take flight, squeaking about the room.

"What am I wearing?" she asked. "Rather than fleeing from the darkness, I chose to hide from it in plain sight. If vampires are abroad, let them think that I am one of their darkling kindred."

"And here I had thought you had dressed as a caricature of the screen vamp Madame Theda Bara."

She picked up her opera-length black gloves to flap them at her spouse, teasing him before she drew them on. "Farnsie, you cheeky lad. It's a good thing that the sea and a continent lie between Madame Bara and you. And here I thought you'd taken a page from that song about only having eyes for me."

"Ah, but Madame Bara cannot hold a candle to the lady of Barsetshire," Farnsie said, taking her hands and kissing the backs of them.

"Hmmm, perhaps after our guests have retired for the night, we might enact the scenes that Mr. Stoker could only hint at in his *Dracula*," she said.

"With you as one of the Count's brides and I as the Count?"

"Rather, with you as the credulous Mr. Harker and I as one of the brides," she replied, with a tinkling laugh.

Moments later, the couple descended the grand staircase into the ballroom. Farnsie had gone for a "minimal" version of fancy dress, donning a simple red leather domino mask topped with small gilded horns and a red satin caplet draped about his shoulders, over his dinner jacket. Lady Bracknell had ordered the servants to open the French doors which opened onto the terrace, so that the night air could waft into the hall, bringing in the scent of a row of bonfires and that the breeze might eddy the candle flames in the chandeliers. Their guests, rather than finding it atmospheric, found it chilly and now stood gathered about the fire on the great hearth.

Carstairs, the butler, approached them, addressing the lady of the house in a low voice. "Ma'am, might I dare to say that your guests would enjoy the dark festivities more if the French doors were closed?"

She tilted her head, pulling her lips into a tight moue. "And yet, it will take away from the atmosphere which I crafted."

"Begging your pardon, Ma'am, but the evening turned colder than any of your staff expected, much less the gardener," Carstairs replied.

"May I speak to him?"

"Certainly, Ma'am, he's out tending the fires."

She turned back to her guests. "Friends and fellow devotees of dark delights, I must convene for a moment with the spirits who walk in the outer darkness." With that, and with the gathered guests murmuring among themselves at this development, Lady Bracknell tucked up her skirts on one side and strode onto the terrace. Despite her thin-soled pumps, she stepped onto the lawn below.

Three bonfires burned on the gravel walk beyond the lawn, under the watch of Klingermann, a tall, saturnine Teuton, black-haired and tanned from working under the sun, leaning upon a long metal rod like Odin leaning on his spear. As she approached, he did not move, save his pale eyes turning toward her.

"And how goes your gathering, *meine Dame*?" he asked

"It would go better if you could rebuild and relight the bonfires upon the terrace."

Lowering the metal rod, he turned fully toward her. "*Wass*? Do you not know what time it took to build the bonfires? I would first need to extinguish these fires, move the braziers, relight the fires and collect more wood, which will disturb your desired atmosphere."

She looked up at him, her head tilted, and keeping her voice sweet but with just a tinge of vinegar in it, replied, "You are the gardener, you know how to handle these things."

He glared at her headpiece, then looked down into her eyes, cold flames kindling behind his own. "I cannot work miracles, not on short notice."

A modicum of her superiority flowed out of her, though she kept this wavering from showing in her face. "Very well, but my guests will lose some of the atmosphere I had hoped for." Before he could retort, she turned and sashayed into the ballroom.

"Carstairs, close the French windows and have the footmen bank up the hearth. My lord husband and I can't have our guests freezing," Lady Bracknell ordered.

"As you wish, Ma'am." He signaled to the footmen waiting by the doors, anticipating the order. The guests breathed easier and stepped away from the hearth, though a few women in lighter costumes rubbed their arms for warmth.

The guests mingled over the buffet dinner, a set up that proved the best idea Farnsie had offered while they planned the party. A fortune-teller mingled with the crowd, improvising the meanings in the lines of the guests' palms or the cards she challenged them to take from a pack she carried.

"How can you host something so wicked at your gathering?" Mrs. Crosswell, the vicar's wife, snipped, glowering toward the fortune-teller, in her Viennese operetta-esque colorful skirts and peasant blouse, as she hovered near a red silken tent rigged in a corner of the ballroom before stepping inside of it.

"Now, now, let's not be cross and rude to our hostess. It's uncharitable to disrupt another's party," her husband, Dr. Crosswell, said.

"Is it so wicked to have some harmless fun, by taking a peek at what the future might hold?" Dyanthe asked, archly. "If you prefer, I will take my turn in our Madame Irena's tent." And so she suited her actions to her words, lifting the curtained entrance carefully to avoid its brushing against her headdress.

Within, Madame Irena sat behind a table covered in a black damask cloth. "Does my Lady Bracknell seek her fortune." She gestured to the crystal sphere on a gilt base on the table. "Shall I gaze into the depths of the crystal? Or shall I read the tale in your palm or in the cards?"

"Hmmm, I've never had my fortune read in the tarrot," she said, sitting down on a stool across from Madame Irena.

The fortune-teller winced at Dyanthe's manner of pronouncing the name of her Tarroque pack. "I would be honored. Is there a question you would ask of fate? Or shall I ask what you need most to know?"

"Hmm, I have no questions to ask, but one can always have advice from the universe," Dyanthe said.

Madame gathered up the cards spread in a half-circle across the tabletop and shuffled the deck. She cut the stack into three piles, turning over the top card of the first. "The Seven of Cups," Madame said, displaying the image of seven cups with peculiar things emerging from them: a star, a crown and gems, a dragon, a tentacled beast, among others. "Seven is one of the perfect numbers and Cups signify love and plenitude. You have many possibilities in love or friendships, many friends and doting relations to support you in all your ventures."

Dyanthe preened. "Oh, that is no mystery: a fortunate noblewoman such as I has many admirers as well as a doting family."

Madame turned over the second card: a queenly woman seated upon a throne, holding a long wooden staff. "The Queen of Wands. A strong and clever woman."

"Obviously myself, yours truly," Dyanthe said, preening again. The cards seemed bent on flattering her rather than mystifying her or boding ill fortune.

She turned over the third card, an image of a page boy, wielding a sword, the image turned upside down. "Hmmm... an interesting card. An energetic man, but one who is quarrelsome, even aggressive, or who stands their ground but may not act reasonable and rational."

"Hmm, I have an idea who that could be. I have a servant or two who could certainly fit the measure," she said, thinking of Klingermann and his prickles. "All together, what does it mean?"

"You are a lady well-loved, but you would do well to make certain you make as much peace as you can with as many as you can, not just the ones you find amenable," Madame said.

"True, though that is near impossible to achieve with some," Dyanthe said. This mere soothsayer seemed far more on the mark than she had anticipated. She could not help a small shiver trickling down her spine as she rose and thanked the fortuneteller before she quit the tent. She would have to inform her friend Rowena Farraday that her prognosticator saw a little too much in her cards.

A small crowd had gathered at a respectful distance from the tent. No doubt some had queued up for their own reading, while others thought to listen in on their hostess's reading.

"Hath our thooth-thayer thaid the thoos?" asked Totty Minchum, her old chum, dressed like a satyr with fur-covered trews in lieu of goat-like legs and sporting the phoniest lisp imaginable.

"Indeed, she has." Dyanthe signaled to a footman passing with a tray of drinks. Once she had moistened her throat and steadied herself with a sip of champagne, she elaborated. "She told me things I knew, and things I needed to know in order to improve myself."

Farnsie leaned in to nuzzle one of the wings on her headdress. "Not that my dark lady needs much self-improvement,"

Dyanthe pulled away from him slightly. "We all have, as it were, pieces in our silver service that require polishing."

"Hmm! If this seer's sayings are so edifying, I suppose it would do little harm for us to engage her services," Mrs. Crosswell said, trotting toward the silken pavilion.

"But does a vicar's wife need more edifying?" Dyanthe said, inwardly dreading the fuss likely to ensue if Mrs. Crosswell had her own soul laid bare by the fortune-teller's revelations.

"Everyone is in need of edification," Mrs. Crosswell said, lifting the silken curtain over the entrance to the pavilion and letting it swing closed.

Farnsie looked from the tent back to Dyanthe. "Why do I have a sense you are trying to shield our vicar's wife from the forces of darkness, Dy?"

Dyanthe took another sip from her glass. "Perhaps, rather, I am protecting her from a little too much light. Shall I say that I believe our fortune-teller truly has the sight."

"Don't be silly, Dy. You probably read too much into her cards or tea leaves," Farnsie said.

"What might she see if she were to read coffee grounds? One has to wonder," Totty said.

"Topham, you dear, clever man, you might have hit upon a novel, perhaps more modish form of divination," Dyanthe said. "If you haven't had your fortune read, perhaps you could broach it to our seer."

"Perhaps I should, though I already know what my future holds: more parties in milady's noble house, more flirtations with whomever wants charming," Totty said, his eyes roaming to a tall girl dressed in layers of diaphanous green with garlands of silk leaves to match festooned about her limbs.

"And our satyr goes in search of a nymph to chase," Farnsie said. As he said this, the vicar's wife stalked out of the tent and finding her husband, blithered at him before he guided her to the French doors for what seemed a breath of fresh air.

"And the vicar's wife has had her revelation," Farnsie noted. "I doubt she suspected whatever the seer said to her."

"Hmm, in which case, shall we pursue some unsuspecting prey of own?" Dyanthe purred.

"As my lady of the darkness wishes," Farnsie said, taking her hand to kiss it before he raised his caplet to half-cover his face and swept off into the gathering.

She went in search of dark company of her own, dancing with many of their guests, playing the dark lady to the nines. Some playfully offered their blood for her delectation, others played up phony but delighted horror at her gracing them with her dark attentions. One guest of indeterminate gender, clad in black garments topped with a plague doctor's raven beak mask and a low top hat, danced a stiff-legged Boston two-step with her.

Well into the evening, the clock on the mantle shelf over the hearth whirred preparatory to striking.

Dyanthe parted with her current dance partner and glided to the center of the ballroom, raising her arms. The clock struck the first chimes of twelve. The string orchestra raised their bows. "Midnight, the witching hour," Dyanthe announced. "My honored guests, the hour of darkness has struck and the power of the night has reached its fullness. But we are safe within the walls of this noble house. However, let us be certain that each person who walks among us is, in truth, a child of earth and not a child of the shadows. Let us take off our masks."

The guests who wore masks or headpieces removed them. Totty Minchum made a great show of trying to pull off his own face. The ladies closest to him squealed in shock, some of their male companions stepped back, surprised, but even in the candlelight, she saw playful glints in their eyes.

"Ah, how disappointing, no creatures of the night have broached our halls," she said, in mock disappointment. "How tragic."

"Who knows what may have slipped in, through different means?" Totty said, with a mischievous leer. The gathering laughed, some playful, some darkly.

"But I would be a poor hostess if I did not follow the rule that I set for my guests." Lady Dyanthe reached behind her neck to lift her velvet hood and unfasten the straps which anchored her headpiece.

The wind rose, slamming one French door open and blowing smoke down the chimney. A gust blew out the candles nearest the open door. The electric lights in the wall sconces flickered.

Farnsie nodded to a footman to secure the door. "It seems the spirits wish to trick us themselves." The guests chuckled nervously, but some eyed the doors askance.

Dyanthe reached up to remove her headpiece. Something gripped her hair. She felt upward. Wings beat against her palms. Sharp teeth snapped at her fingers, grazing the skin. Something squeaked, angry. She tried to look past the edge of her hood but could see nothing.

The guests gasped, some stepping back from her. One young lady, the Fotheringham-Perths' middle daughter, who had dressed as the nymph whom Totty had pursued, screamed, fainting onto an elder gentleman. Dyanthe swatted at her headpiece, but could not dislodge it.

"I've heard of bats getting caught in one's hair, but this is absurd," Totty teased.

Farnsie rushed to her side, flapping a large table napkin at the bat.

"What good will that do?" she cried.

"I'm throwing it over the creature!" Farnsie yelled, finally popping the napkin over the creature which promptly bit through the fabric.

In a bid to shake free, Dyanthe ran out onto the terrace and onto the lawn, shaking the creature, which refused to let go.

From out the darkness beyond the braziers, someone laughed, loud and rasping and sardonic. "Foolish human," Klingermann's voice called from out the shadows. "You would invite the denizens of the darkness to come out to play, till they prove they are not your lapdogs. Be aware that they still have teeth."

She pulled the bat loose, trying to fling it into the bonfire. It escaped her hands, circling her head, before clamping its jaws onto the side of her throat. She screamed, collapsing to the grass in a daze of fear. The bat let go, spiraling up into the night sky. In the darkness, Klingermann cackled again, as if relishing a Halloween prank. She blacked out, her last thought, *Shall the bite of this beast turn me into a true child of the dark...?*

She awakened, sputtering and sneezing. Looking about her, she saw the lush red damask curtains of her own bed. Farnsie paced nearby, while Doctor Slope, the village physician, sat by her bedside, holding a bottle of smelling salts beneath her delicate nostrils.

"Have I become a daughter of the darkness?" she asked. She ran the tip of her tongue along her upper teeth, finding no fangs had grown through her gums.

"You were bitten by a bat, but likely an ordinary one." Dr. Slope said.

She pulled her mouth into a moue "Hmf. And I had hoped something wondrous would come of this night's misadventures."

Farnsie eyed Dr. Slope's leather satchel, sitting on the bedside table. "And you may be experiencing further misadventures."

"I regret to inform you, my Lady, that you will require a series of rabies shots as a precaution," Doctor Slope said. He reached into the satchel, taking out a brown glass vial, then a syringe with a long needle.

"Good heavens," she murmured, closing her eyes and wishing she could faint.

"I'm afraid your Halloween treat became a terrible trick," Farnsie said.

ALL HALLOWS' READ

ALEX EBENSTEIN

THE PACKAGE CAME ON October 30th. A rectangular object wrapped in brown packing paper, postage paid, but no return address. In the center, my name and address written in fat, black marker. Above and below that, in red ink, the words: DO NOT OPEN UNTIL HALLOWEEN. From its weight, corners, firmness, and its *feel*, I knew, quite clearly, the package was a book. Confused and intrigued, I couldn't wait.

I turned the book over to peel away the brown paper, but on the back were the same red words. DO NOT OPEN UNTIL HALLOWEEN.

I hesitated, looked up and down the street, but it was already much too dark to see anything or anyone, even if they'd been standing out in the open. I retreated into my empty house, knowing what I was about to do, yet feeling as if the silence and dust might be watching and judging me. It was ludicrous. Who would ever know?

I ripped the package open.

To my surprise I found the book wrapped in another layer of brown paper, this time covered in several instances of the red warnings. Also affixed to the package: a small square of white cardstock with my name and a message, typed in tight black lettering.

You're correct. Within you'll find a book. A gift, from me to you. But you must wait until Halloween. Or else.

A childhood taunt. *Or else.* Yet it had me glancing over my shoulder again. Except now I didn't feel so alone. As I reread the message, I swear I heard a noise. One that sounded like my name whispered into a breeze over a canyon.

My body shivered, slightly, but enough for my face to flush warm despite my cool, tingling flesh.

Embarrassment.

Paranoia the culprit, certainly. No doubt a product of the season. Nightfall here sooner and lasting longer; leafless trees rising like monstrous skeletons into moonlight skies; and those same dead, dried leaves scraping across the cold ground like a corpse scratching a coffin lid...

I was getting carried away. Caught up in the haunted Halloween spirit and allowing the mysterious package to feed it. Nothing more.

I read the message again, trying to remain rational.

A gift from me to you. But who? It could be any of a number of friends, playing a silly prank. And that rule again? The simplest explanation is often the answer?

I hefted the book in my hands, staring at the warnings to wait, while my inquisitive nature threatened to defy my will, to pluck the message and toss it aside, to tear that final layer of paper free from the book.

My book.

The animal instinct in me, that ancient lizard brain, wanted my fingers to do their dirty work. Yet, the sheer peculiarity of the mysterious package and unknown sender…it was enough to still my hands. For now.

I set the book on the kitchen table. The microwave clock showed 6:30. Less than six hours until midnight. Until Halloween.

Time passed slowly. I filled it with food and a restless nap and TV and a lengthy amount of sitting at the table, staring at the brown papered package. And, of course, messages to my friends to determine who sent the book.

To the self-proclaimed book nerd:
Did you send me a book for Halloween?
No.
Really? Are you sure?
What are you talking about? Of course I'm sure.
I though you were messing with me…
Sorry man. Not me.

More messages, same results. Not a single one admitted to sending the book. More and more it seemed the culprit was a stranger. The word *stalker* came to mind, and once again I felt the sensation of being watched. Not by my untidy house, but whatever presence I'd felt within, perhaps the same that'd whispered my name…

Except I knew that wasn't possible.

Still, despite knowing I'd done so already, I made my rounds around the house again, double- and triple-checking the locks on all the doors and windows, pulling the curtains tight.

Darkness had long since crept in until it surrounded me. The only light came from a yellowy, dim three-bulb fixture dangling over my head at the kitchen table, as I continued to watch the book. *A watched package never opens, blah blah blah*, I thought, a tired and hysterical giggle slipping from my lips. I needed sleep, but what I wanted was Halloween to arrive so I could open the package finally.

I made the mistake of checking the clock again and saw 10:05 blinking at me.

Enough. My patience vanished. The book was from a stranger, supposedly, but a part of me still believed a friend was responsible. Either way, a couple hours to Halloween was good enough, right? What difference did it really make?

I tore at the package, ripping the paper away. I knew what I'd find, but I was still surprised. It was, indeed, a book. But the dust jacket was missing. Just a plain gray hardcover, worn at the corners, faded—clearly well read.

A sticky note was on the cover. Another warning. *Is it Halloween? You still have time to do the right thing.*

I was well past waiting now. I removed the note and crumpled it up with the brown paper. All the same, a twinge of pain hit my midsection, as if my body was attempting a meager revolt, knowing I had, in fact, done the wrong thing.

Dismissing the feeling, I spied the gold lettering stamped along the spine. Both title and author were new to me. *The Hallowed Curse* by A.C. Englund.

Tucked inside the front cover was a bookmark with the words *All Hallows' Read* printed in blocky, fanciful letters across the top. And below:

Happy Halloween! Welcome to All Hallows' Read, the Halloween tradition of bestowing upon a friend the gift of a scary book. Nothing more, nothing less.

Laughter escaped my confused and tight-lipped mouth, sounding nervous and manic, yet genuine. Embarrassment struck again.

All Hallows' Read. Unlike the book, I'd heard of that before. Never participated, but I thought it was a neat idea, and seeing the words had me convinced I'd only been letting paranoia get the best of me earlier.

A book-giving tradition. *Nothing more, nothing less.*

Suddenly I felt ten times lighter. The sender was still unknown, but the heaviest burden of mystery had lifted from my scared, hunched shoulders. The relief that filled the newly created space felt nice, but it came accompanied by the tiredness I'd previously staved off with anticipation.

I admired the Halloween-themed imagery down the rest of the bookmark, then flipped it over. I froze. More text. Handwritten. Scribbled in pen.

You've been chosen. Do you heed the rules? Read and reap. Good luck.

The flesh on the back of my neck ran cold. Like a stranger lurked behind me, blowing chilled air onto my skin. I wheeled around, slapping my neck with one hand to rub it warm, the other arm up in front of me in a defensive pose. But there was no one there. I was still alone.

Was I following the rules? I knew I wasn't, but were these not just words on a piece of paper?

Impulse brought me back to the book, flipping through pages, letting them slide by my thumb, seeing the font, the lines filling each page, knowing if I started now and didn't stop I could have it finished in a few hours.

The clock told me it was long past my bedtime, and I almost did it. Almost set the book down and went to bed. The book wasn't going anywhere. I could come back when it was actually Halloween.

But I didn't. I'd waited long enough, damnit, and wanted to read the book.

I cracked the book to chapter one and read the first lines.

The man knew he was cursed and that death was coming. What he didn't know was how to escape.

I read more, my eyes scanning the lines, devouring each word with the hunger of starved beast. A compulsion bordering on obsession propelled me forward. The story was interesting, but more important, I craved for understanding. Who sent the book and why? What did the handwritten words mean? Was it a trick—something as simple as a book giving tradition?

I had one avenue to find out: read and discover.

The story followed a cursed man forced to live a life underground, running from demons, both internal and external, until survival alone wasn't enough. He had to face his demons or take the permanent escape route from life. The story wasn't overly original—there was even a thinly veiled implication that the unknown demon chasing the man was Death itself. Yet I was compelled in a such a way that putting the book down was not an option. As if by reading the words I'd become hypnotized, and the cure, that final *snap!* to bring me back, would come only when I finished reading.

I barely stopped to take care of the essentials. Partly from desire to continue, partly from fear of stopping. Whenever I paused the air around me felt occupied, unwelcoming. The presence from earlier seemed closer, more real. I blamed the book, which was indeed scary as promised by All Hallows' Read, but ironically, when I read I felt comforted, safe. The words engulfed me, protecting me from whatever spook I'd imagined. The book gave me the power to consume my fears and spit out their remains.

Midnight came and went, and thus, Halloween arrived. I reached the final act of the book and became disheartened. By now I knew the cursed man had been cursed at random, a case of wrong place, wrong time, and his future relied on the thematic question of the book: choosing between selflessness and selfishness. Accept fate and end the curse or perpetuate the curse by passing it off to another innocent soul.

Save yourself and doom another.

The cursed man chose himself. I was angry. He had a chance to end the suffering with himself.

Selfish. Gutless.

When I closed the book it was morning. What I'd read was a flash, but because I'd read it straight through, everything was still fresh in my mind. I wanted to like the book, but I couldn't get over the ending. Was I mad because I thought it disingenuous? Or because I realized I might do the same if faced with a similar situation?

Most importantly, I felt no closer to unraveling the mystery of this gift book than when I received the package. Disappointed, I went to bed. I had to work in a few hours, so I needed whatever sleep I could get.

Days passed and I still hadn't discovered who sent the book. The nightmares started, though. All slightly different but featuring a common plot line: me running, being chased by an unknown terror, ending up stuck for no reason and unable to escape. I'd wake pondering the meaning of survival.

Then the note came, taped to my door a week after Halloween.

I'm sorry it had to be you. Trust me when I say it was, quite literally, not personal. Life is random. We must embrace it or die fighting. I'm aware now that you did not heed my warnings. You broke the rules. I'm sorry for that, too. I wish I could have told you more, warned you more properly, but my hands were tied. You should have listened. It could have ended with you. All you had to do was wait...

Anyway, I'm in no position to judge. But it is on you now. If you don't know what you must do yet, I'm afraid you will soon. Good luck.

Angry and scared, I tried calling the police—clearly dealing with a deranged stalker—but I never finished dialing. I dropped the phone before I could.

Because a visitor arrived. Not the person who'd sent the package. Someone much worse. Some*thing*.

Death.

At my doorstep, but I could have been anywhere. Or nowhere. Like I'd transported beyond the void, approached by a hooded figure with a black hole for a face, scythes for hands. Hell personified.

Death spoke without words. He or she—*It*—spoke in a way that made sound work in reverse, like it had originated inside my brain and resonated out of my body.

You broke the rules. Now face the consequences.

* * *

A year later. A week to Halloween. The package ready to be sent, a stranger selected at random. I know all the rules now, what can and cannot be shared. I'm exhausted from a year of running, pretending to not know what to do, but knowing all the same. Send the book and be rid of the curse, regardless of whether the stranger waits until Halloween, their fate be damned. Or, keep the book and accept my own fate.

I've made my decision. The postage is paid.

ABOUT THE AUTHORS

Kevin David Anderson

Kevin David Anderson's debut novel is the cult zombie romp, Night of the Living Trekkies and his latest book is the horror/comedy Midnight Men. Anderson's short stories have appeared more than 100 times in different publications from anthologies, magazines, podcasts, radio dramas, and in award-worthy publications like the British Fantasy Award-winning quarterly Murky Depths, and the Bram Stoker nominated anthology The Beauty of Death. Anderson's stories have been turned into audio productions on Parsec Award-winning podcasts, Pseudopod, Drabblecast, and on the popular No Sleep Podcast. For more information go to KevinDavidAnderson.com.

Ben Hurry

Ben Hurry is a lifelong fan of all things horrific and spooky, especially the terrifying local content made by his fellow Australians. From his home in Central Queensland he seeks to explore the macabre with help from his two cats, Wordsworth and Cleocatra, and his loving partner Amanda who has somehow put up with him for this long.

J.C. Raye

J.C. Raye's stories are also found in anthologies with Belanger Books, Chthonic Matter, Scary Dairy, Devil's Party, Books & Boos, and Jolly Horror Press to name a few. More stories in 2020 with Rooster Republic, Transmundane and Gravelight Press.

For 20 years, she's been a professor at a small community college teaching the most feared course on the planet: Public Speaking. Witnessing grown people weep, beg, scream, freak out and pass out is just another delightful day on the job for her.

She's won numerous artistic & academic awards over the years for her projects in Communication and seats in her classes sell quicker than tickets to a Rolling Stones concert.

J.C. also loves goats of any kind, even the ones that faint.

Paul Stolp

Paul Stolp is a writer and lifelong devotee of horror and the weird in all their forms. His work has been published in Halloween Horror: Volume 1 and Trembling With Fear. He lives in the Pacific Northwest with his wife and two daughters.

Kelli A. Wilkins

Kelli A. Wilkins loves Halloween and she likes scaring people with her stories. Her short horror fiction has appeared in several print and online anthologies, including Mistresses of the Macabre, Wrapped in White, Moon Shadows, Dark Things II: Cat Crimes, Frightmares, The Four Horsemen, and The Best of the First Line. She has authored three horror ebooks: Kropsy's Curse, Dead Til Dawn, and Nightmare in the North, plus Extraterrestrial Encounters: A Collection of Sci-fi Stories. Visit her site www.kelliwilkins.com to learn more about her writings.

Cullen Monk

Cullen Monk lives in Virginia with their wife and children. Writing is his passion and he tries to write as much as he can when he's not working, hanging out with his kids or wife, or sleeping... and there's never enough time in the day for all those things!

Tim Mendees

Tim Mendees is a writer from Macclesfield in the UK that specialises in unsettling tales of horror and the weird. He has recently been published in Scary Snippets: Sibling Edition, Little boy Lost, Horror For Hire: First & Second shifts, Ghastly Gastronomy, Gruesome Games, It Calls From The Forest, Unleashed: Scary Stories Of Furry Friends, Colp: Black & Grey, Twenty Twenty, Death and Butterflies, Solitude, and has had several short stories accepted for publication in forthcoming anthologies and magazines. His novella 'Miracle Growth' is coming soon from Black Hare Press.

Tim is an active and recognisable figure in the UK Goth music scene in his role as DJ, promoter and podcaster. He also presents a popular series of live video readings of his material. He currently lives in Brighton & Hove with his pet crab, Gerald, and an army of stuffed cephalopods.

Daniel Hale

Daniel Hale is a writer. His preferred genres are horror and dark fantasy, with the occasional foray into more general speculative fiction. He writes mainly short fiction, which can be found in his two collections, *The Library Beneath the Streets*, and the soon-to-be-published *Hallowed Days*. His work has also appeared in anthologies by Mystery and Horror, LLC, Fringeworks Limited, Lethe Press and others. He lives in Akron, OH

DJ Tyrer

DJ Tyrer is the person behind Atlantean Publishing, was short-listed for the 2015 Carillon 'Let's Be Absurd' Fiction Competition, and has been widely published in anthologies and magazines around the world, such as Strangely Funny II, III, IV, V & VI (all Mystery & Horror LLC), Destroy All Robots (Dynatox Ministries), Mrs Claus (Worldweaver Press), More Bizarro Than Bizarro (Bizarro Pulp Press), and Irrational Fears (FTB Press), as well as on Cease Cows, The Flash Fiction Press and The WiFiles, and in issues of Belmont Story Review and Tigershark ezine, and also has a novella available in paperback and on the Kindle, The Yellow House (Dunhams Manor) and a comic horror e-novelette, A Trip to the Middle of the World, available from Alban Lake through Infinite Realms Bookstore.

Joe Kogut

Joe Kogut is a Science Fiction and horror writer from New York. Joe's short stories have appeared in The Monsters We Forgot, Volume one, Flash Fiction Magazine, and other publications.

Erik Handy

Erik Handy grew up on a steady diet of professional wrestling, bad horror movies that went straight to video, and comic books. There were also a lot of video games thrown in the mix. He currently absorbs silence and fish tacos. In his spare time, he works a full-time job he hates. Info about his books can be found at ErikHandy.com.

Patrick Moody

Patrick Moody is the author of one novel, *The Gravedigger's Son* (Sky Pony Press). His short fiction has appeared in several magazines and anthologies, including *A Monster Told Me Bedtime Stories (Monsters Vol. 7)*, *Massacre Magazine*, *Dark Moon Digest*, *America's Emerging Science Fiction and Fantasy Writers*, and has been adapted into audio dramas in *The Wicked Library* and *Campfire Radio*. He lives in Connecticut with his wife

Patrick Winters

Patrick Winters is a graduate of Illinois College in Jacksonville, IL, where he earned a degree in English Literature and Creative Writing. He has been published in the likes of Sanitarium Magazine, Deadman's Tome, Trysts of Fate, and other such titles. A full list of his previous publications may be found at his author's site, if you are so inclined to know: www.wintersauthor.azurewebsites.net/Publications/List

Robert Allen Lupton

Robert Allen Lupton is retired and lives in New Mexico where he is a commercial hot air balloon pilot. Robert runs and writes every day, but not necessarily in that order. More than a hundred and fifty of his short stories have been published in several anthologies including the New York Times best seller, "Chicken Soup For the Soul – Running For Good". His novel, "Foxborn," was published in April 2017 and the sequel, "Dragonborn," in June 2018. His first collection, "Running Into Trouble," was published in October 2017. His collection, "Through a Wine Glass Darkly," was released in June 2019. His newest collection, "Strong Spirits," was released on June 1, 2020. His edited anthology, "Feral," was released September 1, 2020

Jackie Fells

Jackie Fells is a writer living in Seattle where she works all day and spends nights with her family. She rarely has time to write, but when she does, she prefers to write scary stories.

Scott McGregor

Scott McGregor is a new Canadian author residing in Calgary, whose fiction has recently appeared in various anthologies by

Hellbound Books, Oddity Prodigy Productions, Nocturnal Sirens, and many others. He is also a student at Mount Royal University, currently finishing his last year of English and Sociology. His honors project will focus on Marxism in literature and the future of Historical Materialism. Film, board games, and Xbox achievement hunting are some of his other passions. You can reach him at www.scottmcgregorwrites.com and you can find him on Twitter @ScottMSays.

Douglas Ford

Douglas Ford lives and works on the west coast of Florida, just off an exit made famous by a Jack Ketchum short story. His weird and dark fiction has appeared in Dark Moon Digest, Infernal Ink, Weird City, along with several other small press publications. Recent work has appeared in The Best Hardcore Horror, Volumes Three and Four, and a novella, The Reattachment, appeared in 2019 courtesy of Madness Heart Press. Upcoming publications include short story story collection from Madness Heart Press and a story set to appear in *Diabolical Plots.*

Clark Roberts

Clark Roberts writes horror fiction which has appeared in over twenty publications. His fiction collection Led By Beasts pays homage to Stephen King and other influential horror writers from the last few decades. His children's novella Halloween Night on Monster Island is intended for a younger audience and is published through DEADMAN'S TOME. Mr. Roberts lives in Michigan with his wife and two children. Besides reading and writing he enjoys spending time in the outdoors hunting and fishing. He particularly enjoys fishing in the hours of dusk when trout streams whisper, and eyes open in the surrounding woods. Friend him on facebook using the following link: https://www.facebook.com/clark.roberts.39589 If you friend him, he'll confirm; he won't reject you. You'll be a lot cooler for doing this.

E. Seneca

E. Seneca is a freelance speculative fiction author with a strong affinity for horror and dark fantasy. Some of her works include "Harvesters," published in Grimmer & Grimmer Books' anthology DeadSteam, "Light In The Dark," which appeared in The Sirens Call eZine, "It Lives in the Mineshaft," "A Specific Sort of Shared Madness," and "Haunt Me Like A Memory," published by Soteira Press in their Monsters anthology series. She has written original fiction since 2008, and can be found on Twitter @esenecaauthor.

Patrick Meegan

Patrick Meegan's work has appeared in Sanitarium Magazine and the anthologies: Daylight Dims, volume 2; and Crash Code.

R.C. Mulhare

R.C. Mulhare was born in Lowell, Massachusetts, growing up in one of the surrounding towns, in a hundred year old house near an old cemetery. Her interest in the dark and mysterious started when she was quite young, when her mother read the faery tales of the Brothers Grimm and quoted the poetry of Edgar Allan Poe to her, while her Irish storyteller father infused her with a fondness for strange characters and quirky situations. When she isn't writing, she moonlights in grocery retail. She's also fond of hiking in the woods of the White Mountains of New Hampshire, and browsing the antiques shops one finds all over New England. A two-time Amazon best-selling author, contributor to the Hugo Award-Winning Archive of Our Own, and member of the New England Horror Writers, her work previously appeared with Atlantean Publishing, Macabre Maine, FunDead Publications, Deadman's Tome, NEHW Press, Nocturnal Sirens Publishing, and

Weirdbook Magazine, with more stories in various stages of publication. She shares her home with her family, two small parrots, about fifteen hundred books and an unknown number of eldritch things that rattle in the walls when she's writing late in the night. She's delighted to have visitors online via: https://www.facebook.com/rcmulhare/

Alex Ebenstein

Alex Ebenstein is a maker of maps by day, writer of horror fiction by night. He lives with his family in Michigan. He has stories published in Shallow Waters Flash Fiction Anthology, Novel Noctule, and an episode of Tales to Terrify Podcast, among others. Find him on Twitter @AlexEbenstein.

Made in the USA
Coppell, TX
26 October 2020

40075419R00173